GRACE

GRACE

CALVIN BAKER

TYRUS
BOOKS

Published by
TYRUS BOOKS
an imprint of F+W Media, Inc.
10151 Carver Road, Suite 200
Blue Ash, OH 45242. U.S.A.
www.tyrusbooks.com

Hardcover ISBN 10: 1-4405-8578-4
Hardcover ISBN 13: 978-1-4405-8578-4
Paperback ISBN 10: 1-4405-8575-X
Paperback ISBN 13: 978-1-4405-8575-3
eISBN 10: 1-4405-8576-8
eISBN 13: 978-1-4405-8576-0

Printed in the United States of America.

10 9 8 7 6 5 4 3 2 1

Library of Congress Cataloging-in-Publication Data
Baker, Calvin,
    Grace / Calvin Baker.
        pages cm
    ISBN 978-1-4405-8578-4 (hc) -- ISBN 1-4405-8578-4 (hc) -- ISBN 978-1-4405-8575-3 (pb)
-- ISBN 1-4405-8575-X (pb) -- ISBN 978-1-4405-8576-0 (ebook) -- ISBN 1-4405-8576-8 (ebook)
    I. Title.
    PS3552.A3997G73 2015
    813'.54--dc23
                            2014049308

Cover design by Frank Rivera.
Cover image © Clipart.com.

This book is available at quantity discounts for bulk purchases.
For information, please call 1-800-289-0963.

All who go on journeys. You who guided me when I was lost

Each of us creates history. In the work we do and stories we tell. In the groups we join and games we play. The houses we build and gardens we raise. In the things we create and the impressions we leave on the lives of others. Our remembrance of the past. The names of our children.

Christiansen told me this one afternoon, embedded at the hotel bar, soon after I first arrived in the country, when I confessed I was there to bear witness to great events. Write the first draft of history. He snorted into his beer. One day, before I even knew it, he added, I would want nothing but the security of a home and family. Same as everyone else.

He had placed himself in more war zones than anyone I knew, including several generals, so I was surprised when he used that word. Security. I knew that was a myth, but did not have the confidence to question him outright. Still, I wondered if he believed it.

When he was killed a few weeks later, the first thing I thought was that he should have been at home with his family. I realized then the fearlessness I admired in him was nothing but his attempt to provide them security. That he was ordinary.

I believed firmly that lives lived without higher purpose were ill-steered and half-seized, and soon obliterated—by the hours themselves.

That was at the beginning when I was still green and full of ideas. I learned quickly none of it matters.

I had not thought of that brief conversation in years, but the words flooded to mind again the year after my return, at a wedding one morning, as I shared a table on the manicured lawn of a house on a lake with my friends and their fathers. My own father was dead.

"If I were a young man," one of the old-timers said, watching the bridesmaids flit across the lawn in their beautiful summer dresses, "I would go right down there and figure out which of those golden little honeybees would make the sweetest life. And take her right back to the chapel."

"Is that all there is to it?"

"It is at this age."

"Why do young people need everything to be so complicated?"

"Do not listen, boys. There are five divorces between them."

"You're just jealous. Face it. Everyone sitting at this table knows all the women I've ever known look better than any woman you ever knew. On top of it my women are more faithful than your women. Wiser. More compassionate. Run their houses better. Throw better parties. Mother children better. Know more, and do more with it, any way you look."

"If they're so great why have there been so many?"

"There are only four women in a man's life," a tawny-skinned man I did not know, with carefully kept silver hair, said from the other side of our little circle, as the wind gusted the white edges of the tablecloth. "The one who gives birth to you. The one who first stirs and wakens the spirit of love inside you. The one you know is wrong for you, but try to make work anyway. The one who washes your body with her tears.

When you finally comprehend yourself, you will understand none of the others even knew your name."

"For me there was only another," one of the old ones said after a silence.

"The right one is blessing enough."

The conversation was broken off suddenly by cries from down by the shore. A group of women were shouting and running toward the water, past a pile of tiny dress clothes, where a flock of children who had been playing Red Rover moments earlier, had disappeared laughing into the sapphire sea.

"Remember how that felt?" One of the old men recalled, watching the small heads bobbing above the surf. "All of us, every day, should be content as that."

I realized, as the children scrambled back up the beach, how far removed I was from their translucent wonder. In the time I had been home I felt engulfed by a vast numbness, a black hole sucking down a ray of light, and thought the world was nothing but an irrational, hate-filled place I would be forced to suffer until I died. As I sat there that morning, though, buoyed by the well-being of friends, I knew it was only the life I had first chosen that made me different. Had hardened me to the world.

It was then Christiansen's words echoed in my mind, and I began to wonder about starting a family. Hoping if I found someone to share my life with I might discover new joy and wholeness, free of all the claims of history, even if I was uncertain true happiness would be available to me.

When I mused on the idea aloud, the men at the table immediately began opining again. "You might as well marry a rich woman," claimed a friend who had done so and been unhappily married seven years. "At least you won't lose your money when you get divorced." "Marry a young woman," urged another. "Women are all the same," said the old rakehell across the table, who I learned never had wed, smiling with just his eyes. "Like fruit the important thing is to gather them when they are ripe, before some worm has stolen the seed, leaving you nothing but flesh."

Later that afternoon the women I knew added their share. "You should meet my best friend," a married woman said, as we waited on line at the bar. "She's just turned forty, and is dying to have a child. If you're serious that's all that matters." "Marry an island girl," said an island girl I first met under the eaves in a rainstorm, who later taught me what happens when a man does not know his own mind. "When they love you, they love you completely."

9

When my sly old aunt, whom I always tried to spend holidays with, asked, as the reception ended, whether I would be bringing a guest that year, I quickly demurred. "Who knows, maybe next." Besides her I had no other relatives, and I knew she wished nothing more than my happiness. But when I saw her engines firing I vowed to keep the decision to myself. It was, after all, the most serious and private of questions.

If I did not have much idea how to go about it then neither, I thought, watching the intrigue among the wedding guests as the waiters cleared the tables, did anyone else. I simply entrusted myself to the serendipity of the world.

BOOK I

1

"You are fucking insane," the guard muttered under his breath at the television in his guardhouse, before peering out into the early morning darkness as I approached.

"Who's there?" he called, looking up from the bank of monitors, as I reached the wrought-iron gate blocking the private street.

"Harper," I answered.

He stuck his head out from the ghostly glow of the booth, glanced at his watch knowingly as he recognized me, and took a sip of coffee, before clanging open the gate.

I felt exposed by the hour as I made my way up the drive, in the thin blue darkness, before following an overgrown path through the garden at the side of the house that led out to the beach. Inside I could see some of the old people still sitting around the kitchen table, reminiscing and laughing, as I went out through the back fence to the stony shore, where I found my friends sprawled amid the rocks and sounding tide.

Ariel was architecting an elaborate spliff with great ceremony, which he twisted tight and sparked up as I folded myself against a boulder. An old mix tape, from a time before our generation had found its full voice, waxed nostalgic over the Bluetooth speaker, and it was clear they were already high, gazing distractedly into the stars and debating the abundance of life in the universe, between voicing the worries of their lives.

"You talk a lot of mess," Nicola interrupted Ariel as he exhaled a stream of thick white smoke and passed the joint to Rowan. "Both of you. I don't understand how you can smoke that stuff and have the careers you do."

"If I'm going to do anything important I did it already," Ariel replied with eternal innocence. "Being a mathematician is like being an athlete."

"A mathlete," Rowan nodded.

"Now can I *prove* what I just said? No, of course not. Science is limited by the questions it asks, and the tools available to measure them, but math shares a border with poetry, with mystery; and I am absolutely certain there is life out there, an abundant consciousness, carbon-based or not, made of the same stuff we are." He drew on the vanishing joint as it cycled back to him. "Which is starlight."

"So right now we are just starlight contemplating itself. Wow," Rowan said, his eyes half open, as he looked up from the viewfinder of the Galileo to take the joint back from Ariel, noticing me for the first time. "Where were you?"

"He was with one of the bridesmaids," Ariel answered, before I managed to say anything.

"Which one?" Rowan asked.

"The one in the blue dress."

"Dude," Rowan looked to him, high as the moon by then, "they were all wearing blue dresses."

"The one from Miami."

"Thanks," I said, cutting him off before he could continue.

Ariel realized what he had done, and looked to Nicola. Rowan held the smoke in his lungs, stealing a glance as he waited to see whether she would react. I did not have to look. I already knew the expression on her face.

"Why is everyone staring at me?" Nicola countered, peering ahead to the starlit sea. "We were how long ago?"

"I just walked her home. Nothing else," I snapped at Ariel, before changing the subject. "Where did you find the telescope?"

"I rescued it from a box of things my mother put out to be donated, after my father died."

He had gotten the telescope the summer of Halley's comet, when we all received telescopes and spent lazy, monotonous nights gazing up at the sky from our rooftops in the city, where the light pollution made it impossible to see anything, until we came out here late in the season. It felt for a moment, as we sat wrapped in the half-fist of darkness, that time had bent back to us, and we had never left this beach, or known any of the wrinkled years in between.

Nicola took advantage of Rowan's wandering concern to steal a last glance through the lens of the telescope before it grew too light.

"I'm just saying," Ariel returned to his previous topic, exhaling another stream of thick, white smoke. "The universe has not yet stopped creating. Imagine all the implications."

"They might annihilate us," Rowan said. "We might annihilate them."

"Doesn't matter."

"Is this sativa . . . ," inhale, "or indica . . . ," exhale, "we're smoking?"

"Cross . . . ," inhale, "between Kali Mist and Northernlights . . . ," exhale.

Nicola looked up and rolled her eyes with incredulity, pronouncing them too high to take at all seriously anymore.

"Am I the only one here with real responsibility?" she asked jokingly, but with enough call back to reality to break the spell of suspended time, so that the evening and long weekend began to disperse.

I stood slowly, looking at each of them, glad for the hijinks; glad I had taken the trouble to come out here, instead of sleeping the few remaining hours before my flight, to bid farewell to those friends from whom I first learned friendship.

"Hey, I have a license for this," Rowan protested.

"I was just making an observation," Ariel went on, packing the telescope into its case with the utmost care. "I find the idea invigorating."

The sky was ablaze red-golden by then, banishing the final darkness like a jester's robes on the stage, as we began back up the beach to the house, the water receding behind us.

By the time we reached the house the first joggers had appeared on the beach, and a few people practicing yoga and tai chi, making us feel decadent and expansive as we said goodbye.

"My car is back near the hotel," Nicola said. "Harper, you can walk me, if you like. Since you're all of a sudden the protector of helpless damsels."

I went with her in silence through the early morning streets, until her SUV materialized ahead of us. The day was already warm by then, and her nipples were erect against the interior fabric of her dress, extending the material in taut, barely visible circles, like the new snow moon.

She caught my gaze, and a sly smile dashed across her face under the green leaves, until she allowed herself the beginning of a chuckle. She had been my first girlfriend, and we dated from the end of high school until just after college. She was the most substantial girl I had ever met at seventeen, and twenty, and twenty-four when we parted. She had grown into a beautiful woman, and I was a sterling fool. I saw in her smile that she knew she still had an effect on me, leaving me to wonder whether she was upset, and what it might mean if she were.

"I am sorry for how things ended," I said. "I was not ready. I had things to learn." I halted, afraid, like all men who hoard their emotions, that if I let her know how vulnerable I felt she would see I was all vulnerability.

"I know," she answered briskly, her voice quivering with complex emotion. "You still do. It took me a few years, but I'm over any of that now."

"I just wanted you to know."

"And I just wanted you to know I am a husband, two children, a mortgage, and an entire decade over it."

I did the math and did not speak again until we stopped at her car, where we hugged, and parted, then considered each other, and hugged again. Held tight, and did not part, only pulled deeper into the comfort of our embrace and the memory of others deeper still, so that I felt in my marrow what I had been told but never understood before: regret is illumination come too late.

I pulled her tighter and felt her chest heave in time against mine, as my throat clenched around my vocal chords, and remained silent. I did not try to kiss her, afraid what would happen if I did. We clenched each other, absorbing the minute movements of each other's body and the feelings that flowed between us with each circular breath. And in the silence between—all the words we used to say.

2

I was embroiled in a shapeless relationship at the time with a woman named Devi, who worked as an emergency room doctor. A romance? A love affair? I no longer understood its form, only that it felt like an entanglement without a future, which disquieted my conscience. It had never been my intention for it to grow so amorphous or continue so long. We had merely slid into the thing after meeting at a party. I had been standing outside on the balcony and she came out to smoke a cigarette. "I thought you were a doctor," I said. "You smoke?"

"We all have to die of something," she answered, holding out the pack. She was attractive and poised, if a bit high-strung, but otherwise excellent in every way. When we'd gone back inside, so obviously drawn together, the other men in the room envied my monopoly on her time.

We went home together that night, and soon settled into a pattern of meeting each Thursday, whenever we were both in town. We went to the theater and to concerts, and afterward shared meals, wine, easy conversation, the splendor of each other's bed. It was a civilized affair. But our affection never grew and was never transfigured into love.

Our Thursdays had grown familiar, though, chronicling the domestic ups and downs of daily life, and in this way we had gotten caught in a limbo between lust and bliss. If it had broken free of the clay of the affair it had been, it also lacked the breath of a deeper bond. I decided it was time to become more serious or else end things, as it dawned on me how much I was wasting time. I had never tried to imagine a future together, but I admired her and it frightened me to know how pleasant and easy it might be to keep sliding.

When the taxi reached my apartment, the night we first met, I still had not decided to kiss her. "Are you going to invite me in?" she asked.

In the morning when she left, I felt it had been a fine evening, but that would be the end of it. She was the kind of girl who went home with a man she had just met. I was the kind of man who had taken a strange woman home. There it ought to remain.

I called the next day out of a sense of consideration, not intending to signal anything more than fondness, and to keep from adding to anyone's negative experience of the world.

She was careful as well. Telling me she had had fun without regret. We chatted awhile, until she seemed confident again, as she had been the night before. As we talked my interest in her was rekindled. She was not as boring as most doctors, who, because of the way they are trained, usually develop only one part of the mind. Before the call ended I asked her to dinner the following Saturday.

She told me she had to work. "It's not that I don't want to see you. It's just . . . that is when the world goes all to hell and people fall apart. Whatever holds them together during the week dematerializes, then they slip. They spill out of themselves. They crash. They burn. They overdose, or else go into withdrawal. They stab and shoot the people who love them, and generally rage and bleed and come undone all over the place. Afterwards they show up in the emergency room with their regrets, shame, anger, and sad confusion exposed for the whole goddamn world to see. If it wasn't my job I would not look, but it is just as wrong not to do something, so I try to stitch them back together into some human shape as best I can, but what's really the matter is always deeper than whatever wound I am suturing. But it is only an emergency room, so a temporary fix-up is all I can do."

She was beginning to have what sounded like a panic attack, which she managed to prevent. I was not afflicted by them myself, but I was sympathetic to people who were. It was dinnertime by then, and neither of us wished to dine alone.

The next morning we made plans for the following week, setting the frequency to follow, although we were careful never to assume anything, and limited our communication, from one date to the next. Three months into what had become an unspoken understanding, we permitted ourselves to grow genuinely intimate in certain moments, but never beyond the moment itself. An animal baying in the nighttime, that never ventured any closer.

I did not ask what she did the other days of the week, nor open to what she called the box of things that haunted me. I still thought of it as a passing affair, in fact, until one of my friends referred to her as my girlfriend. She was not in the usual sense, but fixed in a state where neither of us wanted to push the other for definition, or press ourselves for clarity. We were simply sliding along in that way that happens in the city.

Whatever we named it or did not, though, after eight months it had grown more intricate, tendrils of expectation, obligation, questions poking forth and hanging in the air. It was this lingering doubt that multiplied our time together, though we knew that was not an acceptable standard. The diffuse, unsatisfied energy of the relationship also kept us from any clarity, and kept us from knowing what our true desire was. It was only abject fear of a muddled, false life that finally stirred me awake.

That Thursday we had tickets to a performance at Lincoln Center, and met at a bar down the street from the hospital where she worked. When we finished our drinks, the early spring weather was alluring and we decided to walk to the theater, chatting idly as we made our way down the rich Westside streets, full of light-hearted ease.

After the show Devi had made reservations for us at a restaurant near Gramercy Park, where we sat out in the garden, which had just opened for the season. The tables had been artificially distressed to look like antique farm tables from the country, and we enjoyed a seasonal meal among the heirloom plants that had provided our salads.

At the end of the meal she suggested a nightcap on the Lower East Side. I still had not unburdened my mind, because I did not like having intimate conversations in public. The weather was still fair, and the food had been satisfying, and her beauty was intoxicating in the candlelight, and I was divided. Wondering if I could will myself to love her. We went for one more drink.

"What is it?" she prodded, testing my drifting thoughts as we walked past a happy young couple, wheeling a stroller.

When I grew pensive, she knifed the silence. "I see where this is headed," she divined, following my eyes after the family.

"What do you see?" I asked, as we floated past the bar and hit Canal Street, where the stench of trash from the fishmongers, piled up curbside, was overwhelming.

"We should break up. That's what you want, isn't it?" She tried to sound clinical and matter of fact, taking a cigarette from her handbag and lighting it. As she exhaled with detached coldness, the emotion it masked made me retreat further into my own doubt. My emotions were at odds, and I still did not understand which to trust.

"I think we should decide if we want to have a serious relationship," I said. "I'm not comfortable with casual anymore."

"You think we should decide," she said tentatively, parsing each word. "Don't you know what you want?"

"We are not in love," I blurted. It sounded awful even to my own ear, and I immediately began trying to reclaim the words from the air and put forth something more decent in their place. "Maybe we can be."

"No, we are not, and no, we cannot. But we are having fun."

"I don't want to have fun. I want to have a relationship."

She laughed, then we both did. The temperature had dropped and she wrapped her arms around her shoulders.

"I did not think you wanted a relationship," she said. "I don't want a relationship. I want to enjoy my youth."

"Alone?" I asked. "You know, serious people have serious relationships. They choose intimacy, and give themselves fully to a passionate connection with another being, even if they make commitments."

"My mother married young," she said. "I've seen what that's like. I'll do it when I am thirty-three," she calculated. "I'll get married at thirty-five and have children at thirty-seven. Until then, what's wrong with this?"

I thought to protest, to pour out the contents of my heart, but I did not wish to turn it into a conflict or risk rejection. I took off my jacket and placed it over her bare shoulders.

"Why now?" Devi asked again, pulling the lapels of the jacket tight.

"No reason. Only that it has been eight months, and I do not think we should continue like this anymore."

"We have a good time together."

"I want more than just a good time."

"Call me in two years."

"What are you going to do if it doesn't work out the way you have planned?"

"I froze my eggs," she looked up at me. It was as much emotion as had ever flowed between us. "I refuse to let my life be circumscribed by anything, including my body. Know what I mean?"

I nodded. "I guess so. But we both know it's not that. I mean, it's not like we fell head over heels for each other."

"Is that what you want? Head-over-heels madness? That is just the brain producing chemicals. You don't let your brain lead you around randomly. You decide. Someone makes sense for you, and what you want in life at that time. The other thing is crazy and frightening."

She touched my arm lightly. "If it took you this long to realize you really want me, maybe it's a sign you really don't." She had warmed enough from walking to turn down the lapels again, and took off the jacket, handing it back to me.

"I thought we would find out," I shook my head, declining the blazer.

"If that's what you wanted, compromise, you would have taken any of the countless opportunities before now. You don't believe it, and are trying to convince yourself. But you can't, because it's too bleak." She draped the jacket over her arm. "If we were meant to have more we would have it by now."

"So we were just—"

"Having fun." She smiled dimly, and took my arm again. "I thought we agreed to that."

We had walked down to the East River by then, and were beneath the Manhattan Bridge, where the air was cool and the fishermen were casting lures under the high moon into the black river. We leaned over the rail, watching them awhile, as I became aware we were on an island in a way I had not appreciated moments before.

"You will find whatever you're looking for," she said. "We both will."

"Yes," I answered, not wanting to drag it out any further. "When you are ready for what you seek, it reveals itself, I guess."

"Is that a theory?"

"I guess."

"So you don't want to continue?" she asked, her coolness giving way to a vulnerable coil of uncertainty and analysis—what I said I wanted, what I really wanted without admitting it, what I was projecting; how she responded to that projection, what she desired, her relationship to her own want—like a complex math problem we knew we would never manage to solve. She took the jacket from her arm and handed it to me again.

I should have taken it and gone home, except the liquor, her guilelessness when she let down her guard, the sheer beauty of her dark face, and the pleasure in hearing the emotion beneath her intelligence when she opened the microphone inside her head to me, all reminded me what had attracted me to her in the beginning, and betrayed my resolve.

"It wasn't so bad a time, was it?" she asked, still holding out the coat and looking across the length of her arms with a tenderness that surprised me.

"No," I said. "We had a lovely time."

"I don't have any regrets. Do you?"

"No," I said. "It's just—"

"Shh. Don't say anything." She put her finger to my lips. "Let's go back to your place and have breakup sex."

"We shouldn't."

"Well, at least kiss me goodbye."

I began trying to explain why we should not, but she planted her mouth on mine.

When our lips parted it seemed to me that her feelings ran deeper, that there was doubt, and it provoked a greater empathy for her as I imagined I saw her human ache.

We found ourselves in bed again. There was, whatever else, a bond between us to remember.

3

She rose the next morning and dressed with a distant indifference that made clear it was the end of the affair, and not the uncertainty of other mornings after a hard night. I found myself hoping aloud we would remain friends, but stopped as soon as I realized I was making one of those *pro forma* statements that ring false even when sincere.

"You mean in case I change my mind. I won't," she said. "I like that we were always honest with each other. Even in what we did not say. Don't change that now. We will not be friends. If you decide you want what I want, you can call me. Otherwise you should delete my number. It's easier that way. Let go the past. Always. Even if it hurts. I always thought we respected that about each other."

I nodded. "I always appreciated what we had. I want more now. As you said, we were honest."

"Oh, Harper, we didn't have claims on each other. That was the point. I was here whenever you asked me to be, and I am not exactly burdened with excess time. I never made demands. We were decent to each other. What else do you want?"

"Not to fight now." I tried to match her coldness. "Why go deeper into it? Why stop being decent now?"

"May I ask something personal?" Devi asked. We were standing in the kitchen, and I made coffee to have something to do with my hands.

"Why not?" I handed her a cup.

She took a cigarette from her purse and raised her eyes to see whether I minded her smoking in the house. I shrugged, and she opened the window, then sat on the sill. "Have you been in love before?"

"Yes. I believe so."

"And it didn't work out, or else we wouldn't be here now. I have as well. I do not need that now. It is too, too unreliable. Know what I mean?"

"I believe so."

"I mean, you think life always works out for the best, if you're smart and work at it. It doesn't. Life makes no sense. You work hard, and you're clever as anyone, and you get banged up despite yourself. If I get banged up again, I at least want it to be beyond my control."

"You think we would hurt each other?"

"I know we would. We would look at each other one day, when we were dissatisfied in general, and wonder whether there was more. Something we had robbed ourselves of. As it is, we have exactly the deal we struck. You call me whenever you want. I answer. Neither of us ever has to say, 'I want you.' Or 'I miss you.' Or 'I feel alone.' Or 'I love you and am devoted for the duration.'" She gestured toward the streets beyond the window. "The messy things that lead to disappointment and worse, when you are still misunderstood and feel alone inside a couple.

"You gave what you wanted, what you could. So did I. And if I didn't give any more, I never gave less. But if you start asking me for more now I *will* give less. Eventually I will hate you for demanding, for needing, and you will hate me for not giving. At least that would be the smart way to feel. But if either of us was emotionally available to the other, we would have owned up to this long ago." She placed her coffee cup down on the sill, and looked out the window.

"It's not a logic problem," I said, still uncertain what I felt, other than we had achieved the clarity of knowing it was over. "It's the difference between what we think—I admire this person;

maybe we can be happy together. What we feel—this is fun; we like each other—and what we experience, which is that we are not in love."

"Maybe we are not emotional people."

"Everyone is emotional. Even us."

"I am a realist. And you? Maybe when it's a war somewhere." She turned from the window to look at me. "Or a disaster, or someone so far removed the camera only looks one way, with no chance of the other person turning it back. Then you understand everything, and feel everything, including your own self-gratifying, morally superior *emotion* of empathy. What about the person next to you? What about me, who was in your bed?"

"You said you were not available in that way."

"Maybe I would have been."

"That's irrational." I was confused, but it was clear our deepest selves were not present, and would not be. We were simply analyzing the end of the affair, shifting the ruins of a vanquished civilization for some muddy understanding of why it was predestined to fail.

"Maybe it would have worked if you had taken the risk in the beginning, six, four, five months ago. You know what I mean? The risk people take when they put everything on the line for what they want. Now you will go chase something else. Why worry about what we had. I don't know why I am arguing about this."

"Because you care? I don't know."

"Because I'm confused. You're confused and confused means no. You don't want me. You've merely talked yourself into it, because you like the idea of me. If you wanted me and I wanted you we would have known. But we cared for each other. It's right to acknowledge that. If you want a family it's wrong that we should settle for that alone."

What she said rang true and I relinquished the argument. What I felt, to my chagrin, was relief.

"Or maybe in the end all we can do is settle. But not yet." She rose from the window, brushing down the skirt of her dress. She came and stood next to me in her bare feet, looking up wistfully.

"You're right." I smiled at her.

"I know," she sighed, moving away to find her shoes. "Yet here we are in this kitchen again. Isn't it the worst?"

"No," I said. "The worst is that more was not given to us." The pain I felt was not only the anguish of separation, but the agony of being at cross-purposes with myself.

I still thought dimly we might figure out how to love each other, not accepting that love was exactly that which refused to be figured. Reason, though, made me want to rationalize that what I had with her was enough, because it seemed to make logical sense, and that was the way of thinking I trusted. The rest of it, the phenomena I could not prove logically, and were threatening to reason itself, I had been trained long ago to shut down. But, as I stood there debating what I was doing, I wondered whether I had not led myself into a trap. What I knew was the uncertainty I felt, which I could not explain, but on some level I think I wanted her because I knew it was a relationship that, even if it did not offer the depths of love, would never produce any sharper pain. I think we recognized that in each other. That we wanted to keep from feeling too much pain. What I accepted that morning, whatever hell it might cost, was I wanted to follow the other part of myself, if it was available—the rest of love.

❧

I cannot pinpoint when I first stopped trusting and following my own emotions; whether it was due to something I witnessed, something I read, or somewhere in my experience. But I distrusted them as much as any false comfort or all-explaining ideology anyone claimed to believe.

The "great events" I witnessed, during the years I worked as a correspondent, covering wars for a small, barely read liberal journal, certainly did nothing to restore my faith once it was gone. The last thing I remembered before changing careers was a nineteen-year-old farm boy with three limbs gone, calling for God to help him, as the bomb blasts still rang in the air. He did not want to die, and he did not want his death to be meaningless.

A cynic would ask which limb remained. I only swallowed my disbelief at the official version of things, spooned out at a press briefing the next day. *Five of our men made the ultimate sacrifice defending their country.* He was a hero, they claimed. I knew they believed it. But it seemed to me to defy the point of life. I was fearful for the future after that, and fearful of the place I was in.

Nights I returned to the hotel, where I drank alone, writing out lifeless copy and searching through the thesaurus for another locution for *lie*, for *injustice*, for *self-serving, self-perpetuating*, until I knew the meaning of every word in the language except innocence, benison, absolution.

When I could no longer abide the world I was in, due to what it seemed to do to the world within me, I understood what danger I had cast myself into, and decided to abandon that path. I quit to earn money and figure out the next part of life. As for war, human rights, and the rest, I had come to suspect they began to be destroyed with the annihilation of the Neanderthals, so deep was murder in our nature.

I was past thirty-five, had few savings from my meager income, and watched as my friends assumed lives of greater and greater ease, while my own plunged into ever-deeper uncertainty. I decided to sell out, if you want to call it that, and get with the rest before it was too late. Not because I had lost faith that anything I did or said or wrote about what I saw mattered. It was because I had come to accept nothing anyone experiences or says matters at all.

I could not get rid of the past completely, of course. Part of that other place remained with me, calling out some days still, in meetings, in restaurants, on the street, whenever I saw people with the same treacherous look in their eyes I associated with greed, suffering, and the nihility in each of us.

I wondered in such moments about Lucifer. *When he was cast down, and transformed from his station as God's favorite, at what point in the fall did he understand himself to be no longer an angel?*

I did my utmost never to be a hypocrite, but comprehended the duality in all our natures. My talisman against my own had been to look to the better part of it. And so keep the more mysterious, equally strong, forces at bay. I policed myself vigilantly in this, as you would a caged panther.

Like Lucifer, though, I knew that I was gifted, and tried to remember all gifts serve a higher purpose, lest I become like the people I saw who compromised, then abandoned, their ideals, until they could justify even the most mortal behaviors. Appetites I shared—I had poured out most of a year in an affair that was too much idle time and empty bottles—but did not approve. It was behavior that belonged to those beings in us who slip free their cages through the ruptures of pain and loss. Until the only sin left was murder.

Sin I learned as a boy, saying prayers every night before bed. I remember reading somewhere that if you said the name of God, any name of God, enough times it would eventually become part of your heart, and only then would you see Him. I came to know rationally where there is no god there is also no sin. In this way I lost my first religion by thirteen. Only to find later what bitter solace reason was for what I had given up.

And like Lucifer, I knew, pride was my greatest sin. By fourteen I was perhaps worse than the devil, who only battled God over His heavenly throne. My war with Him was over creation.

I knew my fortune, though, in being able to choose a life I desired, and the values I would live by. I thought the best way to honor this was to be steadfast in them. I was no longer an idealist, but still tried to believe there was a life of the spirit. At times, sensing it when I listened to music, or read psalms alone on Easter. I left money sometimes for orphanages, for the homeless, for monks whenever I happened past a temple, glad to see their prayer flags chanting against the wind.

Devi left, and from the balcony I watched her make her way down the block toward the subway, her body swaying lightly beneath her printed sundress, the color of forsythia in April. I wondered at the mystery that compels us to feel our entire being awaken to one person and not another, alongside the remorse that the only thing the matter with the person in my bed was nothing to do with who she was, but only who she was not.

I already missed her human company, though, as she slipped away, and the familiarity that kept our affair going so long, the solidity of another person in the immaterial gloom.

As she vanished into the mouth of the subway, I wondered whether if I had said nothing, and let things take their natural course, we might have learned to be satisfied, second-guessing myself again as possible happiness, possible futures collapsed like light switches in an abandoned house with each step she took.

I understood then why the relationship had gone on so long: because I feared there was no such thing as lasting, unconditional love; or else, if there was, I would wake one morning only to find myself unable to fulfill its demands. Her yellow dress disappeared into the subway, and I watched as it swallowed her from my life, alone again and utterly free, as I used to be before I knew her.

4

When I checked my e-mail that morning, I was struck to receive an invitation to Schoeller Mitchell's bachelor party. I knew him from college, as the man I least expected ever to marry. He embraced his debauchery with such zeal and openness, whenever I saw him the word *corrupt* always presented its naked syllables in my mind. The fact that he was finally committing himself to marriage was remarkable, even if it was a woman he'd once dismissed in the most graphic, vulgar terms.

"How did you meet?" A mutual friend had asked, after one of their early dates, at a West Village bar where we were gathered for drinks the last time I'd seen him.

"I was out with Rex, and she was walking down the street with her boyfriend."

"And that didn't deter you?"

"Survival of the fittest, my friend. I knew I was going to marry her."

"You could not possibly have known that."

"Of course I could. Let me show you a picture."

The invitation announced it as the end of an era, which seemed a lucky enough thing for everyone except his future wife. He had organized his life until then unapologetically around self-indulgence, beginning soon after graduation. By the time everyone else had begun to buy houses and settle down, he had bought an Italian sports car with the money he made at his job in a bank.

Around the same time he had also volunteered for a program that helped train aid animals. Rex was a chocolate Labrador Retriever he was helping prepare for life as a seeing-eye dog, but for reasons that were less than admirable. Weekends he would cruise around with the dog in the passenger seat of the sports car, picking up women. "Oh, what a beautiful dog you have." "Isn't he? Unfortunately he doesn't really belong to me. I'm only helping raise him for the Sisters of Mercy. As soon as you get attached, they're gone, and you're heartbroken every time. Rex is going to a blind eight-year-old in South America next week. I hardly know what I'll do." It was nausea-inducing to behold, but impressive for its sheer shamelessness. The only reason we were still friends was our shared history, and the fact that there were so few single men among those we knew.

"Why are you with her, if you do not respect her?" I asked, after hearing more about his new girlfriend than anyone who was not her lover should know.

"Weren't you listening?" He flashed the picture again. "She has an Ivy League degree and screws like a porn star."

"You are a callow man leading a superficial life," I said.

He had been loyal enough, though, to invite me along with a group of our mutual friends to Rio for a final blowout. Whatever else, I was impressed by his optimism and resolve to follow after his instinct. As a general rule I tried to avoid weddings I did not think would survive and declined the invitation.

When I closed the message I realized I was the last bachelor among our friends. I thought about Devi again, and the other women from my past, worrying whether I should have simply chosen someone before thirty, because the heart is only brave early in life. Perhaps I was too coarsened by experience, and my desire to find someone was doomed.

I wasted the rest of the morning flâneuring through cyberspace, growing depressed as I scrolled through pictures of the past staring out from social media pages filled with spouses who might have been me; children who might have been my mine; all the victories, vicissitudes, and compromises of normal life. I decided, by the time I logged off, it was better to regret the past as I remembered it than google up the dead. The past was beyond reach.

I left the apartment, certain again in my decision trusting irrationally that love would somehow find me. But to help it along I also swore off the seductions of the Internet, where desire was reduced to the shallow present, in which you could not smell the perfume in the nest of a potential lover's neck, or scent the summer of your first love, or catch a whiff of your future children.

I was still preoccupied with this as I stopped by the deli for my morning coffee, where Mr. Lee broke my reverie as I waited at the counter to pay.

"Harper," he said, pulling me back from the forest of my thoughts, "why you lonely man?"

"Excuse me?"

"It's Friday. Where Ms. Devi?"

"We broke up," I told him.

"Why on Thursday I always see you with date, but every other morning always shop for one, breakfast for one, coffee for one. Why you don't find good lady?" He leaned over the counter, lowering his voice and tapping the plastic-covered pressboard conspiratorially. "Make love. Make family. Make good life. Happy man."

"It's difficult," I said.

"Difficult when you think. Easy when you do." He made an inappropriate gesture, beaming with avuncular mischief.

He usually sat stoically behind his station, watching the customers come and go, and I did not know he even knew my name, let alone kept tabs on me or had a sense of humor. I thought to ask how it concerned him, but when I realized he saw my agitation that day, and meant it kindly, I took it as another sign, and waved goodbye with genuine goodwill and feigned happiness.

It was near noon, and I had other problems to worry about, as I went to the post office to pick up a package from Davidson, the director of the film I was writing, or had been writing until

Davidson had a breakdown and disappeared to recover. He had only communicated sporadically the past three months, leaving the project and my days uncertain.

Despite whatever financial anxiety it provoked—if I stumbled making my way in the world there was no one but myself to fall back on—I stuck by him, because he had given me an opportunity when I had no experience, except a script I had written which was never made. I was thankful for the chance, and when you have worked with someone in that way you share a bond beyond gratitude, even with the rats who exploit goodwill in others, as well as the ordinary half-rats whose honor runs exactly as deep as self-interest.

Davidson was not a rat. He had talent, but he was also changeable and capricious in a manner that made him unknowable even before his breakdown. When I asked, during our first meeting to discuss the new project, why he had given me the job, he stared at the bare white walls of his office and replied enigmatically, "After I left film school I went into the desert to discover the kinds of movies I wanted to make. For a month all I did was stare into the sand," he motioned to the blank walls, "until I could no longer remember anything I had seen before the sand."

I had no earthly idea what he meant.

"When I had rid myself of everything I had been taught, unlearned every way of seeing not my own, banished every inauthentic way of being, and burned away every single idea that did not rise from my own self, I began to construct a master canon, frame by frame. Whatever rose up from my gut after that belonged to me, and I would serve it. Everything I have done since came from that reel I made in the desert."

I thought I got it. "Where do I fit in?"

"When we met I asked my gut, 'Boss, what do you make of this character?' And my gut replied, 'Boss, give the guy a shot.'"

Which is to say, I should not have been surprised he had gone off the grid and no one knew where he was. But the uncertainty was enervating. The only advantage of the situation had been to allow me to structure my days as I chose.

To keep sane as I waited to see what would happen to the project, I simply kept working. Usually in a café in the East Village, or the Rose Room at the library, or, when the weather was fair, the garden of the Goethe Society, in an old mansion uptown.

At the post office that day I was relieved to find a thick packet, which obviously contained a manuscript, and I thought the last version of the script had finally been approved. I headed uptown to the Rose Room to read.

On the way to the train, one of the shopgirls smiled at me as she raised the metal gate on her boutique. Her smile buoyed my spirits, but I reminded myself how much time could be wasted chasing phantoms and ghosts. Still it made me feel less miserable after the bust-up with Devi.

At the library I found a seat and settled in with my laptop before opening the envelope, which was postmarked Paris, instead of Rome as the last one had been. I did not make much of it until I saw the note inside, telling me he wanted to scratch the project.

I should have seen it coming, and in fact had seen it coming, but had denied the evidence to myself, so was that much more angered and dejected. But as I began typing a tensely worded two-page letter, it occurred to me I might have deserved it for allowing things with Devi to go so long in an unresolved state.

It was only after I had saved the letter to my drafts folder that I read the rest of Davidson's note, and saw the pages in the envelope were not the last version of our script, but a play he had seen in Paris. He wanted to make an adaptation, and asked if I would be interested.

It was an interracial love affair set in the *banlieues* outside Paris, but, as I flipped through it, I thought it was only Davidson being fickle, and the project would eventually evaporate, just as the last one had. The play was translated as *When You Are Weary*, and he had scrawled a list of famous rappers he wanted to consider for the lead.

"On film it should be *Breathless* meets *The Wire*, with a hot soundtrack," he'd written. I could not tell whether he was serious or not—he was pitching—and tried to suppress my sense of outrage at the wasted work I had put into the other project while he flitted around the world like a dilettante.

Inside the package were also several black-and-white stills from the original play to help me visualize what he had seen, but, as I rifled through the photos, I could not imagine what Davidson had in his head, which only increased my pique at him for dropping the other project. I was also having trouble moving beyond the neurotic meanings that would shade everything when it was put on film, and added to my mental notes that in the raced version the betrayal would seem to be because they were an interracial couple.

I was keeping a pretty good list of other things to be pissed about as well, when my computer chimed and I looked up to see an instant message on the screen.

"Sorry," I wrote, mortified when I realized instead of saving the draft I had sent him my unedited thoughts. The damage was done, in any case, but I at least had the satisfaction of speaking my mind, even if it sabotaged me. I could live with that, taking my slip to mean I should just have done with the whole enterprise.

Davidson was all business, though, and ignored the apology, which was clearly insincere. "Thank you for sharing your feelings, my friend. The entire point of the original was how existentially cool Belmondo was—as a crook, a lover, *un type*—right down to the bullet in his back. Other than that it's just a love story, baby. Simple, sweet, tragic. Write it like that.

"He knows about death, in a country that has just lost a generation of its men. She does not. Any other politics are outside, in the tabloids, not inside, where these things, if they are true, tell us about our own world. If it is a shallow desire for the forbidden, it is vulgar if they know it, a petty infatuation if they do not. If it is the signal that goes off inside you it is poetic. If it is profound and real despite great barriers it is ill starred. If they surmount them, heroic. If it is love of the spirit and they cannot achieve it in the world, it is tragedy. Just tell the truth. What could be simpler, and what could be harder?"

He had the upper hand, and not only because he was right, leaving me dangling above the abyss of my own chagrin. Before he signed off, he told me to think about whether I wanted to be part of the project. I was chastened and told him I would read it again, and reply the next week.

"Let's meet for lunch in person, once you've finished," he wrote.

"When will you be back?" I asked.

"Here in Paris," he replied.

I did not want to go to Paris, but felt obliged, and said I would get in touch. My gut told me I was going to get fired in person.

When our instant chat ended I continued to rifle through the material, realizing all of a sudden why Davidson had been drawn to the play. It had been an all-female cast, and as I pored over the photos, I was not sure which of them he was sleeping with, but was positive he was dating at least one of them. He was that way.

I had planned to go to a party that night with my friend Nell, who produced a popular television show, but as I headed home, I no longer felt like going out. The day was jinxed. I called to tell her, mentioning in passing I had broken up with Devi that morning.

When Nell heard this she was even more adamant that I come out. "You were still dating Doctor Perfect? You know there was no *connection* there. Now let it go. Stop worrying, and come to the party." She promised an interesting, beautiful crowd. I was too anxious about work and my conversation with Davidson, however, and bowed out. Instead I spent the evening alone in my empty apartment, making reservations for Paris, to get fired.

5

Despite my misgivings I flew to France two weeks later to meet Davidson, whom I had not heard from again since our chat, and was anxious of what to expect. When I arrived at my hotel there was a message from him at reception, asking that I call as soon as I arrived.

It was still midmorning, and after showering and an hour-long nap, I telephoned the number he had left. When he answered I was relieved to find he was in as good a mood as I had ever witnessed, and invited me to a dinner that evening with a group of actors he had befriended.

It was still light out when I joined them at nine o'clock around a long sidewalk table, not far from the Barbès station. There was a great communal feeling around the table, a mood of perfect naturalness woven through with joy and laughter. An hour later the summer sun was just starting to set, backlighting the gritty streets, and our meal had barely begun.

By the time the dishes were finally cleared it was long after midnight, but our gathering showed no signs of ending, as Davidson ordered Champagne. Several people drifted off after the bottle, but the five of us who remained continued debating, gossiping, laughing around the candles under the streetlights.

When the fifth man left, Davidson was chatting up a dark-haired beauty named Genevieve with quick, hazelnut eyes. Her friend, a *bourgeoise* girl called Florin, had mesmerizing, Athena-gray irises and was fashionably dressed in designer clothes. She was full of whatever she read on the Internet, though, repeating headlines and opinions almost verbatim, which were never as witty or informed as she thought. I did my best to be companionable, even if I was irked by her received opinions; and not because I found those who expressed received opinions and tastes thin-souled, but because they set me on edge as being capable of believing anything that had sufficient followers, and frightened me in the same way crowds at sporting events did, as the peacetime expression of the same latent impulse that caused political mobs.

I also happened to be jealous of Davidson, whose companion seemed fascinating and sparkling with life. I thought to leave, but he seemed transfixed by her, and if I left it would ruin the balance. I tried to be a good sport, making a diminishing effort to engage Florin, as Genevieve leaned attentively toward Davidson while he regaled her with his adventures, and neither of them paid much mind when I tried to interject in the conversation.

I fingered my glass, and humored Florin, masking my boredom, as my attention began visibly wandering when she started talking at length about her problems, and then how great she was, and name-dropping the important people she allegedly knew, and besides that whatever the newspapers said. Her eyes were captivating, though, and I focused on them until their gray mystery turned to ash.

Davidson ordered more Champagne, and I scanned the street, longing to leave, until I had grown sullen. As the darkness deepened I checked my watch, and began motioning to begin my escape, before I became too irritated and unsociable. It was then Genevieve suddenly put her hand on top of mine.

"It is early. You must have more patience. Unless it is not your nature."

"I just flew in this morning," I explained.

"Do we bore you?" she asked impishly.

"Of course not," I replied.

She twisted her mouth with distaste. "I see it all on your face. We were being rude, arguing about work. Do not lie." She let her fingers slide across my wrist, and her touch spread across my skin with the lightness of morning over a familiar landscape, inspiring confidence and the feel of being seen. "Better not to say anything."

I was embarrassed. She saw it. Davidson saw it. Florin saw it. Davidson smiled with bemusement, Florin with pique, and Genevieve unabashedly as my attraction to her began to show.

"Let's talk about something else. I did not mean to say the wrong thing. I thought you knew."

"Knew what?"

"Nothing. Tell me, what is your last name?"

"Roland," I said.

"Do you know the poem?"

"Yes."

"What poem?" Davidson asked.

I began to recite what little I could remember from the *Song of Roland*.

"Charles the king, our emperor and sovereign, for seven years has been in Spain, conquered the land and now no castle against him remains," she translated. "I am impressed. How do you know this?"

"I was caught in a lie by my high school French teacher," I confessed. "As punishment I was made to memorize the first ten stanzas."

"What lie did you tell?" she asked.

"I do not remember," I said. "That's how I got caught."

"I bet I can make you remember," she turned serious. "But never lie to me. I will know."

"You think you can always tell when people are lying?"

"Not everyone. But you, yes." She laughed softly. Her bosom rocked, and her eyes flashed bright like coins from the depths of a fountain, spirits from the bottom of a lake. I wanted nothing more than to see them twinkle again.

"I'm bored," Florin called from the edge of our flirtation. "Let's go. There's a new club nearby, one of my friends owns it."

Davidson looked at Florin, and then at Genevieve's hand, which had made its way back to my wrist, and he was my friend. He began talking to Florin, listening as though she were the most interesting woman he ever met, and the one he had intended to talk to all along. Florin was happy for the attention, and I was happy for the sympathy, and Genevieve was happy because of an irrepressible spirit. Davidson was even more bemused than before, which for him was close to happiness, and we set out for the club.

It was a fine summer night. The club was crowded with people celebrating the beginning of summer, and soon Genevieve and I were pressed against one another.

"I thought you liked my friend," I said.

"No," she replied with certainty. "You are my man."

"When did you decide that?" I asked.

"You are so foolish, and impatient," she said. "Since I saw you. That is why I made you jealous."

"Why would you do that?"

"Why? Because you are my man." She laughed.

I did not usually move fast, but it was a brief trip, and it was clear, so we left for my hotel where we stayed our first night together. In the morning when I woke, she was still curled languorously in my arms, where she remained, as I inhaled the perfume from the top of her head, and did not wake her, because I did not wish to break our embrace.

We went out eventually for a late brunch, then wandered the streets idly, people-watching and talking, before returning to the hotel, where we made love again in the high, perfect afternoon.

She was a beautiful, sensuous girl, with a bright spirit, and I knew it was not practical for us to be together—we did not live in the same city—but was struck by what the Parisians call a *coup de foudre*—stroke of lightning about which little can be said. Silver quick as a message between worlds. She was my girl. Even if we did not know what would happen when we parted, we had the expanse of the weekend like a summer meadow beyond the reach of time.

We did not leave the room again until late the next afternoon, when we bought lunch at Rose Bakery, and farmer's wine from the Jura, to make a picnic in front of the cathedral. When we went for our bread, even the baker could see we were flush with love, and bid us wait a few minutes, then blessed our union with warm loaves of new bread. The wine was good, and the bread was good, and the lawn was filled with couples kissing, as Genevieve curled against my chest like an explosive new galaxy. I did not know what was happening, but I felt fortunate and full of her and thankful.

6

"You know you're betting the long shot," Davidson said, over dinner in St. Germain the following evening. "The improbable. Not to mention impractical. Love rarely works even in the best of cases. You know this, and yet will not help yourself. Either because you crave intensity of experience, a more and more potent drug, or else give privilege to the primal instinct for whom you can love, even when it does not withstand the scrutiny of what you yourself say you want. You wish for reason and desire to be the same, but sense they are at eternal war, Apollo and Dionysus, and know, or should know, misery is when you try but cannot reconcile them. Which will it be? The Romantics chose ardor and were undone. Ancient gods fell into the same divine snare. All perished." Read the myths. Neither will you escape this unharmed."

"None of us will," I answered.

"Lover's gamble. What Olympus would you challenge to palm the fire of gods?"

"It's worth it."

"She will cause you grief. Better to take up a hobby, or check into an ashram, than learn what you are going to learn the way you're going about it."

"I will take my chances."

"Just remember, then, all things tend toward equilibrium. The ending may be as bitter as the beginning is sweet."

"Why are you being a such a cynic?"

"Because I am your friend. Don't get me wrong, I applaud your decision. It is the right way to be. *The way things should be*, so I'm jealous, and not for the reason you think. I wish I could still be that way too."

He told me about his marriage, when he was twenty-eight, which had ended in divorce a year later. He had sworn afterward never to marry again, and, at forty-nine was good as his word, living from affair to affair, some of them longer, some shorter; neither, he claimed, expecting nor seeking more.

"That is the nature of modern life," he argued. "You believe you will find someone who embodies all those things you want, all those things you have been told are appropriate for you, and think you should want. You believe when you find the perfect person your life will be happy. The truth is not that way. You feel a spark, then one day it's gone, leaving you to decide whether to stay on and slog it out, for another kind of idealism you call practicality, but really it is you are hoping the spark might return, or making yourself a martyr to the secular religion of children and family, which is ridiculous on the level of the individual but keeps society whole. Or else you leave and find a new flame. You cannot do what the old gods did, see, under Zeus, which was both at once. So the answer to your future bind rests in whether you can incorporate the thousand tiny failures, or whether the thing for you is the fire itself."

"I thought you were a cynic, now you sound like a romantic."

"Are you an undertaker?"

"What?"

"Stop trying to put people in your boxes."

"That is not what I'm doing."

"No? You're making things binary. They're not. We are all cynics, and all romantics. Stop reducing people to fit little theories and ideas. It says more about the categories in your mind than it does about life. Creating the category is nothing but an attempt to control."

"That means nothing."

"That means everything. Just remember what I said."

He salted his bread and swam it through the olive oil.

"Let's drop it," I said. "I know you are trying to be a friend."

"I am," he affirmed, as we finished dinner faster than usual and parted.

It was late evening, and I went to meet Genevieve at a cocktail lounge near her apartment, where we had drinks on the terrace and debated going on to another place, but began kissing in the open air, ending up back at her apartment, where we entwined until the morning alba spread out over the rooftops.

The curtains were open and the room flooded with light as we fell asleep, but we did not rise until the sun was high over the day, when we enjoyed a light breakfast in the kitchen with the windows open to the ocean of the city below.

It was Sunday and we went antiquing in the markets, then stumbled on a street fair, where we bought Martiniquean food, which we carried down to the river. She took out a white sheet from her bag, which she spread across the white stone, and we reclined and loafed on the banks of the Seine, listening to a Brazilian band play bossa nova standards on the lower banks.

"You are my man," she said, leaning to kiss me.

"I have to go back to New York." I forced myself to be practical, as I considered the uncertainty of a long-distance love affair. "I'm not sure this is possible."

"Because you have fear? So what if we have a crazy love? As long as it is love."

"I have to leave," I said ruefully.

"You do not," she replied. "You can change your ticket."

"Maybe."

"Yes. Stay with me. We will be happy."

"Are you sure?"

"I always know my man."

"I thought you liked my friend first."

"Do not be like that. He is the kind of man who goes to parties where the people ask what his last film is about, which they did not see, and what he will make next, and he explains it to them."

"What should he do?"

"Let it speak for itself."

"I know that is how Americans are. Everyone has to say he is the best. But I only care that he will be a good friend to you. For me he talks too much about money, and pretends to be radical, when really he is safe as a housecat. It makes a little excitement for the *bourgeoisie*, but it is not freedom."

"Davidson is his own man, even when he does what he has to do."

"Yes, that is what the people always say. But he is losing his chance to be a real artist, from being in a business where they confuse money with art. At least he knows it, I guess, and does not lie to himself. And neither should you, even if it makes things difficult. He respects you for that. That is also why he stays here. He hates going back, because in America they only like dead artists and he knows it is making him dead. But you will stay because you are in love, and that is the only thing that makes our lives less alone." She skipped a stone across the river.

"We are all alone. Not even love alters that." I stared up, squinting at the sun.

"True. But it is also true that you will stay for me." She kissed me again slowly as tasting the future. "But you already know."

"Do I?"

"Are you telling me you are leaving? Because you have only to look at me and say, 'Genevieve, I am not your man.' And I will let you go. I will wave my wrist and walk away. Go, say it." She fluttered her fingers and closed her eyes.

I said nothing.

"Good, now let's discover our mystery. Feel how exciting it is?" She took my hand to her breast, so that I could feel how wildly her heart pulsed.

"Yes," I said, unwilling to resist even if I had been able to, which would have taken an effort of will beyond me. I was her man, if only for the time we were together, which is all there ever really is.

She called in sick to work the next morning. We spent the afternoon wandering the streets, and evening in bed, and the next morning as well. Tuesday the museums were all closed, and she had arranged for us to go to the Louvre, which was empty of people except the curators. We roamed from gallery to gallery, looking at the work without any of the usual noise but the crackling energy between the paintings.

"Are you looking at the art, or the naked girls?" she teased, as we made our way through one of the modern wings.

"What is the difference?"

"Don't be superficial," she teased. "The girl and the painter are pilgrim and bridge on the way. The art is a lens, holding still a moment, reflecting it back to us, like a memory we have forgotten. Now do not talk, or else you will miss it if your spirit wants to tell you something better than your own questions."

The pyramid was bright with light, illuminating the world anew, and the rest of the week was the same—the two of us orbiting reality from a celestial perch, until the following Sunday, when I could not change my ticket again, and had to catch an early morning flight for New York.

"Will you vanish, or will we see each other again?"

"I hope we will see each other again," I said, afraid of losing it. "I feel like we might have something."

"Then you should move here." She nested deeper into me, before I could leave the bed to dress. "We are free. We can live wherever we wish."

"I do not know if it is that easy. Let's see what happens."

"We will see what we make happen," was her riposte. I was old enough then to appreciate what I had been given, and knew the sympathy between us demanded I do whatever I could to see if we should be together. What I still did not know was whether I had the faith to trust in it.

7

I returned home plagued with longing, unable to focus on anything besides her. Weeks later our calls and messages to each other continued to grow, leaving me surprised at the strength of my yearning.

"Do you want to come for a visit?" I asked, late one night for me, early in the morning for her, after we had spoken of the strength of our emotions.

"I thought you were against long-distance relationships," she said matter-of-factly. "You are supposed to be forgetting about me, and focusing on all of your important things in New York. I did not want to cross the ocean for an affair."

The sound of her voice over the line always excited me. But I matched her move and retreated. "You are right. I should not have asked."

"You are awful," she said. "How will anyone ever live with you?"

"Who said anything about living together?"

"Do not joke around with what you care about," she declared, present and unafraid of showing herself. "Now you miss me and are sorry for the way you behaved. For your fear." She did not ask, but stated it triumphantly. "Because I know you understand how we must embrace the people who deserve our embrace, without reservation."

Listening to her made it sound so simple, and the distance no longer seemed so great an obstacle. I asked her again to come for a visit.

"I will think about it, but what about your other girls?" she probed. "Won't they be jealous?"

"There are no girls," I said.

"Tell me you miss me then."

"I miss you," I assured her. "I want you here."

"Are you completely certain?"

"Yes. Come over next weekend."

"Before it was simple, now you must wait. You will not catch me again so easily." She gave out the deep, breathy laugh of vitality that had won me before, and it won again. "But if you do, it will be because you are my man."

When we hung up I realized my fear of giving in to what I wanted was not dread of not having it, or of gaining and losing and the resulting pain, only the anxiety of being exposed. As we ended the call I understood why people make such fools of themselves for love. I had no desire to be a fool, of course. But who was I not to be?

∾

She arrived a few weeks later, and I took the train to meet her at the airport, where I found her as beautiful and high-spirited as I remembered, the magnetism between us an electrical storm of attraction. We went back to my apartment, where we made lunch, then spent the rest of the afternoon making love. In the evening we went to Film Forum to see a lost Kurosawa movie, and afterwards walked the sweltering summer streets to Washington Square Park, where we sat on the edge of the fountain to cool off and listen to a jazz quartet, before heading to dinner.

I loved the city in summer, when it metamorphosed from a northern capital to a more southerly pace, but Genevieve had no interest in it. "Let's go home," she said, looking up from her half-eaten salad. "If you don't make love to me this second I will explode."

We taxied back to my apartment, where the unbearable intensity of our thirst for each other was slackened and slackened, but could not be quenched.

"I told you I always know my man," she said, as we lay awake late into the sultry night.

"How many times have you known it?"

"What kind of question is that? I share with you the most beautiful thing, and you ruin it with your petty little jealousy."

I was not a jealous man, but the strength of our attraction made me greedy and insecure even for the past before I knew her.

She soon made it clear, though, that if I wanted to pursue the relationship it would have to be in Paris. After we left dinner with friends at a locavore place in Brooklyn the next day, she told me exactly what she thought of New York.

The restaurant did not take reservations, so our wait was interminable, and I could see she was not going to enjoy the meal, even before we sat down. I suggested we try another restaurant, every place on the block seemed like better or worse versions of the same menu, but it had a meaning to the friends we were with, so we waited.

When we were finally seated the wine was overpriced, and not very good. The food was perfectly fine, but the waiters, and our friends, made too much of it, so no pleasure we received could compete with their self-satisfaction. Genevieve grew antsy, mouthing the word *pretentious* to me when no one was looking.

"What is wrong with Americans?" she asked, as we walked back to the subway. "Everything is 'I like. I do not like.' But it is only opinion, not discernment. All they could talk about was money and food, as though they have never eaten before. But there are more people in pain than in restaurants, and they cannot speak about that, only put money in their stomachs. And then, did you see on the way to the subway, they put books in the street, which I have never seen except in war films, so that is the truth about them."

"It was a fine dinner," I said, trying to take the edge off, and wondering how much I was included in her criticism.

"No, I enjoyed it. Yes, very much." She would not be appeased. "What is not to enjoy? It was like the *ancien régime*."

"That bad?"

"Please do not make me go with them again. We do not have to, do we? No, of course not."

I agreed, but as we exited the subway back to my apartment, she stopped in the middle of the street. "*Amour*, promise me we will never be with the Philistines."

"Okay, but don't be a snob."

"Not a snob. The values I wish to live," she turned intently. "To live, you must be like a simple person with no pretense, or else like a genius, who does not care about convention. Nothing in between. If that makes me a snob, I'm a snob. Not about the things that come from money, but how I live. Democracy is for how to act with other people. For ourselves, and whom we love, everything we do must have a meaning. Only Philistines confuse little pleasure and real joy."

"You mean Americans, don't you?" I asked defensively.

"Not because they are Americans, because they are materialists."

"Well, there was land, then power, and now we care about all the simple pleasures we did not have before. Eventually we will get it right."

"Just promise me we will not be with the Philistines."

"They are just people fumbling through life, like all of us."

"They are Philistines. I do not care. We will not be like that, but like civilized people, who know the difference between the stomach, the mind, and the heart. We will live the right way."

"What does that mean to you?" I asked.

"Like a poet."

I nodded as we came to my building, wondering whether I, or anyone, could live up to her way of seeing.

8

She was a fine, beautiful girl. Spirited, open. Full of love for me. I decided to spend the rest of the summer in Paris. She was there, and Davidson was there. And that was work and that was love and that was most of life.

Genevieve's apartment was tiny, so I rented a hotel room near Canal St. Martin to use as an office, but stayed most of the time in her little flat on the hill in Montmartre. The walls were hung with her work and the rooms suffused with her energy, making the close quarters intimate and restful as a sanctum.

She worked at her studio in the morning, before going to the office where she did temp work. I spent afternoons in my room on the canal, or else worked in cafés, until we met again each evening. It was as she said it would be, I was a free man, and happy as I had not been in as long as I remembered. I felt cared for and I felt free.

"We are on a ship, my love," she declared one morning, opening the windows as high as they would go, onto a narrow widow's walk. "You see, the antennae of the buildings are masts, and we were sailing on a great journey in our red boat." she swept her arms out to the imaginary sea. "Where shall we go?"

"I've never been to Tahiti," I suggested.

"That is a great plan. We can see what inspired Gauguin, and if it inspires us still we can stay. I am a citizen, you know. But in order for you to stay, of course, you may have to marry me."

"Maybe I can get a work visa."

"That will be impossible. You are American, the great imperialist. The only way will be to get married."

We were goofing around, but the sound of the words pleased me. I remembered her admonishment from before, though, refusing to be too light with what we had. "We should not joke about the things that have meaning for us," I said, turning the words back at her.

"You are awful," she yelled over the rooftops. "Here I thought you were so sweet, like a sad puppy I would pick up and take home, and—what is the word?—redeem. Yes. I would redeem you, and then you would be full of life again, and not anxious or afraid, and be my wonderful little pet."

"In your little cage."

"*Mon Dieu, non. Mon amour,* a cage large as the world. Large as love. Strong as gravity. But mine, yes, all mine. Now it is too late."

"Why?"

"Why? Because you second-guessed your heart again. You say you want to be together, but you think there are rules for how to do everything. But there are not, only what we make. You were supposed to say, 'Yes. Let's elope to Tahiti.' Then we would be married. You were not supposed to say, 'Why?' The prince never asks the princess *why*? He knows *why*. She knows *why*. Little babies in their cribs know *why*. Everyone knows this when they are born, but they forget. You are supposed to remember that, not analyze it and be impossible. Your line should have been, 'Genevieve, my true love, I am your knight at your service. I have my armor and my sword but I am lost without you, my grail, my purpose.' Or else, she feigned swooning, 'Let us gather up the threads of our affection and braid a rope to raise a sail on our little ship, to journey wherever we wish.'"

"Okay," I said. "I am your knight."

"Why are you my knight? See how it all goes away? Now, tell me again what you think of Tahiti?"

"I think we should go," I said.

"To do what?"

"Become citizens?"

"I already am a citizen."

"Then I suppose I will have to marry you."

"No. That is entirely insufficient. Don't you know anything? I thought you were my man." She laughed.

"Okay," I said, infected by the idea of doing something spontaneous, "why don't we take a short trip this weekend?"

"A short trip? No one knows how long a voyage will be when it begins, only how far away the place is you are going."

Our playing around turned into plans to spend a few days in Spain. I liked the spontaneity, but it was a spontaneity with which she approached everything, and found it liberating to give in to it.

"I am so happy," she said, giving me a hug. "It will be wonderful. You will see. And, just so you are aware, we do not ever have to get married. It is old-fashioned, unless, one day it comes from inside you, when you have no doubt of your heart and future, and everything else belongs to your past."

9

We spent two splendid days in Madrid, where all our meals were communal, the wine abundant, and the street music came from a time before their Civil War, when the people had killed each other, which they tried to forget and hear as songs of forgiveness, putting aside what they knew of history. When the heat from the *meseta* descended on the city, we took the train north to the emerald coast and periwinkle ocean for respite. The little towns of Galicia were inspirited by pilgrims on the Camino; the food was simple, and the wine tasted of sea grapes and loss. We drank our share, knowing we would overstay our tickets.

When the weather turned gray we fled to find the sun again in San Sebastián. There the locals were clever, leaving the crowded streets to tourists, to enjoy their own vacations by the shore. The wine was fresh and evanescent as we danced with the country folk and ate their offering, which was the best we could hope for.

In old Castile the people were taciturn, starchy as their food. The kind of realists who scoff at Quixotes, so we were out of there by the end of the afternoon.

In Barcelona the locals were self-protective and hard to fathom, but the art and architecture were fanciful, rich, and rebellious, telling us everything the people did not say. Seville was where the Arab gardens were cool, as the musicians played flamenco cautiously, for Catholic ears.

In Granada they fried everything unrepentantly, washing it down with wines sweet as revenge like Phoenician princesses.

On that island we visited last, every female creature except her was pregnant, and before we left the ewes gave birth; the mares in the ramshackle barn, the nannies in the fields, and in the distance, the she-wolves.

Only a new bride in white, sitting on the sea wall every day, like a Cappa-docian vase, mending her husband's nets, had yet to complete her labors. After evening tide her imperiled husband returned from the wine-dark sea in the tiny boat he had named the Argo, *or was it* Arco? *The letters were faded. Fat little goddess, you called her. If only we had been as full. At night, climbing along the volcano, the ocean below shone like obsidian and the stars fused above us. We fought over what we always fought over. Fire from you calling to the fire in me, until the heat of our passion flagged, and we knew what the ancients did when they reached the end of primitive reckoning. Zero, nothing, was unfathomable. The same way we counted on increase. Believed ourselves indivisible.*

೧

What things we fought about seemed so minor that I thought of our relationship as faultless, and by the time we returned to Paris any doubts I may have had before had been banished from my mind. But as we dined in the open air the evening we returned, I realized how much I still did not know about her when we saw her family at a nearby table, and she called nervously for the check.

"Don't you want to greet them?" I asked. "Or are you worried about introducing me?"

"No, I am not," she said. "Let's just go before they see us."

She was adopted, and I knew she was not especially close to her parents, but the reasons she'd given were only the benign differences everyone has with their family. When the waiter next came to the table, though, he told us our bill had already been settled.

"We should at least thank them," I said.

"Fine. We will just say hello, and leave."

We gathered our belongings, and went over to their table, where her parents insisted we join them for coffee. They looked like a model family, genial and healthy, but as we sat with them I sensed a deep underlying tension.

Her two younger sisters talked excitedly about their summers. The youngest was just returned from camp and in the throes of her first crush. The middle sister was in her last year of college, weighing the future.

The mother was a cultured, attractive woman, poised in a manner that comes only with age, but clearly unhappy. The father did not seem to notice his wife's unhappiness, or else did not wish to acknowledge it, though he made all the gestures of a caring spouse, in the old-fashioned way.

Despite the surface of achievement and mirth, as I sat there I kept sensing their deeper unhappiness—the crease of suffering in the mother's brow, the overburdened slope of the father's shoulders as he drained his glass, the nervous, fleeting joviality among the girls, as though performing their happiness for the world and themselves—until I was struck at length by the silent realization the father was having an affair, and not a passing one. Perhaps a whole other family. The effort of maintaining their masks of happiness in the face of their inner compromises strained them nearly to breaking.

Genevieve was eager to leave, and as we finally walked home I sensed her relief to be free of them.

"So what did you think?" she asked.

"They seem like fortunate people," I lied.

"Don't be blind. It is not as happy as it looks," she shrugged. "It is only a pretense. My mother gave too much. My father controls them all with money."

"They are from a different age."

"She gave too much. She should have left long ago. Now it is too late. She will die miserable, and for what?"

"Maybe she thought she was making a sacrifice for her family."

"Perhaps," she said. "And perhaps it is only a lie we tell to make sense of another lie, in order to make a two-faced life seem less cruel."

It was then I began to understand how little I knew.

10

When I went to meet Davidson that Monday I was anxious again
about work, and found things had only taken a downward turn.
He looked as though he had not slept for days, and he was press-
ing me for a rewrite of the draft I had shown him. It was beginning to seem like the project would never be done, even if the
rewrite would trigger clauses Westhaven, my lawyer, had written
into the contract, that improved my terms.

"Forget Paris. Let's move the action to New York," Davidson
argued when we met. "A famous young director is burned out,
and flees to Europe, only to find it a cultural museum. Comfortable, because he has money, but creatively exhausted. What he
wants is not there, and perhaps no longer exists in the world. He
returns to New York deflated, and decides to make one last movie,
then find a new form. It is about a guy from the projects, who has
killed a cop in Georgia by mistake. He hightails it home, haunted
by the murder, trying and failing to escape his own conscience.
One night he meets a beautiful girl in a nightclub and falls truly
madly deeply for her. She is his emotional equal and mate, but
social opposite: a wealthy liberal, who works for a leftist newspaper. The affair plays out as the cops close in."

"Scene two, I will agree to do another revision," I said, "because
it is in the contract, but, scene one, you have to explain to me why
the director wants to make this particular movie, instead of the
one we already wrote, or the one before that."

"Because this one is true."

"How? What's the mirror to life in this version?"

"What mirror?"

"The one that suggests to us, at each point, another possible reality, and, in that slippery depth, challenges what we think we know about ourselves and the world."

"There isn't one," he said. "It is not about making meaning. It is about when there is no meaning, and just trying to hear and follow what comes from the gut so you can find meaning again. It's finding a way forward, when we lose ourselves or get divorced from the meaning in our lives."

"But the way forward has a meaning too," I argued.

"Why? Isn't forward meaning enough?" He tapped his finger impatiently. "Forward because you cannot go back."

"You're using a postmodern device, so you have to consider its implications whether you want to or not."

"What does that mean? Besides theories I buried in the desert."

"Nothing, I suppose. But what if we do it in four panels? He's rich, she's poor, the country is poor. He's rich, she's poor, the country is rich. He's poor, she's rich, the country is rich, and so on. Color as you will. It tells on how local conditions influence character, possibility, choice. The aspects of ourselves visible in different circumstances. What is truly the gut, and what is from outside, and the different narratives available for us to follow to make sense of it."

"That sounds like theory. Do you think it will make a good picture?"

"It will make good art, which is what you really want."

"Just as long as we stay away from modernity. There's no purpose to it anymore, and I am not interested in anything I went to the Sahara to forget, or the Gobi to unlearn, or Sonora to burn and bury in the sand."

I shook my head. "They did not have the kind I am talking about then. It is why you had to go to the desert."

"Okay," he nodded slowly. "Let's make it like that, then."

"Four stories to square the ocean."

"Four dimensions. Four Gospels."

"In the book," I replied.

"What do you mean, in the book?"

"There are four Gospels in the book. In them Christ points to the Father. In the other gospels Christ points to the self. Christ goes back to you."

"Why did they leave them out of the book, then?"

"The fathers did not like it."

"Let's just stick to four."

"Fine, but you still have not told me why you want to move the action to New York?"

"Simple." He held open his hands. "I want to go home."

I returned to my hotel, where I spent the rest of the day in the cool darkness of the shadows cast from the courtyard, trying to work. But I could only think about our conversation and the differences between living and creation it had brought to mind. I decided to break for the next day, and removed a copy of a novel from a pile of books on my desk, then went to the balcony to read awhile. The book turned out to be about a white South African professor who loses his job for taking advantage of one of his black students, then retreats to live with his daughter in the country, where they are viciously attacked in a robbery. As I registered its cold struggle, with violence and postmodernity, I could only think how much the question of redemption for its unsympathetic narrator was the same as that faced by the liberal readers it was meant for, who always believed that by extending compassion to such a character they were demonstrating their humanism rather than the moral vanity of people who have an easier time extending sympathy to those like them, no matter how flawed, than they do giving empathy to those who are not like them in life, whose inner worlds they cannot imagine at all. He is exactly like them. It is only his transgressions are easier to see and condemn. Beyond that there is a false equation of heartless violence perpetuated by and against individuals—placing the narrator's disenfranchisement on the same plane as the African masses—with the systemic violence of the state.

As much as I enjoyed the philosophical inquisition of identity and violence, when all was said and done its concerns were still white and male. Even if they were about unlearning white male constructs, its imagination ended an inch above the author's skin. The question of his salvation was valid, of course, but he was only able to reconcile himself to the country on Western liberal terms, making the ending a false redemption, because it was the same as the answer to all problems liberals face; not reconciliation to the difficulty of life, but release from its muddy depths.

As brutality layered on brutality, and the characters found solace within the constructs of the book's underlying theories, offering their benevolent forgiveness to each other, it became clear why one would not wish to look outside its theoretical framework into the sucking mud of the world. Because reconciliation and redemption there was too bleak to ponder; would take five hundred years.

By evening, when I left to meet Genevieve, I had frittered away the whole day, beyond a single line of direction:

INT. Darkness

❧

"You should quit," Genevieve said, when she saw my angst over deciphering Davidson. "Forget him. Go and make what you want. Let Davidson figure out his own movie."

"It's a collaboration. We'll figure it out."

"How?" she demanded to know.

"It will happen."

"Yes, if you still believe in it," she said. "It will show itself to you. But you should make your own things."

"What do you mean?"

"The film is for the auteur and actor. Write a novel," she said. "That is your form."

"Why do you say that?"

She shrugged. "Everyone has to create; it is the only thing that makes us human. For some people it is enough to build a shed in their backyard, or watch a television show. Others have to invent whole worlds," she said. "And some have to reinvent this one. Maybe we have come at the end of when people cared, but it simply means we did not come too late."

We changed the subject, but I was unburdened by the worry that had weighed on me.

"How was your day?" I asked.

"Superb. I quit my job."

"Why?"

"To make my own things."

"That is fine," I said.

"Yes, it is," she replied, setting a pot on the stove to boil. "Are we not free?"

"We are free," I said. "But free has a cost, too."

"Do not be so *bourgeois*. It is why the world is so miserable. Everybody does false things their whole life, for money or whatever else, but they do not understand it means they then have to live in a false world. We have shelter, and we have good food to eat, and we have each other. What else do we need that we do not have?"

I was struck by her liquid intensity. "Nothing at all."

"I am so happy with you."

When I awoke the next morning she had already gone out, leaving me a note to say she wanted to be alone with her thoughts before the rest of the city arose.

She had left a loaf of fresh bread and pastries, and I made coffee, then dressed, folding her note into my pocket, like a talisman, as I went to hole up in my room.

By the time I sat down, the answer to the previous day's silence was there with me, and I hummed with inspiration all afternoon. By evening I had made enough progress to ring Davidson, who suggested we meet for dinner to discuss the revision.

"In the framing story the director has made three films on three continents in twenty-four months, all for money," I started, "but has spent his first fuel and is exhausted. He is isolated from society, which to him seems to have traded its soul for material things. He is sick in himself to know how close he has come to doing the same, but finally accepts he does not value what it values, does not think as it thinks, or love what it loves, and yet he loves it. He disappears, hoping to discover a new energy and recover himself, not understanding that the *him* he thought he knew before no longer exists. He walks the streets of old Europe, streets he knows and streets foreign to him, rummaging the pockets of his life, thinking of his parents, who were split up by the time he was born."

"What was that like?"

"His mother was a great beauty, who remarried while he was still young, and sent him away to live with his grandparents. When the grandparents die he goes to live with his mother and stepfather, but it does not take. He is an outsider, even when he succeeds. It was the desire for acceptance that fueled his craving for success, so when it does not prove what he thought it would, his psyche presents its cracks and through them, all the rest surfaces."

"He goes to Switzerland and throws himself to pleasure," Davidson nodded. "He sleeps with a woman from every country."

"Seriously?" I asked.

"Did you just roll your eyes at me?"

"Of course not. I only rolled my eyes. The pursuit of material pleasure leaves him depleted—creatively, emotionally, psychically—until, in his collapse, he must find a new purpose, an internal sense of where his true home is. This becomes the movie he needs to make in order to bury the past, and move into his next self. It is the question of how to be when there is no longer an external narrative to guide you, and the narrative you gave yourself in youth no longer holds."

Davidson laughed. "Yes. It was just like that. Everything except the *coup de grâce*. So you think you figured me out?"

"You? No, but I figured out your movie. That is not life as we said yesterday, except maybe slantwise. In a story something happens and there is a reason for it. And if something should happen to blow up, no one is truly hurt. In life things are not that way."

"There are signs in life," he said wistfully, "when we are awake to them."

"Signs, maybe, but that is not the same as meaning."

"Which is why we need stories, and why they must be true, and characters must be true unto themselves."

"Too much," I said, leaving to meet Genevieve. "I have a date."

It was mid-evening, and the city was cast in rose gold as I stopped to buy flowers from a street vendor before climbing the cobblestones up the hill. Someone in one of the flats along the street was listening to Edith Piaf on an old record player, and I felt free and light. I was in my own story, and where I belonged and where I was supposed to be.

This feeling of utter peace and belonging rose in me, I knew, not because I adored Paris, but because I was in love, and that is all I ever need to feel truly home.

11

Genevieve was downcast when I arrived back at the apartment, so I suggested we go to the Cinémathèque to lift her spirits. There was a retrospective of Noir, New Wave, and Neorealism playing, and a Truffaut movie was just starting when we reached the box office. I went to purchase tickets, but she made an elaborate pantomime of standing conspicuously still, like a spy in an old movie, until the usher turned away momentarily and she snuck into the theater. When I found her in the dark she was in a lighter mood, and by the time we walked back into the torpid night air it was as though nothing had ever been wrong.

On the sidewalk out front someone called my name, and I looked up to see Davidson. He was on a date with a blonde named Elsa, who had hypnotic cat eyes. They were both in full eveningwear, dressed for something formal, but had just exited the Fellini film. I asked where they had been.

"We were at a party earlier," Davidson answered. "It was uptight, so we left."

Elsa was stunning in her gown and a pair of emerald earrings that matched her eyes and cost a car each. I know what they cost the same way I knew Davidson's midnight-blue evening suit had been cut for him in London, and that his shoes were hand-stitched for him in Milan, and what they cost, because Davidson told me. He did not buy brands, he had things made no one else had, and took mischievous pleasure in pricing all of it.

They cut a glamorous figure, especially compared to us in our blue jeans, but he suggested we join them for dinner at a place he knew near Montparnasse. We agreed, and the four of us piled into a taxi, through a part of the city. We arrived at what turned out to be a two-star restaurant, where we did not have reservations. But the wool of Davidson's suit whispered power, and the emeralds shone money. The *maître d'hôtel* got the point and seated us at a high table in a corner by a big picture window, which opened onto the street and caressing night air.

We ordered oysters from Normandy, and Champagne from deep in the cellar, then white lamb, with a Burgundy from high up the hill. Our spirits were awake with pleasure and the conversation was interesting and lively, making us feel princely, as Davidson pondered the sweet wines. While he pored over the list Genevieve stood, excusing herself, and Elsa left to go with her, leaving us alone.

"She seems good for you, if you are not still too wise for that sort of snare," I ribbed him.

"We will see. I spent an hour talking with her mother at the party, so maybe she is."

"I see. Next you'll be taking her home to meet yours."

"You jest, but you do not know what you are saying when you bring my mother into this."

"I did not mean any offense."

"It's not that. My mother, my mother is a different sort. Do you know how many women I have introduced to her?"

"No."

"Two. Do you know how many I have dated?"

"More than two?"

"Now why would that be, you ask. The answer is simple. After I brought home my high school girlfriend, Mother sat me down in the parlor—she still calls it the parlor—with the most aggrieved expression on her face. 'You are a man now,' she said, 'or soon will be. And you may do with your days, and you may do with your nights, as you must, and as pleases you. You do not have to explain yourself. Neither to me nor anyone else, ever again. Beyond that I cannot advise you of much. There are, however, things about life you have not yet learned. As you do, you must take them in stride, without complaint. I only hope you are in all things jealous of yourself, and your time, as I am of mine.'

"I looked at her," Davidson continued, "not knowing what on earth she meant, until she said, 'I do not need to meet any more of your young ladies, except the one you intend to marry.'"

"She wanted you to become a serious man," I said.

"She was insane about time. If we were going to the store and I was five minute late she would leave me."

"She wanted you to know what time is?"

"I was seven. But that's what I thought too, until she died and I found a box of letters in her closet, with a bunch of things from her girlhood." He paused. "Things normal people throw away, old perfume bottles with the evaporated residue of their scent, decades-old boxes of uneaten chocolate, ruined pantyhose, every little luxury she'd ever received was there for me to sort out and make sense of. And then I came upon a box wrapped around with ribbons from old gifts. I started unwinding it slowly, feeling I was opening something I should not. When I finally opened it I remembered two stories. Once, when we were sitting at an outdoor café, up by the museum, some kid runs by and snatches her purse from the table. I took out my phone to call the police, and the waiter rushed over making a fuss, but she was perfectly composed and just said, 'Don't call the police. If he stole because he was hungry, let him eat. If he stole because he is bad, God will punish him.' The other was when she wouldn't let me go on a school trip to the zoo, no matter how I cried to see the damn pandas. Finally, she slapped me. It was the only time in my life she ever put a hand on me. I was stunned. 'Nothing in this world belongs in a cage,' she said, shaking her head in a staccato way that I will never forget. Now can you guess what I found inside that box, in the middle of all that crap?"

I shook my head.

"That she had survived the Holocaust. She was interned at a camp called Eschershausen with her parents when she was a girl."

"I have never heard of it" was all I could say into the stunned silence.

"You've never heard of most of them. It's not your ignorance. There were more than anyone knows—thousands and thousands of them."

I fell quiet, thinking of how she must have wanted to protect him from knowing, from carrying her burden. "I always thought of the Holocaust as people's grandparents" was the only thing I managed to say.

"The past is never as far away as you think," he returned, implacable to the point of nonchalance. "Her real point, or part of her point I think, was to understand the difference between passing emotions and situations, and the steadiness of what lies behind them."

"What is that?"

"Every day Zuigan called to himself, 'Master.' And he would answer, 'Yes, Master.' 'Become sober.' 'Yes, Master.' 'And after that do not be deceived by yourself or others.' 'Yes, Master.'"

"It is beautiful. What is it?"

"It is my koan, since I was a boy."

"Do you follow it?"

"We both know I am too vain to go all the way with it. Still, I like to remember it is there."

"Why not follow it all the way, if you have followed it so long?"

"Once you begin to grasp it there will come the question of how sober you wish to be."

"How did you and Elsa meet?" I asked, changing the subject, as I tried to parse whether it was only something he had read, or Davidson actually knew something serious and true.

"Ingo," he answered breezily.

"Seems right." Ingo was one of Davidson's aristocratic investors. "What does she do?"

"Give away money."

"To whom?"

"Orphans. Museums. Needy politicians." He lowered his voice. "You know, she's the tenth wealthiest woman in Paris. She has a title, too."

"She won't anymore if she marries you," I whispered back.

Davidson continued undaunted. He was never daunted. Even in the throes of a nervous breakdown he had greater magnetism and power than most people in their primes. Not just worldly power to work his will, power from faith in his abilities and himself as a man, no matter the company. In his own personhood. That was his security and his charm. "Can you imagine keeping a fortune that size intact that long?" he asked.

"Where did the fortune come from?"

"I believe it marched its way from the frigid, ungiving North Sea into the open-hearted embrace of her Monaco bank."

"How so?"

"Why don't you ask her, if it worries you?"

"It is not my business."

"Then why ask me?"

"You brought it up."

"There was a reason."

"Which was?"

"You still have the didact in you."

"No, I don't."

"Sure you do. Not five minutes ago you liked her. Now here you are sitting in judgment, wanting to know if her grandfather was the Antichrist. What if he were? Would you then be curious to know what is available to her besides shame, denial, or capitulation, and how she obtains it? So long as she is fully within herself, it does not matter."

"It matters."

"To what? To her character, or to your own particular hypocrisy that you do not see."

"I'm not a hypocrite," I said.

"As I said, it is not your fault, but whatever politics they whipped up for you as a boy do not describe the human world, just a momentary politics of relative power. But kings give way to presidents. Priests to painters. Painters to entertainers. Presidents to industry. Paupers to billionaires. All in their turn. The money and power only project whatever picture show is already playing inside the people. Vanity, deceit, insecurity, greatness."

"That is the same as to say what we do does not matter."

"That is to say what matters is exactly what *we* ourselves do. When you come to Hollywood you will see it everywhere, people who think when the world knows who they are, they will be happy. Only to reach their aim, and turn to see themselves unhappy all over the newspapers every morning. The green-hearted ones look and see partway what's going on, and turn gleeful to keep pulling them down, because they refuse any kind of world but their own misery. They look and all they see is imperfection, and they hate it, which is the same as hating beauty. But they do not know that. No one does. We all just sit sharpening up our different hates and hurts until we can point it all back at the world, thinking it is a sword, while calling it virtue. But tell me what you judge and I will tell you what you fear."

"I was talking about discernment of meaning, which is a high thing."

"It certainly is a high thing." He poured us more wine. "It ain't the highest. Sometimes discerning shows what's there; sometimes it veils it from you."

"What's the highest?"

"You know what it is."

"Do I?"

"Of course you do. At least you have the ear to hear it. The question is, do you have the faith to trust what you hear?

"If you like, I will find out who her fathers were, back as far as I can, because fortune like that is not a single instance of luck, but a second and a third; refigured each time history shifted to obliterate them, but did not because of the sheer refusal to die. If they did something in the past I dislike, or that threatens me, should I break with her? Before I have given her a chance? Somebody went to bed one night and decided there in the dark to try for a dynasty, and did not figure she would be on the other side of it all. Maybe she has a mind and will of her own. This play is for the living. Those who do not grasp that are puppets of the past, and the strings are whatever they have been told; and whoever it was who told them that's the way it is, aims to be puppet master. If you wish to live in that mirage, fine, stick to the didactic. But, if you want to be in the present, it will keep you from the brass ring."

"Sorry I brought it up," I said in the face of his argument. "I didn't mean to make anything of it. She is lovely."

"To tell you the truth, I don't want to know. Can I ask you something?" He scanned the room to see whether the women were in sight.

"Yes."

"Would you date a poor girl?"

"Of course. Why wouldn't I?"

"I would not."

"I thought you just said it did not matter."

"That's not what I said. I said, politics do not describe people. There is nothing the matter with poor girls, but one could never understand my worries."

"What worries do you have, Davidson, other than the ones you invite?"

"You will find out one day. Before they make you a boss, you think how fine it would be to be top dog. You wait and wait your turn. You pine all night, and you pine all day. Until at last your day arrives, all gleaming and new. They pick you up by the scruff, and carry you along to the limousine, with all your anticipation, only to find it is for nothing more than to be thrown into the pit, where now, instead of pining, you get to fight. So you claw for the staff, and you bite for the crown, like you do not have good sense; or, if you do, you run from it all, until, exactly one day before you are ready, they catch up to you, or come pull you up from the pit. Next, the barber comes to you, and the tailor comes to you, and all the old king's men, too, everybody come to you now. You are top dog in charge of it all. Boss bitch running the show. You do not sleep much anymore, but that is fine, because you might miss something if you did. So now they get you good and polished, and they put you up in front of whatever little tribe they give you for your own, where you see all your friends, who love you no matter what you do, and you see all your enemies, who hate you no matter what, and all the what-can-you-do-for-me-people, and the what-have-you-done-for-me-lately-folks. Behind them you see all the smile-in-your-face-people, and all the knife-in-your-back-kinds. Know-nothings and know-it-alls. Born-again-people and the won't-never-be-saveds, plus all your good backsliding brothers and sisters in between. Them you beat for the crown. All who want it from you and, way in back, all them you never really saw before. Apart from that, you got all those dogs, and all those bitches who do not keep faith with you at all. You realize then they are all your people now. You own stock and title to a whole restless tribe's worth of problems no one ever told you about, and you did not know before. It is then you figure out if you have it to be boss dog, or just sit in the chair until the king returns."

"You are just seduced by her," I said.

"We will see," he retorted. "But I do not have any preconceived ideas about who it is who might wind me back up in line with time. People like us cannot afford to."

I could tell he liked her, so I let it drop, as Genevieve and Elsa returned to the table. Genevieve looked piqued, dabbing at her eyes, and it was clear she had been crying. Elsa had a worried expression on her face, and looked to Davidson with distress.

"I think we should probably go home," I apologized, bidding goodnight to Elsa and thanking Davidson for the meal.

"Call me tomorrow?" Davidson asked, with an expression of real concern.

"I'll ring around ten o'clock."

We left the restaurant, and I went to hail a taxi, but Genevieve wished to walk, because she did not think she could bear the motion and closed space.

It was the longest night of the year, and music poured from every block as far as the river. When we reached the center, the streets were still crowded with people, and the full moon behind the cathedral shone down silver on the white stone of Notre Dame, and pure and clear on the velvet blackness of the Seine. Below, on the sand, musicians played, and families strolled, and the tourists, and the lovers, and the hustlers; the beautiful in their prime, the powerful at their height, the babes at their mothers' breasts, and the ancients on their canes, all promenaded, alive and pleased the earth was theirs that night.

"Are you pregnant?" I asked.

"No. I am just dizzy. But the fresh air is making it better."

"It is okay if you are."

"*Oui*," she said. "I know. We are together."

She took my hand as we crossed over the river.

"The princess and Davidson are perfect."

"Why do you say that?"

"Because she is so boring, and he can be such a boor."

"He's bright."

"It does not matter. The nice clothes do not matter. The money does not matter. Paris does not. New York does not. Hollywood especially is not important. Art is the only thing that matters, besides an incorruptible love."

We were still holding hands, and in my hand she was the truest girl on the Left Bank, and, when we crossed over the bridge, the river and I had the truest girl in the city in our right hand. The two of us walked the remainder of the way to her house, listening to the music from each block as we passed. When we finally made our way up the cobbled lane again, the people in the same apartment were playing Nina Simone, and Genevieve brightened to the sound.

At her door, she told me she did not think it a good idea for me to stay the night. "I'll be fine tomorrow," she assured me, wiping her damp brow. "I just need to rest."

"I'll come by to check on you in the morning."

"*Oui*, that would be good. We will take breakfast."

"You're okay?"

"Yes, but I want to work. I have not in days. And if I do not, I feel like I will go crazy."

"I'll see you tomorrow," I said, kissing her atop the head, where the walk and the heat had lifted her scent to the crown of her scalp. I inhaled her fragrance deep into my diaphragm, deep as memory, and if I had my way I would have never ceased.

12

I had left my room key at the front desk of the hotel, where I had not been for several days. When I returned that night and asked for it, the night clerk looked at me appraisingly, without recognition, and what felt like undue suspicion.

"*Et, vous-êtes?*"

"*M. Roland.*"

"*Et, quel est votre numéro de chamber?*"

"*Au dernier étage.*" It was the only room on the floor, and the only one in the hotel with a balcony.

"*Et, que faites-vous, M. Roland?*" he asked, attempting to seem nonchalant, but obviously wondering why I did not keep set hours.

"I'm a writer," I said briskly.

"I see," he nodded, still looking confused. "And how come you speak French, you are American?"

I had tried to humor him before, but was unamused by his insolence, and gave him a look to let him know what part of the desk I needed him to operate. His cheekiness may have been motivated by anything. It may have been something specific. I didn't care as long as he got my key, and called me if there was a goddamned fire in the middle of the night.

"Ah, *oui*," he snapped to attention, scrambling to retrieve the keys. "You know, I once saw Miles Davis perform, many years ago at Olympia, when I was a young man. It was raining, and I did not have a ticket, so I wait by the gate. When the usher isn't looking I sneak in, and run, and do not look back.

"When I stopped running, I am in the front, with all the special people. There is a seat free, and I take it. Nobody say nothing.

The lights went dark and it was the most amazing concert I have ever seen. At the end the people next to me, in the furs coats, invite me to another party, because they see how I love the music, or maybe see I listen in a different way.

"The party was in a small, *petit*, *petit* club, maybe the size of this reception, and when Mr. Davis come, everybody shut up. He went to the front of the room, and still does not say anything, and he turn his back on us. It is like, fuck you, my appointment is with the music.

"He create a space that nothing can enter but pure music. He begin to play, and it is even better than at the concert, and no one say nothing the whole two hours. It was the best night of my entire life. And it is only because a spirit see me, and take me from the rain and put me in the concert, and the same spirit put me in the party. Life is like this, no?"

"When we seize it, my friend."

"Or are fortunate and remember what gives us happiness, and see possibility to have it."

We were friends after that, and his words were still with me the next morning when I left the hotel, easy-hearted and centered, to see Genevieve. On my way to her place I stopped to buy bread at our favorite *pâtisserie*, and oranges for juice from the fruit seller. It was still early when I reached the top of the stairs to the atelier, the quiet morning light streaming through the skylight in the hall, where I could hear her footsteps on the other side, so knew she was awake.

When I knocked there was no answer. I called out to her, full of a joy that had welled up inside of me for no seeming reason, but still she did not respond. I knocked again, louder, before fishing in my pocket for the key. As I turned it in the lock I heard unintelligible sounds from the other side, but the security chain was fastened and the door would not budge.

I rang her on the telephone, but could not reach her that way either, so thought she must have been wearing headphones, or earplugs. I wrote a note, and slid it under the door, before leaving her breakfast on the table outside in the hall and making my way back to the street.

When I returned in the evening the pastries were still there. I knocked again, and heard the sound of her moving around inside the apartment. I called out to her. Still there was no answer. I was worried by then, but told myself she was in a mood and just wished to be alone.

I returned the next day in late morning. There was still no answer, and I became consumed with dread. One of the neighbors heard me out in the hall and opened his door to see what the commotion was.

"Have you seen Genevieve recently?" I asked.

"No, but there has been an awful racket in the apartment all night. I do not know what it was."

I tried my key again, but the security chain was still in place, and the door cracked only partway ajar.

"Genevieve," I called through the opening. She did not answer. I pressed my eye to the crack, where I could see a horrible mess inside, as if something had exploded.

"Genevieve!" I heard her sobbing from deep within the apartment. "What's the matter?"

"Nothing."

"Are you alright?"

"*Oui.*"

"Do you want to let me in, baby?"

"*Non.*"

"Why not?"

"I do not want you to see me like this. You will be angry."

"I will not be angry. I promise."

"*Non, amour.* Go away. I will call when I am feeling better."

"Okay," I said. "I'll be at the hotel."

I heard her still crying from the other side. The neighbor remained in the hall, and I asked whether I could cross over from his balcony. He agreed and I went through his apartment with a feeling of slight embarrassment, but offered no excuses.

From the balcony I heard Etta James rising from lower down the hill, and saw Genevieve's windows were open. I sprang over the wall separating the flats, and down along the widow's walk. From my perch outside I could see the extent of the damage in the apartment, and my mind raced with worry. She had covered the walls with paint, and lashed string all around, with pieces of paper pinned to the string, and stacks of what looked like *papier-mâché*, crisscrossing the room in a maze of confusion, where she was seated on the floor amidst it all. She was still wearing the same clothes from two days earlier and obviously had not slept and was in the most awful way.

When she looked up and saw me on the balcony, she shrieked, and threw the water glass in her hand, which shattered against the window frame as I clambered inside.

"What happened? What's wrong?"

"Nothing. I figured it all out, and wanted to make it before I forgot," she said.

"What did you make?" I asked, tenderly as possible.

"It does not matter. I did not finish, and now you are angry because you think I did the wrong thing, and I have lost my concentration, so you have ruined it. I told you to leave me alone."

"I'm sorry," I said. "I did not mean to ruin it."

"It is too late. Do you want to see what you ruined?"

"Yes, show me what you made."

"I know you were worried, because I do not work anymore, and thought I would be like some silly princess who does not do anything and does not know anything except how to wear jewelry, and takes everything for granted. So I wanted to show you all the meaning of everything. Here, see, are the cave paintings and here is the totem pole and here is the primitive perfection, with its ancient sacred magical power, and here is the perfection of the Goyas. Here is Tintoretto, and Michelangelo with all the known universe of God, and the choirs of angels and the saints and the kings and the pilgrims and the penitent and the sinners and the demons. Here is the modernism, and one of Picasso's crying women, because every time he don't know what to paint he makes his woman cry and because the people they love the suffering, and here is the surreality, and here the beautiful light from Corot and the perfect life force from Manet and here is Degas looking at his girls and here is Matisse and all the immaculate colors and the object is here and the form is created and the form is destroyed here by the photo that makes realism into something else, and the abstract is here with pure consciousness and here all the pop things and cartoons for the Americans, and on the wall is Guanyin Bodhisattva and, next to it, there, you will see, is the Virgin, and the suffering the people love so much and here is the creation and it is all the meaning because if you look from here are the eyes that are not gone from the world. Okay I will take the pills again now, and now you know all before we marry but first I wanted to show you this, the entire world. It is everything, almost everything, before the pills make it stop."

I felt knifed through the core and stood frozen with pain; afraid for her and afraid of her, and in awe of the sheer amount of energy that had poured out of her, as I navigated that divine madness, not knowing what I should do. I reached her at last, but she only bit down on her lip anxiously, and turned and went straight away to the bathroom, before emerging with a bunch of pills, which she took with water from the faucet.

"How long has it been since you stopped taking them?"

"Two weeks," she said. "I will be fine again. You will see. But perhaps it is you no longer love me, because I do the wrong thing, the crazy thing. But the crazy thing is necessary."

"I still love you," I said.

"Okay, we go now."

"Where?"

"To the hospital," she answered, as I tried not to cry and kissed her wild, wild eyes.

13

I stayed with her until I felt confident she would be all right alone, before leaving one afternoon, two weeks later, to meet Davidson, whom I had not seen since dinner at the restaurant.

"How are things with Genevieve?" he asked sympathetically.

"Fine."

"You're a terrible liar."

"I know." I was silent after that. There was nothing to say.

"You know it is impossible to be happy when you are with someone who is not well."

"You are not suggesting I leave her when she has fallen on hard times? She will get better. She is ill, not crazy."

"That is not what I said. I only mean sadness is contagious. You see, the educated classes can all be located on a graph, with the queen of England on one end and a renunciant monk on the other. For the creative, it goes from those willing to accommodate the world to those willing to follow art to the edge of the map. It is primarily a function of talent, but the y-axis is fear." He took out a piece of paper and began to draw. "Genevieve is talented and unafraid. I respect my fear, which is why she dislikes me. She fears making the compromises I do. People with modest talent, and reasonable fears, stumble along the axis, there, doing what they can, according to formulas, and thinking the formulas are real. People with greater imagination and either lavish fear or lavish greed do the same, only they know better. People like her have a chance at making something brilliant and changing the world, then again they have a chance of getting lost. You I cannot plot yet, because you have not decided yourself. Worry the koan, it will help. But, what am I saying? I suppose we all fall for the wrong person once."

"You don't leave who you love because she is unwell. I am sure there are other ways of looking at it, but they are not ways to live."

"You love that woman, don't you?"

"Like a blues song I love her. Are you going to tell me to call your shaman?"

"It will not help."

"I thought you said he was a real medicine man."

"First class at fixing things when you get outside of yourself. For what comes to you from your own spirit, nobody can fix, only help you see."

I did not want to discuss it further, and we talked shop instead, then had a glass of wine, but I did not have the taste for it, and went back to my hotel to rest.

The last days had been uncertain and exhausting, with me constantly checking to see she was taking her medication, which she sometimes did and sometimes resisted. She was there, but no longer present, not really, until slowly my faith that she would be well again was sapped, so I was there but not present as well.

I was responsible to her, though, and did not break with her. How could I? I had asked for a great love. They gave it to me.

When I arrived back at her place that evening, she was in a state of tranquility, and we were eating a quiet dinner, when she stared up from her plate all of a sudden. "I always knew you would leave me one day," she said.

"Who said anything about leaving you? I care about you."

"Do not be sorry," she said, "and do not be a coward. Sometimes the people get married, and sometimes the people get divorced. I give you a divorce. You are free. But always remember we were married."

"We still are."

"We are not anymore. *Non*, I was not the right wife for you. It was not right."

"You are the best wife anyone ever wanted. I can wait as long as it takes."

"Yes, I will be better. But no, you cannot wait and see, so don't make me love's beggar. I am too proud."

I felt worse after that, like a weak liar and coward and every mean, worthless thing there is. I did not leave her, though—not that night, or the next one, or the rest of the season.

The following month was September, and things had grown no better. Some days were up and some were volcanic, and I was due to return to New York to attend to my affairs and renew my visa.

"You will call when you arrive?" she asked. "Or you will let all of this fade into the past?"

"Do not say things like that."

"As you wish. Since you are afraid and have doubt, I wish to let you go now, face to face."

"We are still together."

"*Non*. We were. Not anymore."

"Of course we are."

"*Non, mon amour*. Not anymore."

"Don't do this."

"It is done. You wish to be the hero of the story, you tell yourself, but when people tell their own story it is so they can hide what kind of fool they are."

"I'm a fool for you," I said, letting the subject drop, and I returned to the hotel to pack.

When I returned the next morning to say goodbye before my flight, there was an ambulance picking its way down the hill. My heart sank, even before I reached her apartment, with fear of where it had come from. When I reached the top of the stairs, and opened her door, the apartment was empty and squalid. There was no answer when I called, and no note, and no music anywhere to be heard. I saw the neighbor in the hall, but he did not have to tell me anything.

She was a fine, beautiful girl. Luminous. Fragile. True. And she was my girl, and I was broken-spirited with grief to lose her, and our love that ignited all of a sudden to burn brighter than anything I ever knew. And I was hollow and sick with myself for how lowdown it was to give up on her like I did. Haunted every sunless day I crouched low around my own spirit, with no company but all the other ghosts behind my eyelids.

BOOK II

14

The film wrapped in early May and there was a cast party afterward in a club on East Broadway. The club was filled with beautiful people, who made media and fashion and nightlife, and knew, or thought they did, all there was to know about popular culture, and what people wanted, and how to give it to them. The air was clouded with weed smoke, which I never indulged in, but I took a hit from a joint passed to me by a beautiful girl, and had a sip of my cocktail, which I soon finished, and ordered another.

I wanted to abolish the past from my memory, and focus on what came next, which I could not fathom as I leaned against the bar, trying not to look too empty and centerless. Soon the festiveness and laughter washing through the room were enough to numb my worries, as the air began to buzz with electricity and an omnipresent desire—for sex, for money, for conquest—which the beautiful-looking people displayed in their gestures, in their clothes, in the ease of coded references laced through conversations that exuded confidence and spoke of belonging.

There were a smattering of famous faces scattered through the room, whom the regular people, the outsiders, watched surreptitiously. The famous people found each other, while the business people tried to circle next to the players, who manufactured and sold glory they themselves no longer believed in, as they but longed for something new they could hold to a while.

What was left for them was boredom, cynicism, self-deceit. They bullied, they schemed, they manipulated, they threw tantrums. They were broken narcissists who wished to be worshiped. Whatever the chink in anyone else's armor, they looked for a way to exploit it. It was their value proposition. They thought like gangsters, and the only lasting value was survival itself. Whatever happened in the struggle for that, they kept moving forward and never mentioned those fallen by the wayside.

The rarest among them, who had reconciled how it was their world worked and who they themselves were, inhabited that apex of fear and insecurity and uncertainty, like gods walking through a dream. When they bullied and manipulated it was no longer for power or money but to serve some other, invisible truth they believed in absolutely. They were impressed by intelligence, talent, charisma, authenticity. If they could package those things up and sell them, so much the better. That was the game, but they had by then eyes on either side of their heads, one focused on the business at hand, the other turned inward to whatever kept them from losing themselves.

I watched the crowd schmooze, front, hustle, and ordered another cocktail, and took a hit from a blunt someone was nice enough to share as I waited, watching as the reality in the room bent with the force of raw ego and condensed desire in so small a space. My part in it was done. Everything belonged to the machine now, and I did my best to not worry about what came next, and simply enjoy the night.

Our party was upstairs on a balcony, affording us a clear view to the stage below, where last year's pop superstar was making an unannounced appearance to test out the first single from his comeback album, which would be heard all around the world come summer. It was good and catchy the first time you heard it, and still hooked you the hundredth time. But by then you wanted the damn thing out of your head, which is why the machine was busy, even as they listened to it the first time, working up next year's novelty the people did not yet know they wanted.

The tables at the foot of the stage were filled with business people from another party, still in their suits, and their lawyers, still in their ties, ordering bottle service; all wired on coke. They were powerful and connected enough to be in the club, but removed enough from the industry that they served as the first marks, who would start the buzz humming in the next circle out, until the energy from the room rippled across the country, like wavelets across a fishing pond. It would no longer be about the music by the next morning, but an economic reality of mass experience. To be in the club that night was to witness its magical transformation from private art to public culture. And, slip of time, its first step toward the reliquary of the past.

When the superstar left, the crowd was cresting with energy as the next performer, a midget Marilyn Monroe impersonator, took the stage. She did not imitate Marilyn exactly, but gave a pitch-perfect burlesque of the last golden idol to get her ticket punched that way. Unlike the ingénue she impersonated, she could actually sing. Raised-in-church-papa-was-a-traveling-preacher-mamma-used-to-cry-holy-all-the-damn-time-sing. When the black girls in the audience said *That girl can sing*, they didn't qualify it with *white girl*.

She sang like there was something inside her she was on fire to tell, cutting clean through the derivative cunning, the manufactured desire, the Warholian wannabes before her, who had nothing to add but rode the latest trend until it ran out. Hers was a further station, and she knew it, as she tapped at the twin roots of desire and yearning. When I looked her up later there were no recordings from any of her performances, and when I reflected on it, that seemed right too. She sang like she had been here before, and it was the purity and depth she made you aware of in a single, exquisite moment that made you think maybe you had, too.

If she were four inches taller she would have been on every screen in the country. But who knows what the tradeoff would have been? She was not four inches taller, though, and did not get what came with that, but she had that voice. And she had that wanton, unbridled fire; and the people on the screens, and the people who decided what went on them, were watching her with awe and desire and joy that filled them completely and wanted for nothing else, as she made them know what they had come here for, if only for a vanishing moment.

She wore a skintight red leather bodice to complete or complicate the effect, her ass fat and fertile as a harvest moon, so the suits downstairs, who were ginned up, and everyone upstairs, all weeded out, could do nothing but fall under her spell. Downstairs it was to screw her, because she was hot, or because they were freaks and it was something different. She knew that about them, of course; you heard it in her voice when she sang, saw it in the thrust of her hips. She knew everything there was to know. She had been here before. And she teased the crowd, promising any minute now to come down from the stage and fuck us all. If she ever got half a chance she would fuck the whole world.

She never would get her big break, the world is unfair; you suffer that and do not complain. But we were fortunate to be in the room and hear her. Those who were not and knew only what had been put before them by those who did not create, lost out on the chance to know how beauty can overtake you unexpectedly. That is how this world works. It does not give you what you deserve. It gives you part of what you work for, and halfway what you want. Beyond that it gives to you randomly some part of goodness, and all you can take of pain. That is what it was like for her too: somewhere in between. She was still blessed with that sanctified voice, though, and that irreligious fire she copped for herself.

When the set ended I noticed my friend Nell sitting with an animated group at one of the tables, and made my way over. Their laughter was light in the darkness, radiating fellowship, and, as I sat down, a tall, winsome girl in a halter and shorts that showed the long line of her perfect legs saw me notice her, and we traded smiles.

"Oh, you need to friend her up," Nell said, catching the exchange, as we cheek kissed. "Come on, I'll introduce you."

"Do you know her?"

"I will in a second."

Nell was already in motion, homing in on the other edge of the sofa, where she struck up a conversation. Nell was like the pope's confessor, people divulged their secrets to her in order to protect larger secrets, until she was one of the few people who knew how the city—and the people who ran it—truly operated, and could draw the hidden, unlikely connections between all its self-contained worlds. Whether through charm or guile or toughness, she was impossible to resist.

"Fats," she exclaimed, when she had penetrated to the center of the group. At the far corner of the sofa, sitting like a pharaoh, was Clinton Stone, a record producer, who had once been a musician, then president of a label, where he invented a whole new sound. It had made his stars famous, and given him what stars never get to possess, which is power. Nor did he get it by mistake. He knew what a throne was for, and when the suits finally examined the books and realized they had put an artist in charge of the business, it was too late. By the time they separated him from his chair he no longer needed it.

In the years since, he had become impresario to half the town. He knew all the gods, and all the demigods, and all the beautiful, young ones who burned to be gods and demigods. He could tell at a glance who had it to make it, and who did not. Those who had it, he taught to manage it. Those who did not, he taught how to manage that too, until he had aided so many people on their paths he was known around town as Yoda—though never to his face. He was sensitive about his looks.

Nell introduced us, and he asked what I did. I told him I had written the film with Davidson, and he nodded his approval. "He used to sleep on my sofa in Alphabet City, back when we were young and New York was cool. What are you doing next?"

Most conversations about work in the city were a side-winding way to talk about money, but Yoda had the supernal curiosity of the brilliant, and was as fascinated as a child new to the world, which drew me out, until I had told him everything about my worries, and after that how I'd quit my old life.

He nodded inscrutably, asking what had led me to quit, which was simply that I had learned there was nothing unique about suffering, and nothing I could do to stop it, and nothing more I had to say about it. I had asked myself how my life connected to all those others, and the theoretical questions evaporated, and the truth was too much to speak, until I was back at the place I'd started, which was simply: who are you and what do you know?

"It's not just black people they give black lives," he deadpanned, after my brain had flooded through my mouth. He put a hand on my shoulder to shut me up, and told me not to get so weighed down—half my fear was projection, and the other half I created as well.

I asked what he was working on, to change the subject.

"Same as always," he said coolly. "Getting back for what they took from the Africans."

He sent Davidson a text message, telling him to come join us, and ordered another round for the table.

"I bet you date a lot of complicated women," he said when the drinks arrived. "You should meet Estella."

"Because you think I need complications?"

"Because I know you need fewer." He whispered close to my ear. The one you think you like is a hot mess. Estella is grounded. Maybe not a supermodel, and maybe not a supergenius, just real good people, which is its own special thing. If I were you, I would take her out and get to know her."

I was horny and did not want to be alone, but I did not want a relationship and had my eye on the long-legged one who looked like fun. He was talking loudly enough that they both pricked up their ears, laughed, and flowed over to where we were seated.

Yoda made introductions, and soon after slipped away and began politicking with Nell about something in next week's newspaper.

The one I liked was called Anna. She was originally from Texas, had studied psychology, and had just moved East for a new job in branding. She had the wholesome, fresh-faced look of people new to the city, and seemed like a nice girl to know.

"I'd love to see you again sometime," I said to Anna, after we had been talking awhile.

"Next week," she answered, over the noise of the club. I promised to call, and looked at my watch, and cheeked her goodbye.

"Or tonight," she said, wrapping an arm around my neck, and pulling me in to kiss me on the mouth. "You're not leaving, are you?"

"I have an early morning," I wavered over whether to close the deal.

She leaned in seductively. "Are you certain?"

"Do you want me to take you seriously, or take you home tonight?"

"Why can't we do both?"

I debated with myself between how much to trust affection that sprang so spontaneously into existence and my desire not to go home alone. I agreed to stay a while longer.

"Yoda was right," I said, getting up to go to the bar to freshen our drinks. "You're trouble."

"Did he say we should be lovers?" she asked.

"I did not ask him."

"What do you think?" she reached up and pulled me to her again. I had not dated anyone since Genevieve, and had not been looking for anyone—but the feel of her taut body was undeniable. It felt good to have anybody in my arms.

"Maybe." I wanted to be careful with myself. "I'll call you."

She turned her head and smiled as she walked back to her friends, and I returned to the bar.

"That was hot. Did you get her number?" Nell asked, coming over as I waited for the bartender.

"I'll go out with her next week," I answered.

"Next week? Honey, that's a lifetime. Take her home with you. What's the harm?"

I was fairly lit by then, and as Nell voiced her approval I knew she was just trying to cheer me up, but I was still thinking about what I could not hold, and did not wish to be with someone I did not know. Still I did not want to be alone.

"She is still trying to figure out what the world is about. I do not know if I feel like playing."

"Got it," Nell said, turning her alert attention to a commotion that had broken out below.

"Look at that. So typical. So sad." She pointed down to a pair of suits at one of the tables near the stage, each vying to take the singer home.

"Why?"

"Two bankers fighting over a blonde."

The bouncers stepped in to break them apart, but the violence spoiled my high, and I slipped out a side door into the fresh night air to smoke a cigarette.

Outside I took out my phone, fingering it like a worry stone, as I thought of texting Devi, until I remembered she had deleted her number. That should have been enough to stop me, but it was not. I sent her an e-mail as I finished my smoke, before slipping the phone back in my pocket. As the phone reached the bottom of my pocket, it pulsed with what turned out to be a message from Nell.

"Where did you go?" she wrote.

"Having a smoke. May go home."

"Come back upstairs," she insisted. "The party's just getting started." She told me Davidson had finally arrived, along with some others I knew.

I stubbed out my cigarette, and gathered myself to go back inside, as the phone glowed brightly again in the shadow of the street. Devi had sent an e-mail, which I opened, drunkenly hoping she might be willing to come out. "I'm in Jersey," she wrote. "Painting the house with my new fiancé."

I headed back inside for what I still hoped to be a jubilant night.

Upstairs I found Nell and the others engaged in deep conversation. She sensed my approach, however, and took me by the elbow, leading me into the circle, where Davidson was holding court. As we all stood there laughing I felt a hand brush against mine, I took it with firm confidence of what I was doing.

"Anna," I said, "I was afraid you'd gone."

"I'm right here." She laced her fingers through mine, moving closer, so I could hear her over the pulsating music. "Let's go," she whispered.

I saw Nell smile knowingly, as she repositioned herself in the circle so that I had to move closer toward Anna. I was struck again by the sweet brightness of her face, brimming with an easy American confidence. Even as she told of how frantic her first weeks in the city had been, it was with an upbeat demeanor that seemed honest and light and made me take to her.

The balcony was packed, and as our group continued to expand we were pushed near the wall, where we pressed against each other, and her body felt full in my arms, and her eyes twinkled mischievously with possibility that told me to take her home and feel someone's arms around me.

15

Her bare leg brushed against mine as a voluptuous breeze streamed through the taxi window, suffusing us with expectation as we sped along the West Side Highway.

Someone had invited her to an after party in Harlem, which she insisted we go to before calling it a night. It seemed too far away to be worthwhile, but our flirtation had advanced far enough that I went along with her.

We exited the cab and walked up five flights to a rooftop, where all the lights of Manhattan fanned out before us, like a deck of illuminated playing cards. The person who had invited her was not there, and the party was uninteresting, but she seemed to enjoy herself, so I bided my time and took in the view, as she sang along with a rap song I had never heard before.

"Do you think it's wrong," she asked, seeing the look on my face as I registered the words of the song, "for white people to say 'nigger'? Even when they're quoting black people saying nigger?"

"We can express whatever we wish," I said, realizing I was wasting my time, "as long as we understand what we are expressing."

"I agree," she said, missing the nuance of what I had said, and continued singing.

I excused myself to go downstairs, telling her I was tired and ready to leave. "We can share a cab back downtown if you like. But why don't you stay if you're having fun?"

She nodded, her face finally registering the situation. Before I descended the stairs I saw her start to dance with a thugged-out guy, who looked like he had just been released from Rikers that morning. I sighed with relief to be free of her and headed downstairs, stopping in the bathroom before leaving.

When I came out of the bathroom she was standing near the door, waiting.

"I'm sorry." Her pretty face looked up at me. "I hope I didn't upset you."

"Everything is fine," I told her. "It's late."

"You're a real gentleman," she said, "I like that." She pressed her sweaty body against me and wrapped her arms around my neck. "I like you."

Upstairs we could hear the thump of feet on the terrace, dancing to Biggie Smalls. Downstairs our mouths had closed upon each other's, and she trembled in my arms, letting loose a yelp of startling, primal ferocity, as the kiss grew in intensity.

We were both drunk by then and rode back to my place together, making out in the cab, where her cries of passion intensified, her entire body purring beneath me, like a crouching predator. She freed her breasts, which were full in the warm air, stoking the hunger that had throbbed between us all night.

"Take me," she commanded, when we reached my apartment. "Do whatever you want."

Seeing her in the context of my apartment made me realize what a mistake I had made. She was bland, with nothing special about her I could discern, because there was nothing special about her that she had discovered. She was simply part of a certain group at a certain moment, a way of speaking and dressing and looking at the world that was expensively purchased, but less than it wished to seem. Brands and references instead of personality. I did not want to be the kind of person who used other people for their bodies. Her skin crawled with sex, though, and the dull desire I'd felt when I first saw her renewed itself. I was not entirely reconciled to the idea of taking her to bed, and was even vaguely ashamed of knowing what I did and wanting to fuck her anyway. As I tried to decide what to do she coiled herself around me, and I smelled her truffled perfume and salted sweetness, my mind revving until I was sober again with the sudden thought that I did not want her. It was the bone of her hips that when I touched them flooded me with the overwhelming sense she was not my woman. My lust fled.

Her presence in my apartment began to fill me with sadness, and I could not adequately explain to myself how she had come to be there, as I searched for a decent way to bring the matter to a close.

"Take me," she commanded again.

"We should not."

"I thought you wanted me."

"I did. I do."

"Fuck me in the ass," she breathed.

I had no rational objection to what any two consenting adults did with one another, and believed firmly in the universal right to introduce any direct object in any prepositional relation to whatever indirect object so desired. I simply did not want her, and cringed at myself for trying to steal a handful of passion with someone I did not love. *Take me. Do what you want. I do not care who you are, I just want to get off.* Not: *Take me. I am yours. Do what you want. Just be careful what you do to me. I am yours.*

As she reached for me in the billowing darkness we started making out again, the booze and loneliness telling me to be satisfied with the woman in my bed. The voice inside telling me there is no broken blessing like when who is in your arms is not in your heart, and the better part of disgrace too.

"Let's stop." I pulled away.

"Why not just enjoy ourselves?" she asked.

I did not know what to tell her without sounding like a prude. It felt foolish and awkward already, and I issued a limp apology. The bridge of want between us had drawn back completely, as I traced her hips and derrière wistfully beneath the thin fabric of her shorts, knowing what desire there was between us was only the pettiest of lusts; and not the self revealing its true hunger and true generosity that I craved. Not that I was above lust. It was only that if I was to have lust alone I wanted it at least to be the ungovernable lust that would plunge me to the bottom of all wanting.

"You're not going to give me your black cock, baby?" I thought I heard her say. I chose to hear, *You're not going to call me a black car, baby?*

"You'll have to get a yellow cab on the street."

"What?" she asked sharply.

"I thought you asked me to call you a car." Some people belong to you, and you to them—as relatives, lovers, friends, or only kindred passengers enjoying a romp below decks when the ship is in the middle of the ocean and land infinitely far away. You realize how unnatural it is to be there adrift, but the crossing, the defying of what is natural, is what people do, and the holding each other is what delivers you back to the harmony of yourself.

There are people who do not belong to you as well, but sometimes your inborn sense of orientation is dampened, or you think to ignore it. I handed her the rest of her clothes.

"I'll take the subway," she said.

"It is too late."

"Then I'll go down, and wait on the street." She stormed angrily out of the apartment into the hall, looking thwarted and humiliated.

I followed her to the elevator, and rode down with her to the lobby. I had brought her home through some fault in my instinct I was nonetheless responsible to. She refused to meet my eye, and when we reached the street she began walking away in the pale morning light. I went after her, wondering how I found myself in such a situation, until she stopped at last, and a taxi pulled up to the curb.

"Goodnight," I told her, as she ducked in. "Get home safely."

She glowered a moment, refusing to speak, and radiating a look of utter contempt as she closed the door.

I went to the deli for breakfast, hoping Mr. Lee might be there to make light of my troubles. He had not arrived yet, no doubt he was home with his family. I took my egg sandwich and ate as I walked the deserted morning streets back to my apartment, empty but for the pigeons in their nooks, seagulls fishing over the river, and, high above them, a pair of red-tailed hawks, arcing and diving together upon their prey.

16

I was surprised when she tried to reach me the next day, and did not answer her call. I did not know what to say to her, and preferred to forget the entire encounter. I was nagged only by the question of what we owe those with whom we have shared intimate space, even if it's haphazard or ill-advised. Minutes later, she sent a text saying she wished to apologize, and I told her it was not necessary. When she called again I relented, thinking she deserved the opportunity to be heard and unburden herself. The feeling of closure and possibility of atonement.

I had an appointment near Union Square that afternoon, and offered to meet for an early evening drink, thinking it better to handle the matter face to face. She agreed, and asked to meet at the Boathouse in Central Park, at six thirty.

It was eleven o'clock already, and my head pulsed with a self-reproaching hangover, making it impossible to concentrate and get any work done. I browbeat myself to the gym, and afterward went to meet my former editor, Bea, for coffee.

Bea was seated in a booth near the window when I arrived. Her white hair fashionably cut, her dark eyes awake and focused as ever. She looked older than I last remembered, but radiated the same keen presence that struck me each time I saw her. It was an alertness that inspired confidence in whomever she gave her attention to, not merely in her but in a world that could produce such a magnificent person. It was reassuring just to be near her.

She saw me enter, and waved me over to the same table we had sat at when we first met, where she had appraised each new arrival, weighing their merits and defects without seeming judgment, like some wise, ancient elder who had seen all the spectrum of experience. The conversation that first evening went on into the small hours, as we discussed the best of what had been written and said, thought and acted upon. I was twenty-eight at the time, working as a stringer for the Associated Press, and more than a career opportunity it seemed to me the chance to learn from someone I respected.

She had dedicated herself to the same long conversation I joined that night since the sixties, and had never wavered in her seriousness of purpose or way of being, even if that way of being was esteemed differently in the current moment. It was right, I thought, the one, true way, even if by the time I met her it was already clear New York was in the depths of a gilded nadir, from which her kind of questioning, or seeking, had been banished. She wanted to speak "truth to power." It seemed quaint, now. And I saw her for the old hippie she was, the product of another time. Still I respected her as much as anyone I had ever met, because I had learned more from her than I had in my entire educational experience up until the moment we met, loved her in the unique way we love those we admire in our youth, when I thought if civilization ever needed to be remade from the first brick, hers was the hand I would want on the compass.

I knew she was dedicated to a cause she was too old to know had been vanquished, a fact that made me appreciate sitting there again that much more, because even if it was untenable it had been a beautiful, well-meaning vision, from a different time in America, and as a young man it had spoken to me as the only wisdom I needed. She was, I finally realized the day I quit and stunned her into a taciturn silence, my intellectual mother figure.

"So?" Bea asked, her gentle, unassuming voice carefully calibrated to a point midway between professional and personal familiarity. "How are you?"

"Everything is fine," I said.

"Really and truly?" She looked appraisingly at the remnant signs of my hangover. I felt naked and ashamed.

"Yes. I just had a late night."

"You should enjoy your youth." She nodded and waved it off, as we eventually came to what was on her mind, an assignment somewhere awful I had once been before.

"Not on your life," I answered, without thinking to soften it. I had kept abreast of the story, but I did not wish to go back. Witnessing such things did not prevent slavery, or the last war, or the next one; to say nothing of the genocides that did not affect the interests of anyone with the power to stop them. No one was interested in political murder, let alone the soul murder that happened every day. Nothing I had ever done and nothing I could ever do would prevent the massacre she wanted me to report from continuing. The only people who would read such a report in any case were those already constitutionally against such things, and they had no power. Nor did I, so it would only make me suffer, which is what I told her.

She was not the kind of person you refused lightly. I had never heard anyone tell her no, in fact, unless it was someone with something to hide. But she merely smiled at me indulgently so that I immediately understood my own foolishness.

"You're in pain," she nodded, "and world weary. I suppose I should have known. I feel horrible about what happened."

"Things happen all the time. Life moves on," I said.

"Yes and other platitudes." She held me in her eye a moment, then closed her eyelids in sympathy, as a car passed on the street blasting music loud enough to come through the windows. "Why do people listen to that?" she asked.

"It connects with them," I answered.

"Don't they know they are just selling every kind of falsehood?"

"They would say they are winning at America."

"A lie is a lie. All that talent, all that energy. People like that are supposed to be leaders, if I may comment on it. But maybe I'm too old to understand." She turned her thoughts back to the assignment.

I wanted to say yes, and I needed the work, but I simply could not bring myself to agree. I respected her, but felt then she only saw a portion of what we were talking about, and because of that a chasm opened between us, and also another, between what I knew and what I could say.

"Why is it—?" I stopped, on the verge of saying what I should not. I still respected her, even if she didn't understand how utterly narrow her worldview ultimately was. "Why is it—?" I began and stopped again. "Why have you only ever assigned me certain topics?" I broached it anyway.

She nodded, with a slow intake of breath. "I had never thought about it in that way. I thought you were doing what you were interested in."

"Not to the exclusion of other concerns," I replied. "At the moment I'm bored by politics. I'm bored explaining things to people who think they know everything, when all they've ever done is sit behind a desk in school or an office." I stopped, realizing I was answering with a negative. Telling her what I didn't want to do, because I knew only that satisfaction was not available to me in that realm.

"So what are you interested in?" she challenged.

"Art. If someone makes art of politics I will engage it. But only as art, not as some politically correct mission. What I need to know about politics I know. What I need to know about art seems bottomless."

"How do you propose to go about that?"

"I realize it sounds foolish. But do you know why I'm sitting here right now? It's because some teacher made me read *Oedipus* when I was twelve or thirteen, and first learning to read in that way that gives more complex pleasure than story. But the strange and liberating way of seeing that challenges you to look at something foreign beyond what you believe you already know, until it dawns on you: *I am that.*"

"You're Oedipus?"

"No, but I *read* Sophocles: A man unknown to himself, bright, angry, outcast, and blessed gets singled out by the gods for a trial no one should endure, and others could not withstand, or think they could not. Abandonment. Guilt. Shame. Loss. Exile. Friendlessness. Poverty. Blindness. Yet he endures, he endures, through the devotion of the one person who loves him in this world. Not for what he is, but for who he is. That is the only thing between him and death. This is what the gods have devised as his challenge, to know and accept who he truly is—beyond mother, beyond father, beyond status or civilization. Only after he has proven he can endure such a journey do they allow him grace.

"I read that and thought, yes, yes. That's the story of my life. All of it. And also how to live it. I accept."

Bea had been nodding, but shook her head slowly. "Life finds us wherever we are, even those behind desks. It's fine to close a chapter in your life, though. You are at the crossroads now, which I can see hurts in the way everything that makes us human hurts. So never mind work. You will come back to that or not. Tell me how you are in your life."

I recounted the past few months, and she nodded empathetically, asking whether I was dating.

"No. I'm not ready for that."

An inscrutable expression crossed her face. "No. You are not even within your own self again yet, which, of course, can never be the self that was."

"I am moving ahead."

"Good," she replied, finishing her salad, "so long as you understand the contents of your heart, if you'll forgive the advice."

"Bea, I'm sorry. You know I take anything you say seriously. I'm fine."

"Well, I'm sure you will find your sense of equipoise again."

"The film went well at least," I offered.

"I mean the kind of peace that comes from within. Managing pain is not the same as being free of it. Just because you don't want to peer to the bottom of darkness doesn't make it disappear. It only makes us unaware of our course through it, which everyone who would do anything, as you implied, has to thread. But there I go, giving advice again . . . " Her voice trailed off. "I should get back to the office. Call if you change your mind, or if there is anything you need. You know that, I hope."

"I do, and I don't take it for granted." I thanked her for the coffee, and the advice, and the feeling of understanding her friendship always inspired even when we disagreed.

It was six o'clock then, and my head hummed with the restored sense of possibility that comes from being in the company of those who see us, as I left to catch the train uptown to meet Anna.

At Grand Central the subway lurched to a halt in the tunnel, due to track construction, and remained there as six thirty struck and passed. There was no reception in the tunnel, leaving me unable to inform her I would be late.

The woman next to me saw me fidgeting, and gave a compassionate smile. She was reading a book of poetry, which led me to smile back at her, as she brushed a strand of red-dyed hair from her eyes.

I tried to make out the cover of the book she was reading, but the script was Cyrillic. It looked somehow familiar, though, and I asked what it was. "Pushkin," she answered. That made me happy. "I once knew a girl in college who read *Onegin* to me in the original so I could hear its music."

"An opera, or a chamber suite?" she asked; then, seeing the contemplation on my brow, "Was it a great love affair, or more ephemeral?"

"A love affair."

"You haven't had your great one yet." I grew self-conscious. I did not have a type, but she fit neatly within my template of attraction. If not for the previous night I might have allowed myself to take it as a sign.

However, I knew better than to allow myself to get excited about someone I met on the subway. That would only open the door to trouble. People have agendas, or worse, they do not know their own agendas.

"Are you late for something?" She turned to me again, as the train finally started moving toward the station. I looked at my watch: it was six forty-five.

"I may have missed it."

"It's too late for me to go to class, too," she said. "Would you like to have coffee?"

We were at 68th Street, and as we walked up the stairs chatting, she told me she was doing a postdoc in evolutionary linguistics. "Don't you think it's fascinating how you can tell the whole story of humanity through language?" she asked.

I cursed myself for the night before as I asked an anodyne question about whether her family were scientists.

She blushed until her cheeks were the same color as her hair.

"I'm the only person in my family to go to university," she answered, adding she was also the only woman in her extended family who had not had a child before twenty-two.

When I asked why she had not, she told me she had wanted to study, but married at twenty-one. When her husband disapproved, she left him to come here alone.

We surfaced from the subway awkwardly.

I rang Anna, but there was no answer. I began leaving a message, but before I could finish I received an incoming text: "How dare you stand me up," she wrote, full of outrage.

I called again, but she sent me straight to voicemail. I believed in generosity in my dealings with lovers—even former would-be lovers—but her self-importance made me regret again getting involved.

"It was not meant to be," Irina said, when she saw my plans had fallen through. "So—?"

My emotions were chaotic; the last thing I could risk, I told myself, was trouble. I did not know whether she was or not, only that I had a way of drawing to me those who had grown up under dictatorships, in exile, in pain. Girls who had seen people die. Literally. Spiritually. And who had been told they were difficult, ugly, stupid. Too smart for their own good. I did not know what she was about, but the cost of finding out might prove too high. It was the subway. Allure and danger were everywhere.

"It was nice chatting with you," I said, as we parted uncertainly.

But as she walked away, I regretted being closed to experience. She reminded me of people I knew with integrity, resilience, unjaded knowingness.

But as she disappeared I thought of Genevieve and felt what every fanatic, every tyrant, every sad sap in the whole history of the whole world knew instinctively, as he conspired to lock up his wives and daughters behind moats, under custom, under prejudice, under law: When you have lost your woman you have lost your way of life.

17

Before leaving the house the next morning for a meeting with my lawyer, Westhaven, I checked my e-mail, and found a dozen messages from Anna, each more wrathful than the last. "I have the number of the police, and I'm not afraid to use it," she concluded.

Police? I turned off the computer without answering her, and made my way up to see Westhaven, fearful of what I had gotten myself into.

His offices were in an art deco building in Midtown, where the security guard scanned my identification before directing me to the elevator bank, where another guard checked the credentials I had just been issued. I went through a turnstile, then ascended an elevator whose doors opened onto a nondescript office suite of understated good taste. Westhaven's assistant met me at reception and escorted me down the labyrinthine halls to his office, which was filled with books, diplomas, furniture carefully selected to demonstrate wealth without ostentation, and otherwise all the signs and codes you want from an attorney who understands the workings of the world. That it weighs you by a scale of outward signs. That it holds these things to be who you are and what you are worth. But the signs are false. A sign is not the thing. Both the measure that scale takes and the reading it gives are a delusion. But lives are shaped by it nonetheless. I paid Westhaven's crazy fees not because he knew more of the law than others, but because he saw more of the world through his own eyes.

Whatever problem I had he always put in clear perspective. And, as I had neared his office that day, I'd begun to have the sense of calm security I always felt there. He saw life, without cynicism or idealism, and so was a counselor of the first order. Learned, yet respectful of what he did not know. Discrete without being secretive. Shrewd but honest. Sophisticated but never condescending. Skeptical, yet open to new possibilities. Conservative without losing consideration for dreams and those who chased them. Intelligent. Modest. Intolerant of fools.

When I entered his office, he was busy at his computer, which looked out over the park, with his back turned to the door. It was eleven fifty-nine on my watch, and at noon precisely he stopped his other task and bounded energetically from his chair to greet me.

"Good morning, sir." He extended his hand warmly to take mine in a good, reassuring grip. He favored bow ties, and spoke with an easy, Middle American manner and cadence that belied the steel in his eyes, sharp and bright as bayonets, as we chatted amiably.

"You seem well," I said, feeling a peace of mind to be sitting there that morning.

"I had the most wonderful evening yesterday. My wife got us tickets for the entire Henry tetralogy at Cherry Lane. Last night was *Henry V*, and as I watched it, I could not help being struck that all true kings be measured by the hardships they face in order to know the full measure of the world."

"But not all who know hardship become great kings."

"It is the test of the man," he said. "With the best of them, I like to believe all is possible no matter what misstep. Those who are not the best, we are probably wise not to be too entangled with," he smiled, as we settled down to business, "whatever it may seem to profit us. Now, what gives me the pleasure of seeing you today."

I explained to him the situation with Davidson, which was that I had not been paid, as he took notes.

"Interesting, I do think they owe you an additional payment," he said, scanning a clause he had negotiated. "With your permission, I'll contact the production company to see whether that doesn't get things moving along. If it does not, well, it will. Let's assume for the time being it was only an oversight they need to be reminded of." He tapped his hand reassuringly on his desk. "However, that's only business," he looked at me. "May I ask you a personal question?"

"Of course."

"How is everything else?"

"We would be here all morning if I answered that fully."

"Well, I do not have to be in court today."

I explained to him the e-mail I received that morning, as he nodded empathetically, although it was impossible to know what he was thinking, or searching for, as he listened intently.

"Well," he sighed when I finished. "All of it is simply part of human nature. You shouldn't castigate yourself. Let it wash down the stream, and try not to step in that part of the river again, which you will not if you take it seriously, as you should and do most things."

"That is good of you to say."

"I say it because it is true," he replied, "and I see no earthly reason you should be less than fully happy."

"What do you advise that I do?"

"Nothing," he counseled. Real problems do not fire warning shots.

"And people who are unwell always tell us so, if we do not ignore what they are saying." He looked at me, and wrote down a number on a piece of heavy, embossed stationery. "You may have missed what was being told to you. If you are open to it, you might consider a visit to Dr. Glass, who did wonders for me a few years back when I was going through a rough patch."

"Is it obvious?"

"To others? No. To me? I know you."

"All the same, I do not want my head shrunk."

"Read the saints, then. They will put your mind at rest."

I took the phone number in any case, and thanked him, agreeing to call the following week about the contract.

When I reached the street again, I reconsidered his advice and saw no reason to resist being helped. I called Dr. Glass's office. There was an appointment that afternoon, which I took since I was already in Midtown, and I made my way across the park.

When I arrived Dr. Glass had stepped out for an emergency, but her colleague, Dr. Nando, agreed to see me instead. He listened, as I explained why I had come, and immediately suggested some pills for depression. "If Dr. Glass were here she would say it is more complex than that, and you are suffering not so much a mental reversal as enantiodromia, a mind-spirit split, and the only way to heal that is to embrace your deepest consciousness, all of which you know on some level, but which is different from comprehending. That is a question of being. However, unless—what for?—you want to go beating through the metaphysical weeds in search of the roots of your most ancient sadness—ghosts unheard a thousand years—you should just take the pills."

I declined the pills, thinking to get another opinion before submitting to them, but accepted a prescription instead for something to help me sleep. As I folded it into my jacket pocket, I asked if there was anything else I could do besides the drugs. He told me sport, and "Dr. Glass might suggest you follow your heart, and less your head."

I left the office, thinking as I walked of all the things they tell you as a kid, which, by the time you are an adult, are supposed to have worked their way inside of you. If they have not, or if you have discovered the things they first told you are insuperable lies, then through this rupture—between what you believed and what you have discovered to be true—everything else threatens to come tumbling out, until your entire being is up for grabs as you try to figure out what to stuff back inside and what to leave down in the dirt of the crossroads. Let the devil take it all.

18

Westhaven was right; I needed to take better care. He was wrong about Anna, though. The situation did not clear up when I ignored it.

On the way home from the psychiatrist I decided it would be better to get away for a while than to take the medication. I contacted Schoeller to find out if it was too late to join his bachelor party. It was not, but I would have to scramble to make plans.

I was able to use miles instead of buying a last-minute ticket, and the next day I went to see my doctor for a checkup and vaccination. I also wanted to ask about the pills Dr. Nando had suggested.

"Good drugs," he said. "Clean, few side effects. But I can prescribe pills for you. If you ever need a prescription let me know."

"Thank you."

"How is life otherwise?"

"I'm worried about dying."

"Why? You're in perfect health."

I'm not worried about *death*, I'm worried about *dying*. That I have not done enough. That there would be no more meaning even if I had. That the most savage among us, or else the most savage parts of all of us, prevail. I'm afraid there is no sense in life, and if there is I fucked up and missed it. That there are no second chances. "That's good to hear" was all I said.

"Relax. You have a lot of road ahead of you," he reassured me. "You're just a little exhausted. Take a vacation, it will help you regain perspective."

"I'm going to Brazil next week."

"You will need a yellow fever vaccine. While you are at it, you should get diphtheria, and there's a new vaccine you should have too. When was your last hemoglobin, by the way?"

"Eleven years."

"They only last ten."

"What's the new vaccine for?"

"Diseases guys like us don't get."

"Who gets them?"

"Guys who don't take the vaccine."

He was a good doctor, but he was locked in a death dance with the insurance company for every nickel he could charge them. I played my part and took the shot.

The next day I went to get new contact lenses from swaybacked Dr. Nelson. When he hunched over the microscope, though, he was the image of Hephaestus, as he worked a miracle to make me see better.

I was glued together pretty well after that, but I still felt something was wrong. I could not point to anything specific. There was simply something wrong, and I did not know what. When Nell called that afternoon, telling me she had to see me right away, it seemed to confirm my diffuse worries.

"How did you find that one?" she asked incredulously, when I arrived at the restaurant where she had asked to meet. "A real Adela Quested."

"What are you talking about?"

"Never mind. That girl from the club, Anna."

"I don't want to get into it. She's—"

"Crazier than the Mad Hatter on angel dust, is what she is," Nell said, cutting me off.

"She's just dull."

"Did you do anything with her?"

"No. Why?"

"Listen," she hunted around in an enormous green leather shoulder bag, until she retrieved a tiny, white, metallic square. "You know, she's been calling everyone. I don't even know how she got this number," Nell said, waving her hand over the device, which woke up with the sound of Anna's voice defaming me in the vilest terms.

"Oh. Why do you say that?" I heard Nell coaxing her along, in her best Linda Tripp voice.

"Because I can," Anna said. "Who does he think he is?"

"He's one of the most decent people I know," Nell said at length, after Anna had gone on long enough to discredit herself completely. Good old Nell. "If things between you were not what you wanted, maybe it is because you were not honest with him or yourself, and now you're angry. I don't know, Anna. I wasn't there. Then again, maybe it's because of the way you were raised, or the things in your head."

"My last—"

"I'm not done," Nell said. "But I have what I need. Listen, I know you're not from here. I know you don't know what you're doing. But I do, and if you don't stop all of this immediately you are going to find yourself in very serious trouble. Do you hear me, Anna? It's not the kind of attention you want," Nell finished, per- fectly composed and perfectly frightening. "I see through you like a broken window. I just thought you should know that."

"I don't know what to say," I said, as the recording ended. "You taped your conversation with her?"

"I cover my backside," she said unapologetically. "I thought you did, too. Why didn't you tell anyone?"

"I thought it would go away," I said.

"I should have seen through her whole innocent act at the club, sorry. You know what happened to Matt."

"You weren't the one thinking of taking her home. Yeah, I know."

"What did she say to you?"

"Does it matter? It's the risk of taking someone home."

"You know, and I'm not saying this because she's from the South, half of people still live in the nineteenth century."

"You let it hinder you, or you take it in stride."

"I'm glad you can make light of it."

"Thanks to you," I said.

"Fifty percent of people can't see beyond their own experience."

"I'd say ninety."

We let it drop, as Nell read my unarticulated thoughts, at least the ones that were uppermost. The thoughts beneath that were hidden from her. How could they not be? They were still hidden from me.

"Just find someone good and solid. There are tons of great girls. Only be careful," she motioned with her hand to imply the city, to incriminate the Western world, "of the bad ones."

"Well, as my Aunt Isadora would say, you do the best you can. The rest is in the hand of the Creator."

"That is a nice thing to say. You don't believe it, do you?"

"It is what my aunt says."

I was sanguine when I left Nell, but as I rode the subway home I was struck by how horrifically wrong things could have gone, and not only from taking home a stranger; from any arbitrary deed committed or not committed, by yourself or anyone else. A rushed decision, haphazard luck, bad timing. The world was full of disasters-in-waiting. It made me numb to think about, until the only way I could keep from being consumed by paralysis was to grasp that paralysis was exactly the trap laid by my enemies.

Once I saw this I tried to let the entire episode flow into the past. I knew the larger pattern and meaning, but it was not the rope that would hang me. Beyond that, I tried to find in myself the smallest parcel of empathy for Anna. More than that I could not do, but that tiny parcel was enough. From no higher principle than I believed forgiveness a virtue. Not a moral one, simply the self-preserving virtue of knowing the heart that cannot expand in forgiveness—even for those who slight it, even for those who have no claim to it whatsoever—is the most devilish instrument in the world.

19

It had been a wretched spring and, as I boarded the flight to Brazil, I was glad to be putting it behind me for what I hoped would be a new start. By the time I changed planes in Atlanta the hot air felt restorative, and I started immediately to relax, pleased to be out of the city, as the heat made me sweat and aware of my own body. Before boarding my onward flight I checked my messages, and saw Nicola had sent me a text telling me she would be in New York that week. I wrote back to let her know I would be out of town, then downed a sleeping pill.

As I turned on my noise-canceling headphones the artificial quietude was flooded by sour memories and the crippling feeling of a vast, cosmic emptiness. I realized I had lost my orientation, would not even know how to properly describe myself other than the role required of me in a particular context. My present role was traveler on an airplane, and I could neither name any self nor feel anything solid beyond the contours of my seat pushing up from the floor of the suspended flying machine. I had no other beliefs. The feeling attacked violently, from deep within, threatening to overwhelm all my faculties, until finally I plugged my headphones into the jack and turned on the in-flight entertainment system to crowd out the emptiness.

Twenty minutes into the movie, I started to doze off from the pill, and went to the bathroom to remove my contact lenses and brush my teeth.

I do not know what happened next, but when I awoke there was an oxygen mask over my face. The steward told me I had fainted in the aisle, but that it was probably only exhaustion. I nodded lethargically, and went back to sleep.

When I awoke it was morning, and we were over the coast of Bahia. I fell back asleep and did not wake again until the wheels of the plane touched the runway in Rio. I retrieved my luggage from the carousel, bought a newspaper and *café com leite*, then exited the terminal to find a taxi.

I was soon stuck in the morning rush hour, overwhelmed by motion sickness from the stop-and-go traffic. I opened the windows to let in the fresh, humid, air, but was soon choked by the exhaust of whizzing motorbikes and diesel fumes from trucks. I was forced to close the window again, and curled up in the seat and closed my eyes in an attempt to keep from vomiting.

The driver, seeing me fidget, caught my eye the next time I looked ahead, and asked if I was okay. I told him the pollution was making me ill, and he suggested an alternate, if longer, route. I agreed and we pulled off the highway at the next exit. When he saw I had regained my composure, he began to re-create for me an argument he had had with his wife that morning. My Portuguese was limited to the superficial amount I could remember from a college class, combined with cognates from other Latin languages, which was perfect for his purposes, since it allowed me to follow the story only if I kept absolutely alert to what he was saying. He gleaned this, and smiled. He needed someone to hear him, so I listened as he filled the sealed interior with his woes.

We finally pulled up to the hotel, a boxy, glass-and-steel affair from the seventies whose best days were well in the past. Its single charm was in being directly on the beach, with palm trees offering shade all around, beckoning optimistically.

When I went up to my room I found the interior as rundown as the exterior, but was pleased to discover I had a little balcony that opened to the sea. It was still early in the morning, and I opened both the double doors to let in the breeze, then lay down for a nap.

I had only just closed my eyes and started immediately to dream, when a banging at the door blasted me wide awake. From the ruckus in the hall I knew it was my friends, and opened the door to find Schoeller, Freddo, and Doc, who lifted me in a great bear hug. "There he is, in the cheapest goddamned room he could find," Doc said, peeking around the room. "We are glad you came, but why are you so mean to yourself? You live once. Everything is available to you. Why not take it?"

"I flew right," I said.

Doc had arrived in college after a stint in the Navy, where he was stationed in the Pacific doing intelligence. He had spent two years after that living with a tribe in Micronesia, until it was time for him to either take a wife or come back to the West and try to unify his experiences. After all of that he took school with a grain of salt, working hard enough to get into medical school, but not so hard that there was ever a Friday he did not skip classes to play golf. "Come on, let's get this man to the beach," he said to the others, after looking me over. "He needs a sun cure."

They had been drinking since breakfast, and before I could change for the beach someone pushed a *caipirinha* into my hand. I went to get my swim trunks and bathing towel, and we headed down to Leblon.

It was nearly winter in the Southern Hemisphere, but still warm enough for the beaches to be packed, the tourists to be sunburned, and the homeless people to sleep out on the sidewalk. As we passed I gave a *real* to a mother begging with her child hitched against her hip, who was immediately harassed by the security guard from a nearby business, informing her she was begging too close to the entrance of a nearby mall. The way he spoke to her reminded me we were at the southern terminus of the old slave belt, whose northern edge was the Mason-Dixon line.

"You should let those people be," Doc said to the guard: "Beggars are holy. They trust the universe to provide all they may need."

"Maybe, but they're bad for business," Schoeller said.

The city was in the midst of a financial boom, and the air along the grand boulevard at the front of the hotel was charged with the thrill of new money vying against the anxiety of the old.

All of it melted at the shore into the democracy of the sea, along with my own worries. It was my first time in Rio, and the country felt like the New World in miniature, so much so that by noon, as we lunched at a beachfront café, I felt perfectly at ease with what to expect.

We retired for a siesta after lunch, and did not go out again until evening, when we had a lavish dinner atop Santa Teresa. After eating we piled into taxis, and Doc gave the driver an address across town. We drove out through the hills surrounding the city, past the outskirts of a ghetto, which looked like every other ghetto—kids too old for their age, premature sicknesses, somewhere to buy liquor, somewhere to play *fútbol*, a dancehall, no visible means of egress. I felt my earlier sense of division return, and began to watch everything from a remove, trying to decipher the society around me, until we eventually reached an industrial district, where we rolled two levels down a garage ramp, before stopping at a security gate.

Schoeller spoke into the camera at the gate, and the metal barrier receded into the ground, opening onto another ramp, which took us down a third level, where we were greeted by a doorman at a lavish, well-guarded marble entranceway, with a discreet sign above the door that said unironically, *Cielo*.

The manager came to the entrance to welcome us, and escorted us into a sumptuous room with a walk-in humidor and wine cellar stocked with mature wines and aged cigars. In the room next to it was a chef grilling aged Argentinean steak, and in a larger room, girls in every corner, each more beautiful than the last. The room was furnished with antiques modeled after the Topkapi Palace, with rare Persian carpets and Ottoman artifacts. Only the girls were young. Tall girls, short girls, thin girls, buxom girls. Sweet girls, ruthless girls, desperate girls, good girls who had lost all trace of innocence, cynical girls whose experience of it had ended before their childhoods. Black, white, Asian, indigenous, mestizo, octoroon, quadroon, *cafuzo*, *castas*, they only have names for in the local language, and others they just invented with the last people to get off the boat and had not named yet. Whatever you wanted, whatever your unvoiced fantasy, whatever moved through you, dancing together in groups, laughing and winking, as we toured that palace of vice.

"Bunga bunga," Freddo said.

"Technically," Doc corrected, "bunga bunga requires the presence of water."

"Please," Schoeller begged, "don't be a fucking pedant tonight."

"I can't believe you are having your bachelor party here," Freddo said. "You're getting married."

"And when I get married I will be married," Schoeller answered. "I am not yet."

"Do you mean you will give up places like this once you are married?" Doc pressed.

"No."

"He's not marrying for love. Should he also give up pleasure?"

"What are you marrying for then?"

"Because we share the same values, and are devoted to the same way of life."

"That makes it okay?"

"Once I'm married, it will mean something different to come to places like this, is all I mean." He was marked by resignation as he looked around.

"I don't care that he's lying to his wife," Freddo protested. "I care that he's flaunting it, and making all of us complicit in his lying."

"Please shut up, Freddo."

"I can't be here," Freddo protested.

"Why not?" Doc demanded. "You are not forced to do any-thing. What are you afraid of?"

"It is because you see bodies. I see the poor girls I grew up with. I see my sister. My mother."

"That is just a real cry for help."

As much as I disliked agreeing with Freddo I shared his qualms, but for different reasons. Brothels were the nexus of everything I objected to. Besides commoditization of the body, the other interests colliding there were equally nefarious: human trafficking, drugs, violence, and a global network of corruption that flowed back into the legitimate economy. It was in fact one of the points where the legitimate and illegitimate mar-kets mingled, and otherwise upstanding citizens aided all that civil society must necessarily abhor.

I did not say anything, but took it all in as we toured the rooms, more curious than anything else. I had never been inside one before. But the girls were beautiful, in so many different ways, as though someone had assembled a working definition of female beauty until, as we rounded a corner to the penultimate room, it was impossible to know where to focus your attention. There a forty-foot-high waterfall cascaded down from the ceiling, and a group of sirens frolicked in a pool beneath it.

"There," Schoeller said, clapping his hands toward the water, as Doc fished in the interior pockets of his jacket and started passing around pills, "is the bunga, baby."

"What's this?" Schoeller asked, taking one of the pills Doc had passed.

"Molly."

"The others?"

"China. Bolivia. Adderall. Sugarcubes. Valium. Methadone. Morphine."

I knew then it had been a bad idea to come, but simply declined everything, until Schoeller lit a long, thin-stemmed pipe and passed it my way.

"What kind of hash is this?" I asked, exhaling a beautifully exotic taste in a plume of violet smoke.

"The opium kind," he answered.

My muscles relaxed, and soon turned liquid, as the room began to swim pleasantly around me; I found a divan to relax on, while the others fanned out through the club, each in search of his respective desire. The last I remember of any of them that night was watching Doc leave around midnight with a coven of flame-haired she-devils. To do what, I could scarcely imagine.

My mind was swimming happily along the edges of the room, watching the light bend and colors merge, as I fused deeper and deeper into the divan. I had the sensation of falling through a trap door and descending ever deeper, until all that existed was music and color and light. I was completely oblivious to where I was when an Amazonian goddess appeared from the ether, and sat down next to me. She only spoke Tariana, a native language, and our conversation was halting at first, but soon felt completely fluent as she opened an app on her tablet that showed pictures of various poses, starting with starfish, and growing progressively more tantric.

"I do this, and this, and *this* if I like you. If I *don't* like you, I do this. This if you're good, and this if you are wicked."

I wanted all she showed me, as I looked at her and wondered what it would be like to fuck a goddess.

Even if I had decided to leave with her, it would have been impossible, because I could not find my limbs. But as I lay there debating with myself, two other women approached, a tall, light one and a taller, dark one. Both looked like mutants from some further stage in human evolution as they sat down on either side of me.

"What language?" The taller one asked, as she took my head in her lap, while the other took my feet, stretching me out between them. The light one spoke Italian, Arabic, and Spanish; the dark one Japanese, German, Afrikaans, and Dutch. In the state I was in I spoke them all as we laughed and they asked if I wanted to go upstairs. Temptation was wearing me down, and I thought to go, telling myself it would be worthwhile if only for the experience. However, through a colossal and super-valiant effort of will, I declined.

They left and I was proud of my willpower, self-satisfied that I remained true to my discipline, as I watched the lights and color bend so that there were no longer angles in the room, only swooping curves of red and purple emotion until I locked eyes with a woman standing directly across from me, who I remembered seeing when I'd first entered, but had lost sight of amid the undifferentiated faces. When our eyes locked, though, she came to me right away, smiling enigmatically and asking what had taken me so long.

She was a large-eyed, big-bosomed country broad, no other term would do; there was something earthy and old-fashioned about her seductiveness. The kind of woman you hope to find on a lonesome night: apple-bottomed, quick-witted, bewitching, Old and Middle English words from the womb and the milk of the language.

Not beautiful, maybe even a little bit homely if you were slow and missed the point; when I looked at her, there was no explaining it, my dick signaled like a compass. A roost cock, keening and crowing to her soft heat as she sat down and took me in her lap, rocking me back to my first body.

"You work in entertainment," she said perceptively, "but you were in the army before."

"Close," I answered, asking how she knew. She shrugged, and ordered herself a drink and put it on my tab. We began to talk and I poured out my tribulations, my conflicted desires, my whole damn life. She crooked her head to the side, looking down at me, and told me to wise up, I had a grand life if I looked the right way.

"Let me get you a spyglass, Watson," she said. I still didn't understand, and she didn't answer again, only slid down and cradled herself against me to show me what she meant.

"Let's go," she said.

"I should not," I answered. "It is against my code."

"Your what?" she asked.

"My code."

She laughed. "That is because you still do not know what is right for you, or what you want. If you did you wouldn't say *should*. You would say *will*."

"I don't will anything from this place," I said. "That's not what I'm about."

"Come with me, let me find out what you're about," she teased.

"I suppose you will help me know what I want, too," I said.

"Yes," she answered, turning serious. "The body has a knowledge of its own."

"I do not sleep with odalisques."

"You still do not understand, do you? That's not what I am."

"What are you doing here, then?"

"I am a professional lover."

"What does that cost?"

"What is that worth?"

"What is the difference?" I looked up at her, but she was just a light among all the lights.

"The qualia of experience," she answered.

"That's a fine word."

"I used to read in the library, when I dropped out of school and moved to the city to find a job."

"You should have stayed in school."

"If I would have had money."

I had studied enough languages to appreciate the complexity of the verb tense she had constructed. "That took effort to master."

"The compound subjunctive," she said ruefully, "is the story of my life. If I would have known, if I could have done, if it should happen that. If it were up to me. Should it ever be. It's not really the same in American as Brazilian, though. It's the official verb tense of mad visions and inconsolable sorrows, and belongs to poor people and dreamers. This lifetime brought to you by the subjunctive tense."

I laughed at her nerdy joke. At the same time I was touched and knew I was going to leave with her, despite my own rules. Smart girls turned me on.

"So," she said, taking a sip of rum. "The physicalists believe all phenomena can be reduced to the material. The essential concern with all of these things is, of course, how consciousness arises from the body. Whether the consciousness, or soul that makes us human, is only another phenomenon of the body."

I was too far gone to follow, and asked her to clarify.

"Take for example a hypothetical woman, named Maria, who is a brilliant scientist but has lived in a black-and-white room her entire life where her entire life's work has been to study the red of flowers. She understands red is the longest wavelength visible to the naked eye, and she knows how the brain is excited by and reacts to red. She knows, in fact, all there is to know about red, without ever having seen it, or a flower.

"One day Maria decides to finally leave the black-and-white room. She steps out from her little box, and she sees the world for the first time, and she sees red for the first time, and she sees her first flower. Does Maria know what red is?"

"I don't know," I answered. "Does she?"

"It's just a philosophical game," she cooed, stroking me playfully. "Not real life. They like to ask questions like that because I think God does not talk to philosophers very much."

"Why did you bring it up then?" I was confused, still burning to know the answer to the question.

"Because, baby, I know all there is to know about love."

She may have said *you*. She may have said *blue*. I do not remember. I was high on opium, and she had me in her hands.

20

She led me through the halls of that ode to Dionysus, to a room carpeted in silk and exquisitely woven cushions, where she slipped off her dress, and led me to a marble bath. She undressed me and drew the water, then led me in, where she washed me and afterward toweled me dry, before massaging my entire body with rose-scented oil. We went to bed and she laced her legs, long as a country day, around me and I felt perfectly within my skin, undivided in a way I had not since I was a boy. We made love and it was as she said, she was a professional lover.

The next morning, as we sat in bed she kissed me before rising from the sheets, looking down at me still amid the pillows. My head hurt, and my cock, and my conscience as well. "We had something, *meu amor*," she said, rubbing my temples. "Maybe not what you're looking for, but something all the same. You should drop me a postcard from time to time. Come back and see me when you can."

"I do not think I will be back this way again," I said, even as I warmed to the sound of her saying *my love* in the unguarded southern way. "So you don't have to lie to me. I know it's business. Me projecting a fantasy onto you, and you playing it back to get money. It's okay."

"No," she said, smoothing my brow tenderly. "Sometimes I think when people say anything is only business that's the lie. Maybe I didn't choose the best work, but everything is real. I'm still a woman. You are still a man. This is still life. And I'm glad we met, even if you would never let yourself fall in love with a *puta*."

"Come back to bed," I reached for her. Sadly, tenderly. Full of pain and vulnerability that flashed the brighter amid the seediness.

"Just remember what we talked about." She kissed me when she finally left a while later.

"Remind me."

"Oh, *amor*," she smiled softly. "You will remember. It is what you are truly looking for."

I tried to recall what we discussed the night before, but it was all as distant as yesterday's dream. "I can't remember anything," I said.

She hugged herself to me warmly, and rested her hand on my chest briefly and just smiled, before leaving. When she walked away all I could think of was an hourglass.

I shambled back to the hotel, still unable to recall the details of the night before. I felt a tarnished, divided joy, sadness and liberation tempered by self-reproach. All I could remember was a feeling between us of pure physicality, an absolute freedom of being completely in the body and completely at ease. If there was no more truth to it than that, at least there was nothing false.

The only falseness was between me and myself.

It was eleven o'clock by the time I reached my room, where I discovered the maid vacuuming, and my luggage nowhere in sight. When I asked where my things were, she shrugged and pointed a finger toward the roof. I knew what she was talking about, and took the elevator up to Doc's suite, where I found Schoeller and a couple of random guys splayed around the living room in various poses of sin-sickness and suffering. Schoeller was still bumping cocaine from a tiny spoon.

I went to the bathroom to shower and change, then crashed across the bed, where I was fast asleep when Doc showed up half an hour later. He was swaddled in a fresh linen suit, happy as a butter thief, and wide awake as the morning he was born.

He glanced around the room, shaking his head with dismay as he considered us. "Amateurs," he pronounced, before shoving Schoeller aside on the sofa, to open his bag on the table.

"Where have you been all this time?" Schoeller asked.

"Up Corcovado way, to say confession."

"There's a church there?"

"No. I went to speak directly to *O Cristo*. What I did, no priest could comprehend."

"Where did we lose Freddo?" I asked.

"In jail. Here. This will even you out." He was passing out uppers to those who had gone too far down, and downers to those who had gotten too high.

When he reached me he opened my eyes wide with his fingers, before searching them with a penlight.

"First time?" he asked.

I shrugged.

"She gentle with you?"

I smiled.

"Kiss you on the mouth?"

I admitted to it.

"Wrap her legs around you, and rock you in her arms until you felt the heat from the center of the world?"

I laughed weakly.

"Say what you needed to hear? Make you forget your worries, and feel like she knew you? Laugh with you until the darkness shone like diamonds, and make you remember how bounteous loving can be?"

I closed my eyes in wistful reverie.

"Wish you met her under different circumstances?"

I winced.

"You give her all you had? You give her the jailhouse key?"

"I don't want to play this game."

"Circle well done. You found a saint in a cathouse." He grinned at me, and placed a horse pill on my tongue. "Eat this."

"What is it?"

"This one eases the conscience."

He turned back to the room. "We need to get moving. We're driving south to Ihla Grande to surf, and then a little surprise I've worked up."

"No more surprises."

"Mermaids."

"Definitely not."

"Wait till you get there before you decide. We also need to go spring Freddo from the pen, and buy him a new watch."

"What's he doing in jail?"

"He refused to give his girlfriend a present last night, like a good little boy, so she gifted herself his watch."

"How did the police get involved?"

"When he realized it, he lost his cool, then she lost her cool, and security came. He still did not calm the fuck down, so they put him in the tank to chill him out."

"Why didn't you spring him last night?"

"And ruin the party? Besides, nobody told him to check his common sense at customs, and, because he is our dear brother, as all of you are my dear brothers, I decided to leave him in peace awhile to remember himself. Just as someday I will find new livers for each of you. Now, when we get him, he will be repentant, and no longer an adjective-defying asshole."

"I'm fine bailing him out," Schoeller said. "But let him get his own watch."

"We have to," Doc answered, "because he will not have time to do it before going home, and Doris gave him that dumb watch for their first wedding anniversary, when he had no bread and she was making cake. So if he shows up without it she will know something happened, and he will not be able to get himself out of it without lying to her. She will figure this out, of course, and send him to hell. They don't have the kind of relationship where he can simply go home and say honestly: Sugarstack, I know you don't want to hear this, and it's not what I want to be telling you at all, but I was unfaithful to us and as a material consequence lost your watch to a ho in Rio."

"Let her leave him. Who cares if they get divorced?"

"First off, there is no such thing as divorce after you've had children, only nonconjugal polygamy. Second of all, raise your hand if you want him sleeping on your couch. Better to do it this way.

"Why does Doc care so much?" I asked Schoeller.

"You don't know? His father dropped him off in a place like that when he was fifteen, and never came back for him."

"I don't believe you. What kind of father does something like that?"

"His father was a politician."

"How much did you pay her, Doc?" I asked.

He smiled. "You miss the point. It is not about money but her self-worth, and that each time she meets a man like Freddo, a tiny portion of that dissipates, until she has no illusions except what is permanent in the heart, and, she is too young to know this, but by the time she realizes it she will be on an unalterable course she does not control, and to which she has sacrificed herself. Who am I to say what it takes to compensate her for that? Even she will not fully know for years, when she comes to understand what each of you knows, which is the world is brutal and whores do not love anyone. Except, well, me and Harper here."

"How much did it cost, Doc?"

"It does not matter, it was a gift. Not payment or substitute for human affection, but a genuine token of esteem, as she is a person and I am a person, and as our friend was not a person, and as the police, who are not people, became involved, and as she alone has it in her power to press charges or not, I, in the name of all our persons leaving this country come Monday, made a contribution to the scholarship fund for her children, who do not know their father, as well as to the retirement account her guild does not provide."

"Why didn't you get the watch back then?"

"Because, fool, the policeman kept the watch."

It was Sunday, and the stores would only be open a little longer, so Doc, who was fluent in getting things done, went to the precinct to get Freddo, while Schoeller and I went to buy a new watch, which we could do in any language.

We spent two hours after that searching high and low for an engraver, until we were able to track one down to his house, where we paid him to open the shop.

When we met back at the hotel in the late afternoon Freddo was there, sheepish, unable to bring himself to say anything as we loaded into the car for the drive south.

When the city snarl unfurled to the open highway, he tried haltingly to account for himself, looking around at us with battered eyes.

"Don't explain," Doc said. "You have nothing to say."

We continued in the Atlantic silence, and by the time we were two hours on the road his sheepishness had worn off only a little. We stopped for a late lunch at a roadside restaurant, then surfed on an empty stretch of beach, and napped in the waning sun. Freddo's shame was starting to burn away by then, and we presented him with the watch.

"You got it back?" he asked, wide eyed with relief. "How did you manage? Thank you."

"No. We bought you a new one."

"I have to find an engraver," he said, panicking. "If I go home and Doris sees the inscription missing she will destroy me."

"You don't deserve her."

"I know."

"Say it again."

"I don't deserve the woman who married me. She deserves better, and everyone else knows it too."

It was awful to hear, because it was true, and he looked good and miserable and full of self-loathing for one of the few times since I'd known him.

"Okay enough groveling," Doc said. "Look on the back."

Freddo rotated the face of the watch in the dying light, and the timepiece was new, but the inscription was what had been there on the one she first gave to him: "For the only man I ever loved. All my hours. All my life."

We hit Ihla Grande just before sunset, with still enough time to get in a little more surfing. A group of locals had claimed the beach for their own, and when they saw us approach with our boards, one of them threw a rock to warn us off.

"If you were not here since morning, you cannot just show up and have the last wave," he snarled, the sound of heavy metal blaring from a speaker beside him.

"If I am here for the first one tomorrow, then I can have the last one?" Doc asked.

"What language do you need me to explain the concept *get lost* to you in?"

"Whatever pleases you," said Doc.

"You impertinent delinquent," Freddo said in Spanish.

"Did he say impertinent?" one of the kids asked.

"He is trying to stone us to death with syllables."

"Japanese," said Doc.

"As you wish," answered their headman, whom they called Jeitinho, in Japanese, so Doc swore to us afterward.

"You can't just come in the morning and take the best wave," Jeitinho said, drawing from his joint, and blowing smoke at Doc.

Doc looked at the kid and inhaled from his own joint, and nodded to the kid he thought it was a fair rule.

"Sure we can," Freddo said, pushing out his chest. "This is a public beach, and we came all the way here, and this pipsqueak is not keeping us off it."

"Chill," said Doc. "He lives on the wave and that has rights."

"All you tourists come all the way here from somewhere, but you don't know anything about this wave," the kid said.

"I've been riding waves since you were swimming in your father's gonads, you punk." I realized as he said it, Freddo was afraid of the country, which was why he kept behaving like a gringo.

"Punk?" laughed Jeitinho. "That is a compliment in these parts. Cankerous mulefucker, there's an insult for you."

"Why did you call the sheriff a mulefucker?" One of the other kids asked.

"'Cause he ain't good enough for no horse."

Freddo snorted sardonically. "Your life," he said, thinking of the cruelest thing possible he could tell the kid, "is not going to be what you imagine."

"That's enough," said Doc. "There's always another wave."

"There is only one wave," said Jeitinho.

"When I was a young knight errant, I believed the same," Doc nodded.

"What's a knight errant?" asked Jeitinho.

"It is all knights who follow their own path."

"Ain't no knights I know about," said the boy, "but knights who follow the grail. Mine is this wave, and you and your posse of jokers are in my path."

"Admirable," said Doc, "but the wave is not your grail. Still, I will not take it away. What's more, I like you, my friend, and will smoke with you."

Jeitinho smiled and nodded, pleased to be acknowledged with respect, as he passed his joint to Doc, and Doc passed his joint to the kid. When they had finished the exchange the kid asked in earnest what Doc meant when he said there was more than one wave. Doc finished the joint, and told the kid he was failing to allow for either the non-Euclidian possibilities of the question, or the bicameral nature of the body, but would learn it all in time. The kid nodded and told him he had no idea what he meant but he liked his style so he could surf with them the next morning, but not the rest of us. Doc demurred, telling the kid he should surf his wave while it lasted.

We went swimming instead, further up the shore on an unmarked beach, where we discovered a cove carpeted with oysters, which we harvested from the cyan waters. When we had hauled our treasure back to the beach, we began shucking them greedily, except Freddo, who had not brought a knife.

"Where's your knife?"

"I didn't know I would need one," Freddo answered.

"A man needs a knife."

"Can someone open some for me?" The question was answered by silence, and averted eyes.

"The woman shamed you, Freddo," Schoeller said finally. "The lawman shamed you, and even the kid should have taught you something, if you do not see it."

"See what?"

"Freddo, have you ever stood naked before a mirror and asked, if I were dropped, just as I am right now, in the middle of the jungle, what would my place be in the natural world? Could I survive? What would I serve? Who would I be?"

"Never mind." Doc opened his kit bag and retrieved a Chesapeake stabber, which he tossed to Freddo's feet. "We would not want you to starve."

"You can use his, or there is a village up the road, where you might be able to get one of your own," Schoeller said.

"Jerk. I don't know the language," Freddo answered, looking at the darkening, unfamiliar road, and then to the plump, cool oysters and the shucking knife shining in the dying sun, as he tried to figure out what kind of life to have.

When we had opened the remaining oysters, sprayed them with fresh limes, and slurped them down with the arctic cold local beer, the sun had set, and a bonfire appeared on the beach.

It was what Doc had promised, and there began to appear every predictable pleasure.

I refused to join, not wanting anything more than to enjoy the sea and the stars, and not sink any further beneath the waves.

"You're not coming to the party?" Doc asked.

"Not after last night."

"Why not?"

"I broke my code."

"Your what?"

"My code. There is a right way and a wrong way of doing everything."

"And that is your code?"

"Yes."

"And you broke it?"

"Yes."

"So you have sinned?"

"I have no God. I only have my actions over myself."

"Even better. You have sinned boldly. Now you are free. So you broke your code. What happened to you? Nothing is what happened. You did not go to hell. The world did not become any worse or better, except to the extent your own sufferings were added to it. Or were they alleviated? That is in you to decide. You say whore. I say the Magdalene. Jesus's wife."

"That's a historical misreading. Mary Magdalene was conflated with two other women in the sixth century."

"Do you ever let up?"

I knew he meant to be helpful. But I did not know how to let go. How to float in the hands of fate as he seemed to do. Was afraid of what might happen if I did.

"Let yourself make mistakes," Doc said sympathetically. "Let other people make them. Trust the universe a little. You are free to take up your code, or drown it in the sea and make a new code to live by as you wish. Only stop flagellating yourself. You have done it since we met. It drives me crazy. It drives you crazy. First you wear one mask, and so what if then you wear another. They are only masks. But the universe makes everything, and allows all things. The difficulty is only understanding what portion of it all He allows to you. Now did you do something wrong, or only forfeit your imaginary right to judge Schoeller and Freddo? That is for you to answer, for my part I absolve you."

"You're a doctor, not a priest."

"I've been ordained, by the Church of Universal Life, for the wedding. Besides, in my tribe who heals the body also heals the spirit, so if you wish to be in thrall to some rule outside yourself, by the powers of the Church of Universal Life, I hereby absolve you of all sin. Here is your brain, your heart, your courage. Now what happens when you sin again?"

"I will not."

"Poor Protestant. It is part of the journey. The hero's heart is bound by an evil force, he is stuck in Casablanca, trapped at the bottom of the well, and only love will alleviate it. Or else he goes off on a journey, without knowing why, for something mysterious and impossible as the lost ark, which has a hold over him he cannot explain. Somewhere along the way he falls off the path, Siddhartha at court, seduced by the world, or betrayed by his own sad little ego, and has to be helped back onto his path, but broken now of the sin of judging, and off he goes again, in search of his ark, which he now knows is not whatever shadow first set him off, but love itself. Always love. And beyond that, of course, himself. So he is allowed whatever he chooses, so long as it comes from his joy, and not child-ish conscriptions of what you must not do. It will increase his path, and is the only way forward. The path itself flows from that. Maybe she's the woman you were supposed to marry, but you could not see it because you had in your mind some received idea of who you should be with. Suppose now you go back the other way and find someone who checks every box on your list and you get married, then seven years into it you have been having the same fight for all of eternity, and you wake up one morning and understand you are not in love. Will you abandon your wife, or will you find the part of yourself that is connected to her, not because of what you have in common with her, but because of what you have in common with all humans? What if only then do the true depths of love open up."

"Anything else I should know?" I asked sarcastically.

"That is all of it, except there is worse falling in this world than yours, so don't privilege your own. Heaven has always and ever belonged to the blasphemous, who stray and somehow find their way again. Even the Buddhas have to pass through that, and only a fool would think to escape it. Embrace it, until you are done falling. After that fall no more, my friend."

It was well-intentioned advice, however the sadness I felt was not repentance for doing something wrong, rather it was exactly for the freedom he spoke of. The terrific burden of knowing the heart was the only god of right action, and like any god it divined but did not discriminate, meaning if I gave up my rules I had no way of knowing where I would be led. Because my heart did not trust how radiant it was.

All I did know was what I thought I knew before no longer seemed true. I had no more earthly idea what I was doing.

BOOK III

21

On my return to New York I swore off meat, alcohol, tobacco, and sex in a fit of remorse. But nothing I did put me at rest, or made me feel any better. I even went to see Dr. Glass, but talking about my dreams seemed like a waste of time. My parents I had little to say about. My father because we had barely spoken to each other for as long as I could remember before he died. My mother I had no memory of at all.

I realized it had been more than a year since I had seen my Aunt Isadora, and went for a visit, hoping it might make me feel more grounded. But afterward, when I returned to my apartment, I was met by the same gloom. I realized then there was no need for me to be there. If I was ungrounded, I was also unbound and could do whatever I pleased.

The rhythm of life and sense of possibility in the south attracted me, so when my friend Drew suggested I spend some time down in Farodoro, I decided to make an extended stay of it.

In addition to Drew, it turned out I knew several others in the city. When I settled into my rented apartment, in fact, I soon realized the country was festering with expatriates. Some were there for the exchange rate, others for business; several claimed to be helping the world; but in reality all were taking advantage of the special status those from rich countries received in poor countries, unaware of the hidden cost they paid for the illusion by which the middling was called large, and the large declared great.

The only thing less sufferable were those intelligent enough to be aware of it, yet still happy for their different deals, because without that they would be what they were at home: industrious but second best, or talented but lazy. The natives did not complain. They accepted it as the way the world spins.

Yet nothing could mask the fact it was a place for the lost. Those who had let go the thread of their way, uncertain where they should be headed; what path had brought them here; whether they had it within themselves to push forward again; and, for the worst cases, whether forward was a virtue at all.

The things they saw and told themselves were shared delusions, referring to nothing but the world in front of their eyes; their own egos and insular experiences, subject to no other standard but what they themselves knew. These mirages displacing reality were tokens of the things they sought, but never possessed, which pulled them in ever deeper—not into that country, which they never saw—but into their own fantasies, and delusions of their place in the world, so that reality was left ever further behind.

For the permanently lost among them, those who had no meaningful place in that world, and no place in the one they had left, it was where they ended up when the illusion they nursed—that purpose could be instilled from without—finally ran aground. Here they would idle indefinitely.

For those for whom it was a temporary station, there would be a day of reckoning and quiet reproach as they grasped how ill-conceived the venture had been from the start, like pictures from an awkward age or a drunken vacation of which you wish every copy destroyed. They would blame their misfortune on youth, on others, on the country itself, and move to the next station with fanciful tales, painted exotic and glamorous. The past would then become more meaningful than the present. There in the past they had tried to be somebody, had dared something, and that shining fantasy shielded them from the brutality of the present in which they were only ordinary, and not special as they had been misled into believing. In the mind of the lost it is always the world that is upside down.

There were enough stepped-on dreams to bust your own, and they wore them on their sleeves. If I judged them harshly it is because I feared with every inch of my fiber becoming as lost and directionless as they were. Maybe they were right and direction did not matter. How easy it would be to stay there at the bottom of the world. I ran from that scene as fast as I could.

"He's blond," one of the guests, a spook I knew from D.C., with diplomatic cover at the embassy, said excitedly of his son who had been born in the country. "Here it means he can be president."

I met the boy on a later occasion; he was a bright boy, and around other bright children might be shaped into something fine. In the ambiently corrupt hothouse of special deals and special pleading they were setting him up to be something less. Not only were they mediocre, they trained their children to be as well.

"You know the gentleman," another guest, a local, asked after I left the conversation.

"He is an acquaintance."

"How does he have so high a position in the State Department?"

"He works hard. He is pleasant to people, dependable, does not bellyache or wet the bed, and plays the game they give him. That beats most people."

"Yes, but don't they know he's an idiot with no idea what is going on here?"

"Yes, of course, they know he's an idiot. That's why they sent him somewhere he can do no harm."

"You know, they say he works for the CIA."

"I had not heard."

He smiled at me knowingly. "You are a friend of Drew's?"

"Yes. You know her husband, Diego?"

"Since we were tadpoles, this high." He held his hand a foot from the floor. "How do you find the country?"

"What I've seen I enjoy."

"If you truly wish to know a country and her people you must know the land. Our villages in the Islas del Lemuel are especially pleasant this time of year. Tell Diego if you decide to go. I will have my uncle and aunt show you around. It is the perfect place to rest and relax."

It was high summer in the Southern Hemisphere, and the locals had all decamped to the coast and highlands, and after a few more days in the city I decided to follow their example.

Drew and Diego helped me arrange a house on an island up river, which promised good air and the peace of the water. I booked passage out of the city by train, and Farodoro was barely a memory by the time the ferry buzzed to a floating halt next to a dock in late afternoon, as the passengers scampered ashore before the gap between the boat and jetty grew too wide. If this happened, the pilot would go out into the river and back up to the landing stage again, yelling all the while at whoever was responsible, as the other passengers, who were forced into this time-stealing routine every time a greenhorn left the launch, regarded the new arrival with righteous annoyance for keeping them from their holidays and barbecues and sport and friendships and lovemaking.

Mornings I went swimming off the jetty behind my rented cottage. There was also a rowboat for my use that I liked to take out on the river, to fish at high tide. My second day there, though, the tropical rains came and the river overwhelmed its banks. I took the precaution of bringing the boat in from the dock, to tie it up in the yard before the storm, and set out early the next morning to row around the island. Besides mine there were only three other houses, all weekenders and empty, and I was alone that gray, watery morning with no idea or care for what would happen to me when I went back to New York. I was a free man in a free country, my own life in my own hands, and I was content with how simple and beautiful life could be, the way certain mornings make you want to live forever.

When the high water receded I discovered a trail that circled the inner perimeter of the island, which made for good exercise and nature-seeing whenever I was in a less amphibious mood.

I kept more or less to this routine, until I was told after the storm, by Doña Iñes, the woman who kept the market on a neighboring island, to be careful because someone had spotted a jaguar on one of the islands. They were native to the area, but no one had seen one in years. Whether it was a rumor or the truth, her warning had the opposite effect. My curiosity overrode my fear, and the possibility of spying such an elusive animal on its own terms made me add evening walks to the morning ones I already enjoyed, hoping to catch a glimpse.

I never saw the jaguar, only the woodpeckers and herons singing their Magellanic morning song, and sometimes a Pampas cat or two in the feral loneliness of dusk.

After my second weekend the other houses all closed down for the season, their inhabitants returning permanently to the city from the winter holiday, leaving me with the entire island to myself, which pleased me fine. I had brought books, and there was also an athletic club and bar on a neighboring island, which I would row to on those evenings when isolation overcame me and I required company. But mostly I swam and fished and enjoyed the watery sunsets and walked the land, trying to tame the hollering tempest within.

❧

In the middle of my fourth week I made a trip to the main island to get supplies. I was back home, still in the kitchen after putting away my groceries, and reading to myself aloud from a book I had been trying to get through since college—watery consciousness, dirty language, fall from grace, a writer's journey, a wife's journey,

golden bonds, a rock a tree a river circle and alchemy of life—
when I saw a silhouette out beyond the screen door.

"May I help you?" I asked.

"Señor Roland?" A woman's voice called.

"Yes," I answered in Spanish. "How do you do?"

"We are friends of Diego's family who live at the other side of
the island. We saw your lights, and called the owners who told us
you were still here. I'm Mrs. Saavardra and wanted to invite you
to our place for an *asador*."

"That's kind of you, Señora."

"Any night you wish, just come by. We usually take dinner
around nine o'clock."

"That's very good of you."

"This weekend we will have visitors from the city, so perhaps
you might like to come by then. It should be a marvelous time."

"Thank you," I said. Señora Saavardra set back out for her side
of the island, as I tried to decide whether she only meant to be
good mannered, or was being busy, or whether it was the local
custom and I was obliged to go. I thought to call Drew in the city
to ask, but decided in the end I could not be obliged to do anything. I was there to be with the reality within myself. I no longer
cared about how I was expected to behave, or what I was obliged
to do, but simply where I was and how I would be with myself.

22

The local market was poorly stocked and I had taken the rowboat downriver toward the sea to try and earn my supper. By the time the sun began setting over the brackish water I still had not had any luck, and was dreading another meal of rice and lentils as I rowed back upstream.

When I reached the island the Friday ferry was docking at the little pier, and I bobbed in its wake while the passengers from the city came ashore. It was a bank holiday in Farodoro, and the residents of the other houses had returned for the long weekend, waking the island again with the buzz of laughter and activity. As I tied my boat and came ashore I saw everyone had left the dock except a woman sitting on top of her luggage with her back to me, looking around for her host.

I was so used to spending my time alone by then it did not occur to me to help her, and I walked away absent-mindedly, until I saw another resident stop and offer her directions and help with the bags. Her host, a white-haired gentleman in late middle age, had arrived by then, though, and they embraced familiarly before starting out for the other side of the island.

When she stood I saw clearly how striking she was, and the flash of beauty reminded me of what vanishes, time past and what was in it; and in the embrace I saw what remains, also time and what is in it now, and what might be in the fullness of the future for those with courage to seize and hold fast. I realized how much road was ahead of me still, and it was then I was stirred to go to the Saavardra's party and no longer simply shut myself away.

The island was crisp from a breeze blowing in from sea, and the evening light the color of old cognac as I walked through the forested interior to their place. The lights from all the other houses were aflame, and every so often the sound of merriment was on the air. Other than that it was only the cerulean sky above.

The Saavardra spread was built facing the water, with a high, formal gate that led up a path on the island side through the landscaped grounds. It was overgrown with vegetation, blending so discreetly with the surroundings that I had not noticed it on my wanderings. There were two outer buildings immediately inside the gate, between them the blood-red clay of a tennis court, and then a wide expanse of manicured green lawn, still sodden from the last rain. There was no buzzer or knocker on the front door, and I rapped my knuckles against the hardwood, listening as it echoed inside the house.

"*Buenos tardes, Señor Roland. Bienvenido,*" Mrs. Saavardra greeted me. "You are just in time for drinks."

She walked me through a set of pleasant rooms, grand in proportion but comfortably furnished in a way that attested to freedom from care. Out on the veranda at the front of the house, Mr. Saavardra sat alone smoking a cigar, listening to Beethoven's *Moonlight Sonata* playing softly, and watching the birds flock in the diminishing light to nest.

"How good to finally meet you," he said convivially.

"Thank you for the invitation," I replied. "I hope I am not too early."

"No. I am always happy whenever we have guests. You see, this house was my wife's idea, and it is always lonely for me here." He lowered his voice conspiratorially. "I detest nature."

He was in his early seventies, with a dignified, easy manner which I liked immediately. "Why did you build the house, if you do not enjoy it?" I asked.

"Because my wife told me to," he sighed, pouring two glasses of chilled red wine, and handing me one. "Men who want peace do ninety percent of what their wives ask them. The secret to happiness, of course, is finding a woman who wants from you mostly what you want from yourself."

"And the other ten percent?"

"Five percent is eternal mystery," he said. "The other five percent depends on the type of man you are."

We drank our wine, which was good, and I complimented him on it.

"My father and uncles used to make this wine," he told me, not without pride. "Now my cousins make it. The wine is the same. Only the people change."

He freshened our glasses and we went down the veranda to the front lawn, where there was a pitch of dry sand and bocce balls, which we picked up and started playing.

"You are a journalist?"

"I was," I said. "That part of life is behind me."

"It is good for young men these days to have more than one career," he nodded. "There is so much to be curious about. You are in your prime, and so you must embrace all of it. Young men should want to change the world. Old men need it to stay the same."

"I try as best I can."

"Don't try, *caballero*. Do. You are in your prime, and master of your horse. You know its power, it knows the power of the rider, so will finally go wherever you instruct. Jump as you command. In five years more, if you have not already, you will have taught your horse to somersault and fly. Five years from there you will no longer need the horse."

"What business are you in, Señor Saavardra?"

"My grandfather poured his life into a piece of land in a desolate part of the south. My father hired men to work the same land for him. Now my brothers manage a company exporting what comes from that land. When I turned seventeen I knew I did not want anything to do with the dirt. I left for university, and later

joined a bank, where I spent the next forty years of my life buying
and selling companies that farmed and mined the land."

"Fate. Was it a good business for you?"

"It was not bad. I have no complaints. I married young, though,
and now our children are all abroad and my wife somewhere made
her own life, so now I am just another old man who does not
know what to do with the days."

"You did not have things you wished to do in your retirement?"

"No, that is a problem, you see. In my family the men all died
young, and I never considered the idea of retirement. I know now
that eventually I must end up back on the land."

He had lived in Boston as a student, and when I asked if he
enjoyed his time there he frowned faintly. "Yes. It was a very
pleasant city," he answered diplomatically. "Beautiful, clean. The
people were a little racist, but what can you do? That was when I
was there, of course. I do not know how fast such things change.
Always they hear an accent and think certain things about you,
and you are not supposed to notice, and if you say something
they will deny it. Or they see that you have some money, and then
you are a man, or only another dollar. They wish to do business,
but it is a sullied affair by then and they do not even know it, so
you must decide if it is worth it. Whether you will exercise your
indifference, or decide to demonstrate the superiority of your discipline, or else show them the magnificence of your heart."

"I am sorry you did not enjoy it."

"No, on the contrary. I enjoyed my time there immensely. But
I quickly saw the lie of the country, so was happy to return home,
and then, for what I sought to do, and people I needed to prove
myself to, no one would be impressed if I earned another degree
or not, only that I had something of value to contribute. It was the
middle of a financial crisis, and the problem I wished to solve was
not theoretical, but that my people were suffering. I hope you do
not mind my frankness."

"I find frankness refreshing."

"I am too old. I say what I think because it no longer matters to the world, or my place in it. When it mattered I kept it private. Do you think that was cowardly?"

"I think you did what you had to."

He was beating me soundly at bocce, and we debated the relative merits of different countries as he told me how his name came about when his grandfather landed from Sardinia, he thought it sounded illustrious. It was an enjoyable conversation and I was sorry when it ended.

"I had better prepare the *asador*," he said, after taking the third game from me. "Thank you for humoring me."

"You flatter me, *señor*."

"No, *caballero*. I have been playing this game a long time."

We went to a side porch, where he stirred the burning wood for the barbecue, before turning a crank to lower a heavy grille over the flames, and began placing thick cuts of meat over the fire, explaining to me where on the cow each cut was from, when he saw I took an interest, and that the wood was from a tree that had been cut down in his family's vineyard. I admired the joy this simple pleasure gave him, and the care he took in what he was doing without being showy, as he distributed the embers and tested the heat of each part of the fire before placing the proper piece of meat over it. I realized it was part of his atomic unit of being in the world.

As he cooked, the other guests began arriving from the boat launch, and other houses, beginning with the Maldonados, who lived on one of the nearby islands. Both were psychiatrists in their early fifties who radiated intelligent wakefulness. "It is a mixed marriage, and shouldn't have lasted this long," Mrs. Maldonado said slyly, after we were introduced. "Pablo's a Lacanian. I'm a Jungian."

After chatting awhile, she went inside to seek out Mrs. Saavardra, and Mr. Maldonado came to the grill, taking a glass of wine with us around the fire, and asking how I was enjoying the country.

"It is pleasant here," I remarked.

"Well, you must come back one day," he said. "All the young people have left to find something new. Not knowing that we do not have to seek experience, it finds us whether we desire it to or not."

When the meat was ready, we ferried it to the dining table on the veranda, where Mrs. Saavardra and Mrs. Maldonado were deep in conversation with the other guests. "*Olé*," they all exclaimed, when they saw the platter piled high with the steaming meat.

"*Gracias,*" Mr. Saavardra said humbly.

We sat around a large wooden table in the open air, and began to pass bottles, bowls, plates. "Sylvie," Mrs. Saver, called into the house. "Everything will get cold."

"*Momentito,*" a cloudless, self-assured voice called from inside the house.

"Don't wait, Harper," Mrs. Saavardra insisted. "It is best when it is still hot."

"I will wait," I said.

When the door opened a few moments later it was the woman from the launch that afternoon. She was a few years older than she had seemed from afar, with a presence that suggested character, and a guarded watchfulness in her eye.

Mrs. Saavardra had seated us next to each other near the end of the table. She was American, down visiting relatives, but made it clear from the outset she did not care for my attention, which was fine since I was not looking for anything with anyone, but to be myself. After the perfunctory politesse, we barely spoke through the rest of dinner. "I know you don't offer help to strangers, but do you mind passing the salt?" she asked.

"I was lost in my thoughts." I did not offer any further explanation, only put myself on guard to let the meal pass without incident. I marked her down as judgmental, the type who thought her experience of things was all of it. She was an attractive woman to make small talk with at a dinner party, nothing more.

We ignored each other for the remainder of the meal except, *please pass the salad, thank you,* and other conversational bibelots.

Mrs. Saavardra saw we were not getting along, and looked disconcerted. Mr. Saavardra looked at Sylvie and looked at me and looked at his wife and chuckled to himself.

"Tell me," asked Mrs. Maldonado, to break the tension, "what brought you here."

"I came by accident, really," I said.

"There are no such accidents," she replied. "This place must have called to you for a purpose. How do you spend your days?"

"In recreation," I said, careful not to betray any more than that.

"Or re-creation," she replied. "The natives thought all thoughts, and all words, remain in the universe forever. Some points on earth focus the vibrations. These islands were an enchanted gateway to the netherworld and the cosmos, and the center of their place in it. They held their initiation ceremonies on them, because only in such places was full knowledge of, and access to, both worlds possible. They came here to remember their place in the universe and reconcile themselves to it."

"I never knew that," Sylvie said.

"Jung said man is indispensable to the completion of creation, is its second creator, giving it objective meaning. It is this consciousness they were tapping, the one that gives us our place in the process of being. So it is exactly when we seem to do nothing that we are really returning to our most primary function, which is to experience our place in existence."

"It's a second active principle, activated by the first in the same system," her husband mused. "The idea of god can only resonate if you believe in god. Naming it presupposes its existence."

"Maybe," Mrs. Saavardra added, "or it means what King David meant when he told his people, 'You are gods.'"

"What is the difference between that and what the rishis teach in the Vedas?" Sylvie asked.

"What do they teach?" I asked.

"That there is full consciousness, then a higher, or deeper, consciousness; beyond that is all of consciousness."

"That is an interesting construction," said Mr. Maldonado, who mostly listened and rarely spoke.

"What allows us to construct it? What allows us to figure out the laws of nature? To make music? How strange is it they should be comprehensible, and we are the only animal on the planet the universe has given the ability to puzzle over and understand it."

"So far as we know."

"We are simply the universe looking back at itself."

"Or," said Mr. Maldonado, "characters in a text someone has written."

"But isn't the text just an image, to focus the mind on the idea of god? To bring it home that god makes all things, even his own reflection?"

"I am not a believer."

"Why don't you believe?" Sylvie asked.

"When I went to church as a boy—"

"Don't tell me you let the church get between you and God."

"Still, you mean *an* idea." Mr. Maldonado corrected.

"No. *The* idea," Sylvie interjected. Mr. Saavardra gave me a fresh glass, which he filled with a different wine. "Like the feeling you get in Rome when you realize even gods die. Or are consumed. And see the clock of life and the clock of history, and understand that there is another beyond that."

"I have never been to Rome." I drank the new wine.

"He means wherever you were the first time you grasped time," Mrs. Maldonado said.

"Go to Rome."

"Yes?"

"If only to see how thin are the things we tell ourselves are permanent."

"He had a girl there he almost married. Tell him about the girl."

"It did not last. Was is there to say? I was young, headstrong, even careless. She was beguiling as she was proud and reckless. We had a divine affair that burned everything all up. There is nothing remarkable to tell." His voice was sad with remembered happiness and unbearable knowledge. "When I left I am not ashamed to say I wept. I still do not know whether it was the perfect agony of a divided love, or only the melancholy of leaving Rome."

"You think there is no difference between their story of god and our own?"

"I think, for the most part, there is only an eternal masculine, an eternal feminine, and a demi-divine human."

"And you think it is experienced the same by everyone, or are there ten billion ways?"

"What I'm curious to know is whether anyone here has ever had direct experience?"

We all contemplated the question in private silence.

"Have you heard about this new man in America," Mr. Maldonado asked when no one answered, "who has a theory that all of us, and all of the different ways of being, are just different organs in the same body?"

"I don't see what's new about that. Don't the Buddhists say since forever any path is only a path?"

"Do they include their own in that?"

"Yes."

"That is honest of them."

"Do you have to follow a known path, or is it permissible to create your own?"

"Even if we follow a known path, aren't the steps we make our own?"

"I'm not that advanced yet."

We had a lively debate, and I was impressed by their learnedness, and the seriousness with which they took their inner lives, and the inner life of their society, as we talked under the stars until the embers faded and the bugs on the patio grew too fierce.

As we began to move inside I was overcome with drowsiness and made motions to leave. My days started with the sun; they were all still on city time. They were adamant I remain, though, to keep even numbers as we split into teams to play a card game, and later, charades with the names of movies, which was difficult since I did not know the local films, and also because some names were completely different in translation.

I feared making a fool of myself, but my self-consciousness quickly gave way to laughter, although Sylvie took glee in ribbing me.

"Señor Roland is clever," she said, as I mimed a title. "For a gringo."

Her aunt began to reprimand her, but stopped when she saw Mr. Saavardra shake his head in bemusement. We played the levitation game after that, and everyone was full of pleasure and the oxygen-rich ocean air increasing our majestic mood.

Mrs. Maldonado, who reminded me of Bea, was inspired to sing, and soon we all were. When I heard Sylvie sing I was surprised by the strength of emotion in her voice. Not for the first time that night, I found myself trying to reconcile the qualities about her I did not like with the feeling here was a person of substance. As I listened to her sing I also wondered what shelter she had lost, what child of hers murdered, or gone astray, what husband she witnessed wither with work, to make her sound so ancient and wise.

"Harper," Thiago asked, the formality having melted hours earlier. "Do you by chance play tennis?"

"Not well," I said.

"We have a lovely court," he offered, "which you should feel free to use."

"I saw it when I arrived, it is a lovely court. Thank you."

"While the weather holds, please feel free to play whenever you wish."

"Would you like a game?" I asked. "As long as you don't beat me as badly as you did at bocce."

"I'm afraid my knees do not allow me to play much anymore, and when I ignore their advice it is my pride that puts an end to it. Sylvie is quite accomplished, though."

"You played competitively?" I asked.

"Not seriously," she said modestly, "but I played."

"When did you stop?"

"When my father lost all his money."

"I'm sorry to hear that."

"No, it made me know something about life." She looked me directly in the eye with the full, steady gaze of someone who has done copious self-reflection. "What it means to have things, and what that is worth. What it means to lose them, and be without, and what that teaches you. But mostly, what it means to dream and to chase recklessly."

"He get what he was after?"

"It cost him a family."

She did not say it with bitterness, but a matter-of-fact evenness that touched me that much more. I did not know whether her sadness was in the past and healed or permanent, but she seemed sterling clear, without either illusion or anger, and there was no question that I liked her. Not with lust, simply the way some women make you think about family.

"Do you still enjoy the game?" I asked, turning the conversation back to tennis, and our plans for the next afternoon.

"I enjoy what it shows about people," she answered, with what seemed to me a challenge.

"Don't be lulled," Mr. Saavardra cautioned. "If she offers you a wager, don't accept."

"I won't bet," I said, "but I'll play."

She and I talked in the airy living room a while longer, sometimes disagreeing strongly, but whenever she laughed I saw how alive and free she could be, which softened any edge.

When our conversation broke off we looked around to see everyone else had gone to bed. Realizing we had talked so intently, we grew awkward and I stood to say goodbye. She looked at me full and steady again and smiled with the transparency of those who might see us fully, and I was arrested another moment, sensing some unseen possibility and abundance just out of reach.

There was nothing dramatic; a tiny lunette opened—unformed desire—until our shared question—fear, uncertainty, caution—was whether we would leap through the high, small pane or flee. It was a feeling I knew not to trust. The pain of erring was too much.

We broke apart—the tension between us alive enough to name. The current was soon replaced by awkwardness, as I thanked her for her family's hospitality and excused myself to walk back around to my own side of the island; feeling, as I made my way through the dark, the quick pulse of want and hope from some other body hidden within me that wished to override the rest with its own certainty. I silenced it with the simple, rational knowledge that I did not know her. It was merely something in my subconscious that had caught and fought back irrationally, and difficult to resist.

23

Thiago answered the door the following afternoon when I arrived.

"I hope we did not keep you up last night," I apologized, as we waited for Sylvie in the vestibule.

"I am sorry we did not say goodnight," he said. "But we did not wish to interrupt your conversation. You know, Sylvie is an excellent person, a deeply good woman." He nodded thoughtfully. "The women on that side of the family can be real forces."

"Friends should not be involved," I said.

"True, but men and women need each other. What are rules in the face of that? Some of them matter some of the time, and others are arbitrary. Even those that matter become irrelevant when you have in mind the thing you must do in work or life. There is no authority above that. Power, consequences, perhaps. Authority? Not for people who know what they are about. You elect your values and burdens and way of being after considering carefully the options available to you, and their cost. Who is great serves what is great, and pays the cost. Who is less, serves something less and pays for that. But I think you know this already. It is something we hear in the first part of life, and only understand in the second.

"I trust you, in any case, to know what you are about. If you do, everything else is in compliance. Things will work out or not. The rest, only the two of you can determine: whether she is whom you would be responsible to, and entrust with your life, and vice versa. If so, the only thing for me or anyone to say is, *Olé, señors.*

"If she is not, you will know in an afternoon, and she will know inside an hour. Whatever this true voice says, you will abide by. That is the way to be gentle with each other. You are young, enjoy your game."

"Thank you," I said, as Sylvie entered the hall breathlessly. His exhortation in another context might have made me apprehensive, but here it only made me glad to see her so well loved.

"Whatever my uncle said, don't listen," she said, looking at each of us as he went back to his study. "He is old-fashioned and patriarchal. Did he tell you I'm an innocent virgin?"

When she alluded to sex it made me flush and as we walked to the court, where we hit a few balls to loosen up and get a feel for each other's game before we started to play. She had beautiful form, and beautiful instincts for the game. She could not out-hit me, so worked patiently, waiting for my errors. I had weight in my right arm, and relied on my harder serve and forehand to make up for any lack of finesse when she tested my other wing. In the end I took the first set, not beautifully but I won.

Midway through the second set my legs began to cramp, but I played through stubbornly until the end of the set, which she won. As I tried to stretch out the cramp, she came to see if I needed help.

"I am fine."

"Don't be macho. Tell me if you want to quit."

"No."

She smiled and laughed, and we started the third set. The cramping did not let up, however, and she showed real concern for me. But I was determined to play through.

She was mindful of my situation in the beginning, until I gloated the tiniest bit, after a long rally. After that she was meticulous and relentless, making me run as much as she could.

"Don't worry," she said, "I will still respect you when you lose."

"It's not important to me."

"That you win, or that I respect you?"

"Either."

"So I see." She laughed.

"What do you see?"

"You're in a bad situation either way."

"It is only a game."

"That is what my ex-husband used to say, and he meant it. But I don't believe you think anything is only a game."

"You were married?"

"Yes. I thought I mentioned it last night. It was what you were supposed to do at the age I was then, which was also old enough to know better."

"Who did you marry?"

"A man I thought was the right kind of man to marry."

"He was not?"

"He *was* the right kind. He just was not the right man. Uncle Thiago is the only one who saw that, and questioned why I was doing it."

"You didn't know?"

"I didn't listen. I was doing what I was supposed to do, because I did not know what *I-me-myself* wanted to do. And even if I had, I might not have known how to do it, let alone how to be in a real promise with someone else. I went ahead with it, and it was just right, except for the voice somewhere saying, are *you* sure? Are you *sure*? Of course I wasn't. How could I be? But the people had been invited. The hall was reserved. I walked down the aisle to the wrong prince, and the wrong castle. They all look the same from the *outside*. But once you get *inside*, oh boy little boy, that's a whole other story."

"How long since you divorced?"

"We separated three years ago. We just filed the final papers. I came here to get away from all of it. The papers had a meaning I didn't expect, and the lawyers were a way I did not know."

"But you're a lawyer."

"Not that kind. I know about hammering together constitutions, not chiseling apart marriages."

"Sorry it was difficult."

"No harder than it should be. But no one ever listens to that part of the fairy tale. They tell you all these little girl lies, and I'm sure they told you little boy lies too, and then you are living to fulfill the lie, not knowing what else there is, and so you are stuck in a relative life. I have this in relation to that. But still need that over there. Once I find my prince, my castle, my pot of gold everything will be fine. For men, it is probably just: be tough and work hard. That is the only thing you think is required of you. But you think I'm just justifying my mistake."

"How do you know what I think?"

"I'm sorry. I should not assume. All I meant to say is if you have just a partway idea of yourself, how can you have a wholehearted relationship to anyone else? Does that make sense? It's too hard to understand what another person goes through, if anyone ever really does, if you don't know what you yourself have been through, so that was the hard part of it for me."

"You think you know now?"

"I see the look in your eye. Maybe. I just hope someday, some wise kindergarten teacher will take all the boys and girls into the coatroom, right after they have heard their first fairy tale, and tell them the score: Okay, now forget everything you just heard about the end. You are going to keep hearing it in everything they tell you from now on—how beautiful the princess is, how rich and handsome the prince, all about the gold standard. Just listen to me, kids, and pay close attention. First you will get lost in the woods. Or waylaid by ogres who sell you out to the witch, who is going to put you in her pot. Or else you will spend the best hundred years of your life fast asleep. And for you poor coyotes who think you are clever, Acme has special traps they are going to use to fix you up like Ozymandias. If not that, it will be the dragon who catches up to you and singes you to within an inch of your life. You will have to spend years in psychotherapy explaining why you can't go into the kitchen, because you are afraid of fire, and that's why you're so goddamned thin."

She took a drink from my water bottle, before finishing her thought. "So you might as well do your own thing starting now, and live your own life in your own way, because I promise you this, whichever way you head, and whatever it is you're after, if it is worth anything at all, sooner or later it's going to hurt like hell."

"Can't we all just stay out of the woods?"

"What, and turn into the dragon one scale at a time?"

Our game was long since ended, and we were sitting on the red clay, next to the net posts, careless of anything else. I wanted to spend more time with her, and invited her to join me on the river later in the week.

"I return to the city tomorrow," she said. "I can come back on the weekend, and we can go out together then."

"I would like that," I said.

"I see what you are thinking," she smiled. "Don't worry."

"Don't worry about what?"

"You are wondering whether I'm available."

"I am?"

"That's what I would wonder if I were a sensible man and had met a random girl I liked. But you should not. I have paperwork to take care of in the city that will dredge up old feelings, and I'll be sad and probably cry. But that will be to clean it all out. Hopefully you won't get insecure, or run away, because it will just be the sadness, complex but complete, you feel for what is vanished and gone. I will be better than new after that because I know something I did not before. Some of it I wish I did not, but I do, which makes me wiser and perfectly available. And if you play your cards right—who knows? So, second date?"

As I listened to her the idea lodged in my mind, and with it that joy of anticipation and new possibility. I was impressed again with her forthrightness and self-possession, and not anxious as I had been the night before, as I commanded myself to meet her steady gaze, and tried to observe what I was feeling, which was that perhaps it was not only my subconscious that was being snagged but my spirit.

Still I only did not know what our next meeting would hold.

24

A torrential rain was falling in Farodoro and predicted to sweep over the islands by evening, lasting through the weekend. Sylvie postponed, and I rowed to the main island in the afternoon for supplies to last through the storm. At the counter I asked Doña Iñes for batteries, but she had already run out, so I bought candles and extra matches, hoping if there was a blackout I would not burn the place down. There was only intermittent Internet on the island, and I had not read anything of the outside since arriving, so I put a stack of days-old newspapers in my basket as well. I scanned the headlines as I waited on line, saw the world was unchanged since I'd left, then put them back.

"*Oh, mi niño,*" Doña Iñes said, pushing me aside and packing my rucksack with the groceries, when she saw how ineptly I did it. She was from the Canaries, and had married a local man who died on her three years after she arrived. She never remarried or had children and called everyone "my child." But I thought she was especially fond of me, because I knew her island and all about how the sea was there, and the fish and volcanoes and the light of first day in the middle of the Atlantic.

"*Buena suerte con la tormenta,*" she waved, as I took my supplies out to the dock.

"*Gracias.*"

Outside again I could see the pregnant, swollen clouds up river, and hurried to get back before they burst. As I loaded the boat the unmistakable sound of a child's crying reached me, and I turned to see a nine-year-old girl, in a navy dress, bawling on the other side of the wharf.

"*¿Por qué lloras?*" I asked, looking up from the boat. The child did not answer me, but kept bawling, and I was helpless of what to do until Doña Iñes ran out of her store to check on the commotion.

"*¡Su hija!*" she exclaimed. "*¿Perro, por qué llora?*"

"She is not my daughter."

"*Ich kann nicht meine Vetters finden,*" the little girl wept, explaining her misery.

"No? But she speaks English."

"She's German. Have you seen her before?"

"No," Doña Iñes said. "And there are not any Germans around here. They go to the south."

I asked the child her name.

"Lenore," she said.

"*Und hast du einen Nachname, meine kleine Dame?*"

She giggled. "*Ja. Himmelstein.*"

"That's a funny name you have," I said. Lenore laughed.

"Is there a Himmelstein family on the island?" I asked Doña Iñes.

"Ah, she must belong to Juan's family. They live on the island just there," she pointed across the watery flats to a spit of land with a single house perched on it.

"Can you telephone over?" I asked. The clouds were gathering more quickly, and I was anxious to get back before the downpour.

"Why don't you take her?" Doña Iñes asked, incredulous. "It's right there. You can see the house."

I did not want to be responsible for a child, and made the excuse that I had left my house open and did not want it to flood.

"What is there to flood?" She laughed at me. "Ah, *mi niño*, you do not wish to be involved," she gleaned. "Here we may not be rich as in your country, but at least if someone loses a child we do not worry they will sue us if our boat capsizes. Ferry the child."

"Call to the house, and ask them to meet us at the dock," I agreed reluctantly.

"*Sí*," Doña Iñes smiled. Lenore beamed, and climbed into the boat. "You are doing the right thing."

Lenore was sitting near the prow like a creature born of the sea, happy to be going home. I was never around children, and as I rowed her toward the island, did not know what to say, so asked the usual questions you would a stranger.

"Who do you think will win the elections?"

"I don't know. I can't vote."

"What are your teams for the next World Cup?"

"I do not like sports," she answered. "You seem sad. If I had such a wonderful boat I wouldn't be sad."

"You think so?"

"Yes. No one would be able to tell me where to go, or make me go anywhere I didn't like, or ever be able to leave me."

"Where would you go?" I asked, wondering about her parents.

"Oh, everywhere," she lit up. "Even the moon, if I could row there. But everywhere on earth."

"You'll go lots of places, Lenore, when it's your time for it," I said. "When I was your age I had never been anywhere yet."

"You think?" she asked, hopefully.

"Absolutely," I assured her.

"Which place do you think is the best in the world to see first?"

"It does not matter," I said. "It is just the land, the language, and the people that change."

"Well, I can't wait," she hugged herself.

We neared shore, and she brightened to see her mother waiting on the dock. The mother was a handsome woman, but tipsy with drink and beside herself with worry, as she stooped down to lift Lenore from the boat.

"What happened?" The mother asked the child.

"They left me," Lenore told on her cousins' mischief. "And this nice man brought me home. Thank you." She turned to me.

"Would you care to join us for a coffee?" the mother asked. She was ringless, and I might have been curious to hear their story on another occasion, but I realized I was uninterested in anyone but Sylvie. Besides that she had used the formal tense, and I had been in nature too long, so the remove seemed dissonant with the landscape itself. I shook my head, pointing to the clouds, which had already begun to open.

25

An Egyptian blue sky unfurled overhead, clear to the edge of space, and the prelapsarian air below fluttered with a clement, pure breeze to inspire the blood. The usually muddy delta waters shone like a mirror, rippling gently each time we broke the surface with our oars.

Near the market we crested alongside another couple, out rowing for sport. Sylvie began to pull with a quickened pace, and I followed suit, and they smiled at us, like-minded, pulling even again until we had a race.

"To the next island," they cried.

"*¡Vale!*" we answered. We sprinted prow to prow, exhausting ourselves, until they seemed to flag as we opened enough of a lead to be sure of victory. They took advantage of our slacking off to surge again, though, and soon began pulling even, but we had by then reached the island, doubled over from the effort.

"*Bravo,*" they called, and waved in a gesture of fellow feeling. We were all drenched with sweat and our hearts beat quick and glad, as we floated down near the sea basin, relaxing again. Sylvie and I smiled at our victory. I still felt the bliss of physical exertion and the bliss of being with her, making me never want to leave that little corner of the world.

"We make a good team," she said, as we neared the open sea. She saw the fishing tackle under the seats and maneuvered it out through the slats. "May I?"

I took her oar. She baited the hook with a lure, then cast an expert line into the sterling water.

"You cast well," I said.

"My family used to go when we were young. I did not like it, but it was always nice to be on the river with the people I cared for. I felt we could be anytime in all of history, and it would be just like that. I would cast my line, telling myself if I caught a fish I would get to the next epoch in history."

"That was a lot of pressure."

"I know." She laughed at herself and her amber eyes shone, as her bare arms arced over the water with a sensuous poise.

I idled the boat on the current, letting us drift around toward one of the seaward islands in the full midday heat, though it was not as hot as it had been in previous weeks, so I felt the season beginning to ebb.

As we reached the open sea, I rowed around the island, the fishing line tensed.

"We caught something," she said excitedly, the breeze playing in the folds of her white summer dress.

The fish leapt, and the line played out until I thought she was going to lose it, but she pulled up expertly and it was snagged sound. She began to reel it in toward us, but too quickly, and gave way when the line tensed tight to the point of snapping. The fish ran free again, fast toward the open sea, but she had it with both hands and all her might, so it was clear how big it was. She opened the line, letting the fish run until it seemed to tire. When it swam less furiously, she began reeling in intently. From the curve of the pole I was afraid it might snap, but she loosened it in time, as the fish ran back, in a mighty struggle I would not have imagined she had in her.

"Is it too much?"

"No." Her face was furrowed with sweat, and I could see she took pleasure in the contest. But the fish was massive, and I put one hand on hers to help her steady it, helping her coax it hard or slack as the fish kept struggling below.

"Yes, you can help me now."

We saw the fish down in the clear water, close to the boat, and began to haul it in, as the beast lunged angrily into the air. Sylvie let out a shriek of fear and surprise at the sheer size of it, then surprise and joy. The fish dove under again, and we pulled up again, one final time, to claim it silver and glistening into the boat.

"What do we do now?" She laughed, proud, but drawing away from its convulsive final moments. It was a giant river creature, but I managed to pick it up soundly by the gills, and hold it against the bottom of the boat, where I so took up an iki stick.

"Don't look," I said, seeing her agonize, as I prepared to kill it.

"Yes, you can do this part," she said.

"It will be painless." I kept my voice calm, though it was something I had only forced myself to learn since I was on the island, and did not look forward to it.

"Do we have to kill it?" she asked when she saw the spike.

"We can throw it back, but if you want to eat it, this is the best way to end it."

"It looks cruel," she wavered.

"It is your fish. You can do whatever you wish."

"It is our fish. We should cook it for dinner."

"Then this is the best way."

I got it over with quickly, and we rowed directly back to the Saavardra's dock, where we carried the fish into the kitchen. There was no one about, as we cleaned the fish in the sink, then packed it in ice, and put it in the refrigerator for later, before cleaning up.

"You think it is okay we took the fish?" she asked.

"It is terrific we took such a fish," I said. "It will be a great dinner."

"Yes," she said. "We can do it on the grill. I don't know where my uncle and aunt are, but you will come for dinner tonight, and we will make a fire for the fish."

I nodded.

"Then one day it will be our turn for the fire."

"Eventually. It is the second law of nature, or so they say."

"What do they say is the first?" she asked, though I think it was just to hear me say it.

"It is the radiance and connection of all things."

"Have you ever seen it?"

"No, but I've been told."

"Yes, they told me that, too. Do you believe it?"

"I want to believe it."

"I don't know that I can anymore. I once did, but you go out and give your heart to doing things you think matter, and find out how little all your efforts are worth, and it weighs on you. Does that make sense?"

I looked at her in the diminishing light and nodded, and felt a great uprush of kindredness and the desire to continue with her.

She had walked with me toward the river, and we were still on the verandah of the house. I put my arm around her waist and she did not move it. But when I bent to kiss her she turned away.

"Don't you feel what I do?"

She looked at me with the full force of our attraction, before turning back to face the dock. "I'm not sure I know exactly what you feel."

"Yes you do. I don't want to name it yet."

"Then we won't."

"So that means you feel the same way?"

"Yes. I think so."

"That makes me glad."

"It scares me. You don't live here, so we may suffer, and even if you did, we might still suffer."

"That scares me less than missing an opportunity for happiness."

"Me too." She said, looking away. "Do you have another woman?"

"If I did I would not kiss you."

"Do you swear?" she asked.

"Of course," I nodded, and she cried. It was then I kissed her the first time, careful because I understood why it was she always played so godforsakenly hard.

26

The southern summer passed too quickly. We left our little island and returned together to her apartment in Farodoro, where I caught up on my affairs and balanced my accounts in New York.

The film had enjoyed a good opening, and the final wire from the production company, a bonus Westhaven had negotiated, had reached my bank. It was as much as I had ever received at one time, enough to not worry for a couple of years, if I was smart with the money, so I felt flush and brimming with energy.

As I was logging off, my cell phone rang with a call from Davidson, who was out in Los Angeles. He told me he had been trying to contact me for weeks, which I was happy to hear because I needed to get back to work.

"Well?" he asked expectantly.

"Well, what? I need work. Where have you been, by the way?"

"In the Gobi Desert, where I had the most amazing vision. I asked the universe to show me the future."

I took the bait. "What did you see?"

"Television."

"Of course."

"So, did you get paid?"

"Yes."

"And?"

"And what? Like I said, I need work. I have expenses, plus catching up to do."

"What are you going to buy? A house? An electric car? A car with bad gas mileage?"

"Nothing."

"A man Friday who drives and build houses?"

"Nothing."

"Nothing?"

"Maybe a little more time for myself to figure things out."

"You cannot buy time, my friend. Time cannot be created, only used up. Compensation is for time you have spent. They give it to you to make you forget for a moment you're going to die."

"In that case buying something will not help."

"Trust me, it will. Go buy yourself something that has a meaning for you, Harper. Anything. So long as it is something you will continue to enjoy."

"I will think about it, but my pleasure is in the work."

"Interesting. I did not know you had that in you."

"Had what?"

"You don't know your own power. Remember when you were a kid, before you ever got some, and you were walking around, all nuts, because you were tired of being a no-name chump virgin? Then one day, at last at last, you get some. You got some. But it was not how you imagined it would be, or what you heard it should be, because you were a no-name chump virgin, who would believe anything, and she was a no-name chump virgin, who knew nothing, so neither of you knew what you were doing. But you got some—alleluia—and were still marked by the newness of her skin; of the experience itself. You smell every electron in the room; feel every hadron, every boson; sense every tau in the air and it didn't even feel like you were doing it. It was not bodily, but ethereal as innocence. Afterward, you don't know how you feel, or how you are supposed to feel. Part of you wishes you had waited and were still a virgin, but you walk your half-virgin self through the streets, over the hills, across the lawn, down the beach, not knowing you just entered the hall to the big dance, and you do not know the steps. You just float through the subway, down the highway, over the hills where the dew has not burned away yet, like the baby fuzz on your upper lip, looking at the little kids playing tag, as you hear music and voices drifting from the houses you cannot make out. Everything has a new feeling to it. You got some. And you don't know what or how, but something is different, take-me-to-the-river changed, because Time just looked out over that field, down that street, up across the sands, and noticed your chump self for the first time—putting a hand on you in a way you will not understand for years.

"Later that day, you see your friends, and one of them looks at you strange. He knows. 'I hear they gave you some last night,' he jibs.

"'They did?' another asks.

"'That's what I hear.'

"'Who?'

"'Seraphine.'

"'Which Sarah? Black Sarah? White Sarah? Asian Sarah? Spanish Sara?'

"'Not Sarah, Seraphine.'

"'You mean those two supernerds are trying to make Godzilla nerd.'

"'How do you feel?' they ask, when they tire of ribbing you.

"'Feel about what?'" You play it cool.

"'Feel now that you did it, and ain't a no-name chump virgin.'"

"'I don't know what you're talking about,' you insist. 'I ain't never been a no-name chump virgin. I been doing it my whole life.'"

As the call ended I agreed to meet him and Elsa on a ski trip out West, if I made it home before Easter.

"Don't disappoint me. We made something good. We should commemorate that."

After hanging up, I went out to the kitchen, where I found Sylvie standing next to the sink motionless.

"What are you doing?" I asked.

"Nothing," she replied.

"It looked—"

"It is kayotsarga pose," she said. "I was practicing non-attachment."

I took up a knife to start chopping vegetables for dinner.

"I can do it." She pushed me aside, taking up the knife.

"What is wrong?"

"You're going back?" she asked. "You should just leave now and get it over with, instead of drawing it out, letting us get more attached."

"Who said I was going?"

"I overheard your conversation."

"I agreed to go skiing. I thought you enjoyed skiing."

"I don't want to go back to the States."

"Don't you have to at some point? We can't hide down here forever."

"Who is hiding? Maybe it started that way, but now it is living. It is choosing a different way of being."

"We'll figure it out," I said, but she would not be put off.

"We could be happy," she argued. "But New York does not make sense to me anymore. People there live too asymmetrically. The only important thing is work. I do not want that anymore."

"You want?"

"A family."

"We can do that anywhere."

"No."

"Why not?"

"It's too soon for this kind of talk. We're not going to have it. If we were having it, though, I would say everything there is so competitive, and I could never find myself in the middle of it. I was always suffocating. See, it provokes all my insecurities."

"That is why you left?"

"No, I can handle my insecurities. It is because we will end up doing things we do not like, only to support a lifestyle and values which are not how I want to raise my children."

"You think should have a family together?" I probed.

"Maybe," she said. "That's not what I said, though."

"Why don't we just go on the trip, and decide the rest later?"

"I don't want to grow closer until I know how I feel."

"That's a little bit complicated. About where to live or whether to have a family?"

"I know I want a family."

"So do I." It came out before I knew what I was saying. Before I knew it was what I had wanted to say. I felt exposed, but also a feeling of contentment I could no more explain than a leaf could explain why it loves the sun. I wanted that as I wanted my next breath—to keep multiplying until time commanded me stop.

"Do you know what you are saying?"

"I think so."

"You should be certain. You know, I was not looking for anything, except minding my own business in the middle of nowhere, until here you show up, and made me fall all in love."

"Is that what I did?"

"Yes."

"Then I am happy," I said.

"Me too. I think. But I don't know if we can be equal to making something together, or even whether you are careless or not."

"That's fair," I said.

"What do you mean?" she asked.

"I mean, I will consider anything you say."

"Let me know when it is not something you consider, and it just is."

I nodded. I felt linked to her, like a golden chain uniting my past and future. The feeling, poor, dumb Adam must have had that made him listen to his woman instead of his god; instinct that whispered this is what was truly available of life.

What Eve, that defiant queen, knew when she woke him from slumber—*Eat this, Adam. There's suffering all around this menagerie. We're going to suffer, too. See the lion. See the lamb. Wise up, baby. It's just me and you. To hell with Yahweh. We can create ourselves*—was, if the price was to suffer and toil and try to create, and fail, and try again, sometimes to win, but always to die, then that is what it meant to be human and alive.

God knew it to be the same.

It was dark and we had gone to the roof to grill, but a gusting wind made it difficult, and by the time our meager fire was finally lit the sky was already crowded with stars.

"Look how many constellations you can still see in the city."

"You can't see any in New York."

"Look, there is Taurus, and there is Orion, the hunter, and those are his two dogs. The big one, Canis Major, was a present from Zeus to one of his lovers. There is the boat *Argo*. Over there is the clock. They all used to have a meaning to people. Their whole lives written across the sky."

"Isn't it sad, for us it's just balls of burning gas, and no more than that?"

"They still mean something. Maybe just beauty."

"Beauty is not enough. I want meaning, Harper Roland. A whole life of it."

"Yes," I said, turning the vegetables on the flames, and looking up. "Taurus, the bull, was the form Zeus transformed himself into when he was courting a mortal woman so exceptional she made even the gods love her. That's you. She was charmed by the bull, and accepted one day when he offered her a ride on his back; then Zeus stood and spirited her off to his cave."

"What a brute. Is that you?"

"No. The hunter, Orion, sprang to her aid. He's more ancient than Zeus, and was called Gilgamesh in the first writings, before they were lost in the fog and meaning of a different time. But all stories are still written on the sky. Maybe he was the first person ever to lose his way, or go his own way, and have to wrestle the world for his soul, to return to where he belonged. But stronger, wiser. And when he returned he was the first hero. That is more ancient than any god we know."

"That's nice. But I don't want either of us to lose our way again. And the only way for that is if you stay with me."

She looked over to me with unguarded eyes, and my hand reached out to her before I had thought about it and embraced her and pulled her closer to me and that was the whole truth.

27

"Wow, look, Mommy, the whole world," a child in the seat ahead of me exclaimed, as he stared at the earth from above for the first time. The barren Andes stretched up, otherworldly and jagged in the evening sun. Nothing else stirred or seemed alive in the firmament around us, as the plane taxied through the gloaming.

I disembarked, and hurried to catch my connection. As I rounded the corner from security a stoop-shouldered old woman stopped me with her eyes.

"You are not traveling alone," she said enigmatically.

"What do you mean?" I asked.

"There is an energy traveling with you, protecting you."

"Thank you," I said, lost. "You see such things?"

She looked at me mysteriously again before smiling and moving away, as I made my way to the next gate. I was still perplexed, but pleased for her blessing as I embarked again, the mountains quickly invisible and the lights of the city rapidly fading.

I awoke in the gray early morning, banking through snow clouds over New York. Ours was the first flight to land that day, so the customs line was empty when I made my way through, only to be stopped by the Homeland agent who examined my papers.

"This passport is full." He scowled his disapproval. "I shouldn't stamp it." His display was meant to provoke uncertainty. I knew he would let me pass.

"I'll get a new one first thing tomorrow," I said, performing my part in the drama, as I waited for his foul morning mood to pass. At length he went through a great kabuki of mercy, before relenting, and stamping on top of another stamp. "Next time I won't."

My suitcase was the only one on the carousel when I reached baggage claim, and I moved efficiently through the automatic doors, past the people holding flowers and signs for whomever they had gotten up so early to greet.

It was soon rush hour so I took AirTrain. The train was at the platform when I arrived, and whisked me to Jamaica Station, where I caught the LIRR to Atlantic Avenue. There I found a cab, but was thwarted by traffic near the Brooklyn Bridge. I asked the driver to leave me at Fulton Ferry, where I picked up the first water taxi of the season, and made it across the gray river in the fluttering snow.

The empty apartment needed dusting, but was otherwise as I left it. I poured myself a glass of water, which was the only thing in the refrigerator, set a kettle to boil, and went to shower.

When I returned to the kitchen I ground coffee beans, which I measured into a filter and bloomed with a bit of the water before pouring the rest slowly over them for three minutes. I finished my coffee, unpacked my luggage, and stored it away.

That evening I ordered a movie in English over the computer, and American dinner over the phone, and ate my meal as I watched the movie, and drank a nightcap of Kentucky bourbon.

When I went to sleep I was happy to be in my own house and not some strange shore for the first time in months, and snug with my own comforter around my shoulders, in my own bed, and to fall asleep dreaming American.

By midweek, though, I was aware only of the emptiness of the rooms, an incompleteness that stayed with me until Sylvie arrived a few weeks later.

I was curious to meet her friends, and pleased to find I got on with them without undue effort. But by week's end she was spent from the city, and happy to get away when we headed west, under the great sky again.

Other than Davidson and Elsa, we were joined by Ingo, one of the film's backers, Ingo's fiancée, Ola, who worked at a bank in

London, and Gabriel, a cinematographer, and his wife, Renata, a famous Hungarian dancer and beauty.

Everyone besides me was an accomplished skier. I had planned the trip mainly because I thought Sylvie would enjoy it, and was glad to see she did. The snow was fresh and powdery; the mountain not too crowded; and when I fell, as I took my first lesson, I learned to take it in stride.

"Your ski edges are set at ninety degrees from the factory," Sylvie consoled me when I grew frustrated. "Mine are bent to eighty-eight degrees. It makes it easier to carve the powder."

"Yes, that is why."

"Don't worry, you will get better."

"How long do you think it will take before I can go off trail?" I joked, after falling down again.

"You're so sweet in the country. But I'm afraid you'll never be a good skier."

"Because I started too late?"

"No, because you don't love it. You'll plateau, and lose interest."

"We will have to find another hobby, then."

"Diving. Bookbinding. Cooking. Gardening. Tango. Would you take up tango with me?"

"We will do it all."

"But what happens when we lose interest?"

"We will find new things."

"What if we run out?"

"We will be happy and old by then. Don't you think?"

"Yes."

The third evening we were at the bar in the lodge, playing pool with a group of locals, who lived all season on the mountain and were telling the others about the best trails. We had dinner in town that night, and afterward were in such high spirits we decided to drive to the casino on a nearby reservation.

We left in two cars under the Easter moon, over the empty roads, through the darkness in the country with nothing but the white headlights reflecting back off the white snow, blue evening stillness, and the wine-dark forest against the twilight.

When we neared the casino red and orange neon lights burst through the darkness to meet us on the highway, breaking the spell of a lunar landscape, but transfixing us with how tawdry they had made that part of the wilderness.

"It all seemed so innocent before," Ingo remarked, unhappily. "Like the America one imagines."

"It was a way of bringing hard currency to a poor country," Gabriel told him. "They did not know what came with it."

"What is the difference between innocent and ignorant, anyway?"

"Ignorant means not knowing. Innocent is intending no harm."

"Ah, so they overlap, and pull apart, as in our language."

We were on the casino floor. Renata and Gabriel had never been in a casino before, and looked around with superior awe, the way Europeans always try to condescend to Americans in the heart of the country. As we fanned out toward the tables, the others tried to egg them into gambling, which they refused.

Davidson and Elsa were dressed to the nines, elegant as always, even amid the whirling slot machines, with everyone else in ski vests and blue jeans, as the speakers piped in Johnny Cash and Joni Mitchell.

We settled down to the roulette wheel in pairs, playing alternately the red or the black, so none of us was up or down very much, and as a group we were not leaving too much behind. Davidson and Elsa grew bored with the small stakes, though, and put a pile on seven, which they lost. They bet another stack on four, and lost that, too. Ingo and Ola were calculating the odds, which they did not like, and did not deviate from their calculations, win or lose, so did not move too far up or down. Neither did we, leaving the only excitement in watching Davidson and Elsa blow their chips in spectacular fashion.

After an hour, Sylvie and I were up a hundred, but the game had grown tedious, and she wanted to raise the stakes. "May I?" She took a chip from our stack.

She bet a street on her birthday, and then a corner on our two birthdays, and we lost both. Next, she went with her number, which was not the dealer's, and so we lost fifty bucks in short order. We were still up fifty, and it was fun, so she took half what was left and played the centerline. We lost again.

"I am blowing all our money," she said, as she took another chip.

"How are we betting the final one?" I asked, as she placed the last of our winnings.

She played it straight up on the day we met, and the dealer spun. The ball jumped up and the ball jumped down and the ball spun over the wheel, as our eyes followed the damn thing, projecting our desire and superstition, losing our money but having a blast.

Davidson and Elsa hit, and the croupier paid them out thousands, which was a nice pile of chips that they put right back on the table.

"Our dear friends are rich," said Ingo.

Sylvie and I were down to what we started with, and Sylvie did not want to bet more, but we were having so much fun I insisted. She took it and played another street, but wouldn't tell me what it signified, and the dumb little ball danced over the big dumb wheel, and we laughed with merriment and joy when one of her numbers fell.

"Look, we won everything back," she said. "Let's stop now."

"What did you bet?" I asked.

"Isn't it crazy," Sylvie replied, "how the brain looks for meaning, and looks for meaning, even where you know there is none."

"So you bet?"

"I'm not telling, you. You would know too much."

"Well, we are lucky," I said.

"We are lucky," she said.

"It's randomness," Gabriel chimed in.

"We were having a moment."

We turned back to the table, where Davidson and Elsa had let everything ride again, and lost it all again.

"Our dear friends are poor." Ingo shook his head with exaggerated sadness.

They went further down from there, and wanted to play a new game with less chance. Sylvie went to cash out our chips. Ola went with her to find the others, who had wandered off. Ingo and I went with Davidson over to the poker tables to keep an eye on him, as he settled in against the dealer.

"When you were up thousands, why didn't you take some chips off the table?" I asked, after he had cut the cards.

Davidson took his gaze from the deck, and trained it on me. "I lost a woman once. You know what I mean?"

"We all have," vouched the prince.

"I lost her when my chips were down. I did not have no chips, mind you. I had those on the table I was letting ride, to make the things I dreamed happen. But I was willing to follow that down past my bottom dollar, and off the edge of the earth if needed. That frightened her too much."

"She was not the right girl," I said.

"Too selfish."

"No, she was the right girl. Lover's gamble. Whenever someone wants something as much as I did, part of it is about the thing, the rest is about the want. And, brothers, I wanted. No, she was an absolute champion of a girl, who had already run a pretty rotten race they cooked up for her. She had the head for it, and she had the legs for it. She just was not nervy for it again. She knew it about herself, too, and when she saw her chance she broke first thing for the exit."

"Did she win her race?"

"In a kind of way—you can read about it in the papers—but she sold too soon to claim all she should have. But she was then more girl than woman."

"Like you said, she was a girl."

"Yes. A woman is a whole other order—.

"Yeah, she was the right girl, but she was just a girl, and never understood it was not the chips I was playing for then, but the whole crooked casino. Then again, maybe she did.

"Still, she got her chips, and she got in the papers, and I got my movies. It was not my time yet, and not the right one for us. Now it is my time. I have as many chips as I ever need. And I have a queen for a woman. Now I am going to spin the wheel, and spin the wheel, and play and win, and win, and win and never stop."

"Elsa is good for you," I said, as the next hand was being dealt. She had grown on me, which did not matter. What mattered was my friend was happy.

"Sylvie is good for you, too. The French girl—"

"Genevieve."

"Yes, that one was too immature and self-involved. She still needed what I used to."

"No, it was neither of us knew then that whatever we achieve pales next to life."

"Whatever the case, Sylvie is more nurturing. She appreciates your interior life. For men like us that is the most important thing. She is smart and curious, too, so you will not become bored. Not that smart tells you anything about her heart. Trust me. I used to go with a genius. The woman knew everything but herself. Sylvie feels closer to the goddess. If I were you I would stick by her."

"Davidson, the what?"

"The goddess. I can see these things. You do not have to understand them. She will give you a run for your money whichever way."

"I'm glad you like her," I said, falling into a melancholy silence.

"You still got it for Genevieve?"

"No, just thinking how unfortunate all of that was."

"I hate to tell you, but you were not unlucky, my friend. You were unhappy, and the moral of that part of the story is when we are hurt we draw the damaged to us."

"No," I said. "It is that before we understand real compassion, everything good tilts away."

He put a hand on my shoulder, and told me he disagreed. "There are all kinds of unsympathetic people who have the whole world sticking to their greedy little fingers.

"But, you know how it is when you are in a monastery, and you wake one morning from your dreams to walk in the gardens, and realize all of a sudden it is not your garden?"

"No."

"Or else you are out in the desert, tripping your balls off on peyote, and you have walked across half of Potosí, and your shaman materializes to tell you look up into the night, which if you ever have the chance you should not pass up, and there you see them. All the luminous thousand faces of the gods, pulsating at you from the very depths of the universe. You search up in that sky in awe at each face and still you search and search, until you realize none of them is the god face you are looking for, the one your life has prepared you to see. Because, wouldn't you know it, the universe has a sense of humor. What it chooses to reveal to you are the Aztec gods of that desert. So there you are, looking up at the gods, and the glow of a love that has been there all your life and ever will be, and you don't even know its name."

"That's too Delphic," I said, watching his face to see if he was putting me on. "What do you mean?"

"It means I was searching the wrong desert," he said. "Love is that way too."

"I do not presume to know all about how love is."

"That is what Paul said. 'Though I speak with the tongue of men and of angels, and have not love.' So you do know."

I pondered this new koan as the others arrived at the table. Sylvie squeezed in next to me to watch Davidson play at the high table. It was midnight by then, and Sylvie began to worry about getting too late a start on the slopes the next morning.

The two of us left the others there, and took one of the cars back to the hotel, under the still high moon, perfect as the sky is in the West.

The next day it was as she feared, and none of the rest made it out to the mountain, except Ingo, who wanted to get in as much as he could, since he claimed it was better than the skiing in Europe. But he had made plans with a group of ski bums we'd met the first night of our trip, the Kings of the Mountain taking the Prince to the wilderness to test what he was made of. Sylvie went with me down the intermediate slopes, so we could spend the morning together.

"I have finally found something you are not good at," she said, as we prepared for our final descent of the day.

"I am terrible, but give me a couple of seasons."

"Maybe I'll give you more than that," she said. The snow was icy and no longer pristine, but the moon rose cold and high, as the fat red sun sank over the horizon. We kissed before launching off the mountain between the two. Sine and cosine of our daily bread. The sun was still impossible to look at full on as we made our final run down the slope. The moon was bright and irresistible as molten silver. Our blood swelled like the tide when we reached the bottom, where we stood watching until the sun was finally gone, the moon at full height, and the sixty seconds of perfection on the horizon, after the sun has disappeared and you can look at the whole sky and still see as much of the sun as you can bear.

28

We returned to join the others for dinner. As I waited for Sylvie to change, the telephone rang. It had been three days without it, and the sound jolted me in the deep silence of the countryside. In another day I might have realized I could go without it at all, but I was not away long enough yet and so still addicted to the thing, answering from the daze of habit.

"Hi, Bea," I greeted her.

"Are you still done with the serious life?" she asked.

"Forever and ever," I said. "I ran away, and I'm never coming back."

"I heard something about L.A. Well at least don't forget the way back."

"I'm out west now."

"Where?"

"In America. The golden land of opportunity, where we will all make a new life."

"Nel mezzo del cammin di nostra vita, mi ritrovai per una selva oscura, ché la diritta via era smarrita."

"I don't speak Greek," I said, "only American."

"Let me help you. It's Dante."

"Sounds Greek to me."

"I won't insult you by translating, because I know you'll look it up. Just as I know, when you get tired of all the fun, you'll be back. Just you watch. You'll be back before you even know you left."

"Why would I ever do such a thing?"

"I still have an assignment for you."

"Not interested."

"There was a village razed last week, by the guerrillas you were following in a past life. Everyone was left for murdered. Except the killers went about things in too much of a hurry, you know how mass murderers are, they have no eye for detail, so they never quite manage to kill us all. In the morning there were several people alive who had hidden away in the fields, including one young man who witnessed everything. He was shot, hacked, and thrown into the grave with the others, but bless him he was still alive. When the soldiers had gone, he crawled from beneath all the dead over him in the grave, and later walked five miles, through the night, until daybreak, when he appeared at the medical tent of a refugee camp. He was so bloody with machete cuts, and stricken with absolute fear that the white vest who first saw him thought he was a ghost. But he was alive."

"Who was behind it?"

"I thought you might go and find out what's going on."

"Oh damn it, Bea, I can't," I told her.

"I'll pay hazard rates."

"It's not compensation enough."

"Compensation? Since when is that the first thing on your mind?"

"It is what you get to make you forget you are on the losing side of the war. I'm sorry, Bea, but even your highest rates won't make me forget."

"You've gotten cynical, my dear."

"Yes, I went into my first war when I was twenty-eight. I was thirty-five when I came out, and by God, I was cynical."

"It is just a phase you're going through."

"That part of my life is over."

"Someone has to bear witness."

"Yes, and it is someone else's turn. Listen." I held the phone aloft.

"What am I supposed to be hearing?"

"The sound of quiet. Of quietude."

"I hear it, honey, but I'm not sure you do. Go on, though, have fun in your new country. Have as much fun as you can bear, and for as long as you can stand it. You deserve that much. Call me when it wears thin, and you're ready to do something meaningful again."

"I may have found a different meaning, Bea."

"Yes. I know. You'll get your fill of it."

"It may take a while."

"However long it takes you will tire of it, because your standards are too high. At least they used to be. You used to have such beautiful standards, you know that? Too beautiful. Now you're disappointed with the world, because it did not live up to them and prepare something better for us all. So you're burned out, and hard of sight for a spell. You got burned bad is all, and it may take a while to recover. Is that it, honey?"

"Sounds like you know."

"I do know, and it is also fine if you never go back. But one day, I think, at least it is my hope for you, you'll see how perfect the world is again, even with all its lousy standards, and even if it is full of brutality it forces us to know without succumbing. It's still a perfect place, and you're perfect, and Bill, you remember him? That pompous nitwit? He's perfect too. And Jen, who has no self-esteem even though she is just perfect. Steve is a hopeless lush, and he's perfect. Joe is a sanctimonious boor; Jane is a prude and a snob; Mary had two abortions, and Gil is such an unhappy bastard he has something malignant to say about every man he knows, and every woman not in love with him; and because he is brilliant does not excuse it, but because they are all perfect human beings does. Phil would do whatever he thought he could get away with, if he thought no one was looking, would just rip your throat clear from your neck if it would help him get ahead. Simon thinks the problem with the whole world is he doesn't run it, and boy if he isn't just the answer to a problem none us know we have, poor thing. Leah has nothing at all she believes in, and not a friend left, because she hit on all their husbands. That's just how it goes, and they are all still perfect."

"Things here are pretty perfect, too."

"Got it. I'll call you with the next one. Tell me, who do you think I should assign this one to?"

"How about that kid who wrote that piece about the death penalty?"

"He's too green for this one, dear."

"Only because he hasn't been seasoned by the fire yet, Bea. Give him the assignment and, when he comes back there won't be a part of him still green. He'll be baptized by fire, by darkness, by the hellacious heat that consumes the darkness. He'll go and he'll come back just glowing where the green was burned off, because he's been so near the fire and not goddamn in it. Ask him then if he's sure he wants to pour his life out in it."

"Just make sure you don't let it consume too much of you," Bea cautioned. "The space in your heart for deep living. People kill, and they are the demons, and others do what they can to stop it, and those are the angels, unless they fall. But everyone, angel or demon, suffers, and a demon is only an angel turned upside down who refuses to be righted. Look at any revolution for proof.

"If the angel does not first understand the demon in herself, she will never understand evil, and so it will happen again and again because we do not see the suffering in others, all others, even still not fully our own. That is what dooms us. Be an angel for me, dear, and trust in that. Even when you doubt the rest. And, yes, the angels too suffer. They suffer more than anyone because they suffer *for* everyone, which is why they fear, and why they fall sometimes, and why they are angels to begin."

"I just want to enjoy myself now and live my life, like any other human being."

"Have fun on your holiday, dear," Bea sighed, giving up when she saw it was hopeless with me. "Enjoy being in love, which is the gateway to the spirit, and enjoy the end of your first youth, and all the fine rooms, and the fine things in the fine rooms, and all the fine people there are. Call me when you reach the last room, and you are feeling beautiful again on the inside, and you want to know what's next, because you are sick to the gills with beautiful wine and what all. Call me when you can laugh at yourself and the rest of it, too. I will take you to lunch, and we'll talk about what matters, and have the most beautiful time. Promise me?"

"You're the angel, Bea, and a real friend."

"Off you go. Enjoy Candy Mountain. I hope you eat the whole rotten thing, if that's what you want, and no bellyache."

"*Ciao bella.*"

"*Ciao bello.*"

As I hung up, Sylvie asked who I had been talking to.

"An old friend."

"It sounded like work."

"My old editor."

"You love her. What does she want?"

"Nothing. She dialed by mistake, trying to reach someone else."

"I don't buy it."

"She offered me an assignment."

"Where?"

"Gabindi."

"I've never been anywhere in Africa. If you took the assignment we could make a trip of it."

"I have friends in Nairobi I'd like to see, and a safari might be nice."

"Safaris aren't in Africa. They're in parks."

"All the same it would still be grand to go to one of them. You don't have to do it for me, though. But if you decide on the assignment, because it has a meaning for you, I would love to see the elephants. I mean, wouldn't it be absolute bliss to see them so magnificent in the wild, before there are none left."

"I will think about it."

"Don't do it for me, as I said. But if there is part of you that wants to do it for your own reasons, I could meet you and we could visit friends and make a special time of it."

"Why do you make everything sound so pleasant?"

"Only if you want to. I can also go by myself, before I have to take my next job."

"No," I said. "It's me who doesn't want to keep traveling alone."

We were late to meet the others for dinner, and rushed to join them in town for a meal of buffalo burgers and old-school California wine from Mount Eden. Dinner was perfect, and our lovemaking too that night.

Before bed we soaked in the hot tub, luxuriating in our last hours before going back east. We were surrounded by the ancient forest behind the cabin, simple and unspoiled. I felt like a perfect Philistine.

29

We dropped off the rental car in the predawn light and boarded a regional flight to Salt Lake, where our landing was delayed. When we finally reached the next gate, the agent told us our connection had been canceled, due to a storm back east that had closed down most of the coast.

The terminal was filling up with stranded passengers, and fearing we might be stuck there the rest of the day, I asked whether they could fly us into Philadelphia instead. The flights were all full. We put our names on the standby list, then went for breakfast, before going to the next gate to see if we were called. Our hopes were dashed when we saw they were asking for volunteers to skip the flight. By then the airport was jam-packed, the agents beaten down, and people were setting up camp for the long haul. We went back to the information desk, where there was an infinite line and only two agents on duty, one of whom told us there was nothing else east that day.

"What about ATL?" I asked, dreading the prospect of being stranded.

"Traffic is backed up there for hours, and if you get in, you will not make it back out."

"What do you think?" I asked Sylvie.

"I think we should stay here another night."

"There are no hotels. We'll have to sleep in the airport."

Sylvie scanned the desk to see where business was done, and approached another agent. "We need your help," she said, the gentle certainty of her charm cutting through the chaos with quiet command. "I know you have all these other people to deal with, but we need to get home."

"Detroit is open, but there is only one eastward flight from there."

"Do you have room?"

"No, but you would be first on the list. If you land before the storm moves in."

She booked it, and printed out the tickets. "Can I have your ID?"

I handed her my passport.

"No, your crew ID."

"We are not crew."

"I thought you were."

"No, I just always like to have a way home."

We went to the gate for the flight, and, as the plane began boarding, exhaled with relief when our names flashed green.

We landed in Detroit half an hour late, and the onward flight was already boarding, but when we reached the gate there was an old couple there in wheelchairs, the husband breathing from a respirator. Sylvie and I looked at each other, her face twisted in a wry smile and her eyes brimmed with I-told-you-so as we gave up our seats.

"Let's find a hotel," she said, sitting down at the empty gate, despairing of what to do. When we called around, they were all booked, so we were forced to camp out in the airport after all.

The only places open, other than the lounges, were a record shop, with old Motown drifting into the corridors, and a soul food restaurant called Brother Leon's, where a line of people out the door waited to be fed. The sign in the window announced worldwide delivery, with a cartoon picture of the couple behind the counter leaning out of an airplane, riding in a speedboat, sitting in the jump seat of an old Ford.

Life taking you places? Don't even know where you are? This is Motown. We understand people move. We deliver. Coming from nowhere? Don't know how long you'll be staying? We will feed you.

Feeling out of sorts? Headache? Heartbreak? Midlife crisis? Meno-pause? Double-consciousness? Plain ole vanilla angst? Let me put it to you this way, who's going to bury you where? Here, have some pie.

Ready to order? *You do know what you want, right? Maybe some-thing to take along for the kids? Their kids? Come on now, what are you going to feed them? Big, corn-fed American babies? Or smug little brats, in need of being separated from their sushi money? A man has to know what's worth holding on to, or else it will surely slip away, my daddy used to say. Don't take it the wrong way. I'm only asking because time is passing.* What do you want with the world?

Cornbread with that? 'Course you do. *Why you at it, might as well figure out how are you going to bridge your past, which you barely understand, and your future, which you have no way of knowing. Don't mean to burden you. Just fiddling time in a snowstorm. But do you hear me? Define yourself on your own terms. What happens when you are only the content of your own character in the dark heart of the great American story?* Sweet potatoes or plantains? *What's the secret to the oxtail stew? I'll tell you the secret, youngblood. It all hangs on what you feed your ox.*

What binds you to the spirit that flowed through your ancestors? To the others who are not connected to the same ancestors, and sometimes maybe ain't connected to nothing at all? How do you carry on, and keep yourself open to the spirit that sustained them as your life melts into the wide-open world? Leon's Soul Food. We deliver, baby. Soda? *Just another current in the river, feeding the open sea, a tributary to draw on when times require. Maybe not even in your own lifetime but your children's and their children's. What place for them in the corny American song? To the spirit? Do you still hear it? Or have you gone over? Don't tell me. Ain't really none of my business. This is a question for deep in the darkness when you are in that place where the world does not matter, and even the one you love does not matter, but when you focus your prayer, and all that matters is who you are in eternity.*

"Stay or to go?"

How long does it take you standing there, recalling your grandfather, before you understand what the old folks, all old folks, really meant every time they asked you anything—why don't you come here and let me get a good look at you? Do they take you to church? What grade are you in now? What are you running so fast for? What did you just say?—is: How is your soul fixed? *Are you strong enough to keep it right no matter what happens to you out in the world? Strong enough yet to tend it yourself long after we are gone?*

30

We wrangled a flight home late the next afternoon, and cabbed back to my apartment over the treacherous snowpacked roads from the airport. The driver caromed down the highway faster than was advisable, sending us skidding, slip-sliding the entire way. I hectored him to slow down, but the roads were unsafe at any speed and there was nothing we could do but clench our teeth, lock hands, and try not to think about it.

When we finally pulled over the bridge onto Canal Street it was one in the morning. The eerie white streets were completely snowed in, and the only thing moving were the traffic lights, flashing red against the banked whiteness as the blizzard continued to lash the city. My apartment was not far away, but the snowdrifts were as high as the roof of the car and the taxi could go no further. We exited near Broadway, and were immediately whipped by the arctic air catching the oversized gear bags like sails, pushing us back with each violent gust of wind.

"Look," Sylvie said, turning to face Broadway. "Have you ever seen the city so empty?" All that was visible were our tracks in the snow behind us, the flashing red streetlights, and nothing else astir.

"Only once," I said.

All day we had tried to make the best of it, but as the buildings on lower Broadway focused the wind into a tunnel, and the snow pelted our faces, I told her how sorry I was for my lack of patience in insisting we return.

"I forgive you," she said. "But we could have done it my way too, you know, and stayed put."

My building was in sight by then, and we pressed into the warm sanctum of the lobby, and were home.

We left our luggage in the living room, found food in the refrigerator, and drank hot tea, before falling into a bone-deep sleep.

That night I dreamed I was climbing a great set of stone stairs carved from a cliff. At the summit was a lake, which I dove down until I nearly drowned, before emerging on the outskirts of a majestic, red-golden city. When I emerged in its castle I ascended into a vaulted room, and walked around until I came to a kitchen, where I saw my mother cooking. She was young in my dream and happy. I approached and she told me sit down and tell her what I had learned, as though I had just come home from school. The dream dissolved, and I awoke in the middle of the blue night as the tempest continued to rage outside.

I could not go back to sleep, and went to the kitchen for water. When I returned to bed Sylvie was awake. "You were right," she said, the tempest outside beating against the glass. "It's good we made it home."

"No, you were right. We should have stayed where we were. The risk was not worth it."

"But now we are safe and snug." She nestled against me in the predawn and fell back asleep. I remained awake the rest of the night, but stayed in bed watching her sleep. When she woke we rose to make breakfast, then returned to bed where we spent the rest of the morning. By late afternoon the snow began easing up, and we went out to explore. The plows were out on the avenues, but the smaller streets were pristine with snow, and we made our way over to the Battery, and we followed the bike path along the Hudson before taking the subway up to Hell's Kitchen, and then made our way across to Central Park. The edges of the park were full of people sledding, and making snow angels, but the interior was silent, and the tops of the buildings scarcely visible, so it felt like an otherworldly forest, as we crossed east and headed back downtown.

We walked down the middle of Fifth, quiet and still as a blanket of new wool. The lions outside the Met were frozen over in a clear sheet of ice, and the doormen guarded their posts in the cold, draped in greatcoats.

By the time we reached the southern edge of the park, we were shivering with cold, and decided to have drinks before heading home. There was life out front of one of the hotels, and we made our way toward it.

There was no one inside except a handful of young guests and their chaperones, all dressed up for a birthday party, looking worried no one would make it out in the weather.

We were seated in a window bay, looking out from our perch over the emptiness of the streets.

"Aren't they just the best waiters in the world?" Sylvie asked, when our drinks arrived. "They are not playing at waiting. They are real, first-class waiters from a different time, when people knew to wait for things."

"Which era was that?" I asked, and we played the game of choosing which epoch we would best like to live in, and drank our toddies, and decided it was the perfect time to be alive.

There were no cabs when we left, and it had begun to snow again, so we took the subway to Canal, which was barricaded, due to a blaze that had broken out in the apartment blocks along East Broadway, forcing us to walk through the snow-blanketed streets, which had turned to a wet, sooty slush.

As we trundled home the needles of swirling snow began to blind us, and everyone else around was coated in the falling flakes, which looked gentle where there was no wind but were ferociously sharp to the skin, reminding me of things that used to be.

Everyone's eyes were asquint, with scarves pulled around their noses and mouths for protection, as we maneuvered the confusion of the barricades, wondering which way to go. We clasped hands in commiseration, then shoved them in our pockets for warmth, nodding sympathetically at passersby who did the same, everyone afraid and confused and anxious to get home.

A water main had burst on Chambers, sheeting the street in ice, and snapping over the few spindly trees, forcing us to double back again with the crowd, willy-nilly out toward the river, as the ghostly snow fell over us.

Sylvie tucked against my shoulder and we leaned into the howling onslaught, miserable and frozen to the core, and it felt we would never be warm.

I was too cold to talk, but when we reached John Street I thought to get some groceries, so that we would not be forced to leave the house the next day.

The shelves were empty, and the cashiers stared at the flashing television screen for information, wondering how they would get home at the end of their shift. They looked like they had not slept at all, scanning the screens anxiously for information. The announcers in their hyperbole kept calling it the Storm of the Century, but had no more information than that, except that there was no longer train service, and no more taxis, and nothing moving into or out of or through the city at all.

"Look, you're all covered," Mr. Lee said when we entered, handing us towels. We thanked him and asked how they were faring. "We all slept at the store last night," he answered. "We may be here again. But we have food at least."

We got what we could from the shelves, and stepped back out into the whipping gusts, until we finally reached the heat of the lobby, where we felt safe. The power in the building was out, so we climbed the stairs to the apartment. There was gas, so we made hot chocolate and lit candles and camped around the kitchen table.

It was still snowing the next morning, leaving the city frozen as the final ice age, and even the hum of white noise had disappeared into true silence, with nothing but winter all around.

"Look how easily even New York is made fragile," Sylvie commented, looking down on the frozen city. "Just imagine what happens when a storm lands, or a drone strikes, in some place still half-made or half-defeated from being taken over."

We stayed the next day in bed, under the comforter, reading to each other out loud, and only left the warm covers in the evening to cook.

"I will make dinner," I said, going off to the kitchen. "Is there anything in particular you want?"

"Whatever you're in the mood for."

"There is the roast we bought last night, and some parsnips."

"It sounds like a fine winter meal, but a vegetable is also sometimes green. Why don't we make a salad of the fennel?"

Outside the power had not been fully restored, but the yellow sodium lamps glowed on the frozen snow, and beyond there were little flickers of light coming from the windows of the buildings with generators; but mostly there was darkness, the world reduced to the size of my apartment and everything beyond distant and meaningless.

"You know what this reminds me of?" she asked.

"Yes," I said.

"Were you here?"

"Yes."

"Me too."

She did not say anything else for a long time after that, but simply stared out over Lower Manhattan into the storm. "You know, there are kids in grade school now who were not even alive then."

"Time moves so fast."

"And if we have children they will never know what it felt like here then. They won't know what it was like before, at all."

"Before the murders."

"I did not know you could be like that."

"Like what?"

"So narrow with hate. Look at your face."

"Neither did I."

"But our children would not know any of it. Nothing except what they read in history. They'd never have to nurse from that shapeless fear and rage, neither ours nor theirs, or the knowledge of what we forged from our sadness and fear and tarnished with shame. They wouldn't know any of it. Wouldn't that be glorious?"

"Yes," I said. "Except they will know, if only from the effects, or else they will know something from the same root. They cannot escape that."

"No," she shook her head. "I mean if they did not know anything like that at all."

"Yes," I said. "That would be glorious, but it's not possible."

"I did not ask you to weigh it, just to think if we could make the world again. They would be brand new, and the world would be new for them. We could make the world again for them, and they would not have to know anything like that at all. Wouldn't that be divine?"

"Yes," I said.

From bed we could no longer see the lights of the buildings in the distance, but watched whiteness cover the invisible city, and the people below, with all their burdens, and it just kept falling over us, like ash.

31

I accepted the assignment from Bea and we flew from winter back toward warmth, taking the PATH train from World Financial Center to Newark in the early evening rush. Our plane lifted and tacked out over the bay, then up the Hudson in harmony with the boats and the evening traffic along the West Side Highway and Midtown skyline. The entire city was aglow with activity, and the silhouettes of the buildings were a calming sight, and we fell asleep peacefully.

We woke the next morning with the Atlantic sun over the Netherlands, and changed flights in Amsterdam, where we stopped to buy buttery Dutch pastries, and the European papers. It was always refreshing to see the news from a perspective beyond the information firewall of America, and shocking every time to realize how thick that firewall was. Sylvie said much the same, as we scanned the papers from around the world in the free Dutch port.

"Which do you want?" I asked.

"Let's take them all." She gathered up a stack. "We can compare them and sort out for ourselves how much truth is in each and what's really going on."

As we fastened ourselves in for the next leg of the journey I told her how much I was looking forward to the trip.

"That's nice of you to say, sweetheart," she said, turning from the window. "I know you're only going to make me happy, and it does make me happy."

"I have my own reasons, too. Did you ever wonder why us, though?"

"No. I know why." She pulled her pashmina around her neck and leaned against me.

"Tell me what you think," I said.

"A lot of it is stuff you don't believe."

"Try me."

"A shrink might say our neuroses match. A believer would say when we are open on the deep level the universe sends to us what we need, always. A pragmatist would shrug and say it is the causal outcome of a chain of factors we can never know completely, and probably shouldn't worry too much about. A traditionalist might say people like us belong together. A mystic, that it is only mutual submission to what is happening to us. The Greeks would say it is *éros*. But ask, is it also *philia*? *Pragma*? *Agápe*? My mother just wants to know if you are good to me. If I am good to you."

"What do you tell her?"

"Yes." She laughed with her eyes and kissed my cheek.

"And the rest?"

"I think if all those ways of looking at the question exist it must be rich and complex enough to sustain so many different ways of looking; the richest, most complex thing there is, which we know less about than we do the cosmos, so only a fool would think to say anything definitive. Maybe when gods walked the earth and showed themselves to us, there was certainty. Except they retreated from us, or we from them, and now—thinking that by knowing the laws of the universe we know the universe—we celebrate our reason as all there is, like little baby children who believe themselves grow. And still, it is there for us. And somewhere, I like to think, they are smiling, watching lovingly while we bumble about, claiming to know their intent, except it really is just a great mystery. So what do I know? I have given up on theories of love. All we can have is the experience and practice of it, allowing the rest to work through us. That is enough. We were willing and ready and submitted. That is what matters. Unless we decide to go all the way as seers do. But for us it is probably best to simply accept it." She squeezed my hand.

I did not tell her I did not agree with all of it. I had no theory of my own, or anything more adorned than that she made me a better man. That was satisfaction enough, as we lifted through the sky, and fell asleep against each other.

When we woke again the Rift Valley had split open below us, ample and lush. We had a five-day safari planned. After that I would report my story, and eventually we would meet back in Farodoro. Beyond that we did not have plans.

"Where would you like to live?" I asked, as the plane descended.

"With you. Wherever you wish," she indulged me, not too convincingly. "Let's just enjoy ourselves, and not talk about it yet, because if you wish to live somewhere I do not, we are going to have a fantastic little fight. You will begin with whatever argument you have readied in your mind, and it will be some kind of tautology or other, which I will tenderly deconstruct, for your own good, with actual facts, so there is no winning for you that way. Next, we will start psychologizing, and after that it will be all down to the emotions. You will throw up both your hands, and say, 'Please. Just listen to me, woman.' Of course you will not say the last, because you are not stupid that way, but you will think it, honey, and I will overhear.

"I will calmly point my finger, right here." She poked my chest playfully. "And say, 'I heard you plenty. Is that the best you got? Cause if it is, you just see here, man.'

"Yes. It's going to be an exquisite little fight. I wish we could have it now, but I'm too tired, so just you wait. We'll argue, and eventually get through it, as soon as we agree. But in the end, you'll see you will agree with me, and everything will be beautiful again."

"When I agree with you?"

"Yes. And you know why you will?"

"Tell me."

"Because I would follow you—if you had somewhere to go with meaning for you, even if it was simple as, 'This is where I truly wish to be right now.' You do not, though, and I do. But you are going to make us go through that awful fight first. That is fine, as I said. I'll win, and off we'll go happily ever after to make a real home for us."

We had been going twenty straight hours by then, and were boarding our final flight over the dense, red valley and equatorial vegetation, then up into the spindly mountains, where the engines of the plane could be heard laboring to clear the peaks.

We landed on a narrow, old-fashioned airstrip beside a tin-roofed terminal, and made our way through customs behind locals laden with oversized suitcases and appliances brought back from the world beyond.

Whenever I arrived on the continent what I first noticed was not poverty, or the customs agent's thinly-veiled request for baksheesh, or even the heat. What I felt when we disembarked in Africa was the sense of ease I always re-encountered upon arrival. Where in other countries I always met, or feared meeting, some occluded notion of who I was, in Africa the things that clouded the distance between others and myself was more subtle. If someone who did not know you needed to casually question your intentions or intelligence or humanity, he would find a better reason than your skin. Where there was enmity it was over real resources, or judgment against a true offense caused by some legitimately fucked-up thing about you, or your tribe.

Beyond that I was expected to wear the mask of my social self as everyone did, understanding these were merely masks, and only those who took them too seriously, with no space between self and mask, were harmed. Everyone else knew there was an interior beneath the surface of everything. The outside mattered, but only just so. I observed the sense of release I felt as an invisible burden lifted. Then I noticed the heat, and soon after that my own foul temper.

We had emerged into the humid arrivals hall, where the air was oppressive as a truncheon, and I retrieved my mental list of everything that drove me crazy about Africa, all of which boiled down to the fact that generations after decolonization, the electricity still did not work. Maybe that's blaming the victim, or maybe it was a reasonable minimum standard for an international airport; in whichever case the air-conditioning and lights in the hall were out, and we were lost in the sea of people.

Sylvie's mood was undampened and I tried to keep mine to myself when I saw how invigorated she was by the new landscape beyond the glass doors. "It's so beautiful," she said. "It's like an Eden."

"It's like hell," I returned, as we searched for the driver from our tour company amid the bustle of the hall.

"Relax, we're in paradise. Besides, you must know by now how sad it makes me feel when you criticize everything."

I was uncertain how to respond as I realized she was serious. "I did not know."

"You don't know everything. Maybe sometimes, not even yourself and what you are feeling. How much sadness and anger— outrage and indignation at the world, but also just pure leaden rage—you carry. Or how much that weighs and space it takes up."

There are seemingly insignificant things people say in close quarters, whose substance takes a while to come clear. Maybe it's something they've said before, maybe you disagree, but you stop and hear it fully for once, because you realize it is bound up with, if not everything mean in the world, but a radius you can affect. She was not angry or skeptical or annoyed. She was hurt, a thought I could not bear. "What do you want me to do?" I asked. "Tell me how you would have me be instead."

"Like I said, just relax. Stop weighing and comparing and ranking and judging everything you see. Only take it in and experience it every once in a while, the way they did in Eden."

She gave my hand a quick squeeze, and released it when she spied our names on a neat, hand-stenciled sign across the hall. We began toward it.

Our driver was a jauntily dressed man in his mid-twenties, named Ali, of mixed African and Indian extraction, boundless energy, and morbid good cheer, as he helped us with the luggage and led us to a waiting Range Rover.

"I see you survived the flight," he remarked as we exited the heat of the terminal. "You know they crash sometimes."

We loaded into the truck, where he had been listening to bangra at full volume, which he quickly cranked down. "Sorry, boss," he said, not fully apologetic. "It's my theme song."

I eyed him warily, still undecided how reliable he was, as I realized I had forgotten to exchange currency, and announced I was going back to the hall to buy some of the local money.

"Don't bother with the touts here in the airport," Ali advised. "The bank machine will be broken, and the brokers will only offer you ninety percent of the bank rate."

"What is the right rate?"

"I can get you forty percent over the listed one any day of the week. Fifty on Sundays."

I told him I was going to go to the restroom before the long drive, and ventured back inside, unconvinced of his claims. When I checked around the hall, though, it was as he said: the powerless ATM had a cardboard out-of-service sign affixed to it, and the currency kiosk took too large a markup. I exchanged two hundred dollars to be safe, and returned to the car.

"Did you check?" Ali asked.

"Yes, Ali," I said.

"I would have checked, too," he replied. "It is no offense to me, boss. But I can get you the best rate. Anything else you require, just let me know. I am the man for the job."

"Thank you, Ali."

"Air conditioning or window, boss?" he asked, as we pulled away from the curb.

"Ali. Don't call me boss."

"Whatever you want, sahib. *Hakuna matata*," he turned and winked to me. "Means, don't worry."

"The window, please," Sylvie laughed gaily.

He powered the windows down with the push of a button on his console, and hot air suffocated the interior of the car, until we cleared the parking lot and sped out onto the dense, new black road, which he navigated expertly through airport traffic, skirting the edge of the city to point us up toward the cool, green hills.

"How is lady boss?" he asked. "Is the air too much?"

"I'm fine, Ali. Thank you for asking." I caught Sylvie's reflection in the side mirror as she smiled, and I began to relax at last.

An hour later we were in the bush, with nothing around except an occasional zebra or giraffe herd by the side of the road, which by then had turned into a pretty improvisational affair. We continued climbing up over a range of hills, where the sweet air cooled enough to begin to hush our jangled nerves.

The vegetation thinned once we reached the other side of the hills, near our base camp on the plains, a set of low mud-colored buildings, with a brick-lined walkway and sparse garden, which, like the rest of the vegetation on the plains, was in the midst of a drought, though not so parched as the wilderness.

Our rooms were airy and simple. There was a sitting area with a sofa, a large bed draped with mosquito netting, and two night-stands. Out back we discovered an open-air shower, where we bathed in the cool waters and dying sun, before heading to the dining room. The beer at the bar was stored unrefrigerated in a dark pantry, but was cool to the touch, and refreshing when we drank it.

As we sat, the chef could be seen in the outdoor kitchen, and when he noticed us he came to let us know there would be eland for dinner, and offered something to tide us over if we were hungry.

We were, and he provided bread and fruit, along with some roasted peanuts, all fresh and good. Out in the field beyond the kitchen there was a commotion from the camp *askaris*, who could be heard chanting energetically, arranged in a circle, moving in turns in the distance.

"What are they doing?" Sylvie asked, trying to get a better glimpse. The barman demurred to answer, but Ali, who had come into the dining room, told her.

"Drinking the blood from the eland."

"Why?" she asked. "Don't they get meat too?"

"In their tribe they drink the blood first, because it is life, and it is a sin to them to waste it."

He offered to arrange for us to try some, but we stuck with our bread and fruit.

That evening we had a supper of the just-butchered eland, with garden vegetables, then sat around a fire on the broad lawn, where we were joined by a group just in from Tanzania. They had all been traveling awhile, but had met each other in a bar near Kilimanjaro. They were already sick of each other, though, and after not too long we were sick of them, too.

There were three couples: one Australian; one British—she was Scottish, he was an Englishman; and an American couple from New Jersey with squeaky voices, who worked for an NGO. We called them the Coalition. The Americans we named Higher and Higher, because of their voices, which were like brittle glass. I did not like their politics either—their beliefs were State Department boilerplate and not their own. But mostly I hated them because of those voices. The Aussies I disliked because they were Australian. I had nothing special against the Brits yet, besides the ostentatious understatement the English specialize in, and Edward's red pants—the leisure uniform that year of men who did not work for a living and their acolytes—and the fact that they were riding with the others.

All of them were full of talk about what they had seen, and—after a few beers—what they had heard about the rebels on the other side of the mountains. After that, they were full of "Who do you know in London?" and "How about New York?" and "Where did you go last year?" "Where did you study?" "Isn't the Aussie dollar surging?" "Hasn't the price of classified Bordeaux just gotten crazy?" "It is the Asian speculators." "It buoys the Aussies as well, though" and "Now even Everest is gone all to hell."

"Say, have ever you met the queen?"

"Why, we see her every year at Ascot."

"What's Ascot?"

"A horse race."

"Oh my God! You guys hang out with the queen?! Like how awesome is that?!"

"Like totally awesome!! How come you get to go to the races with the queen?"

"Not exactly with the queen, dear."

"Well, no, not exactly with her, dear," Effie said. "But we are more than just in the stadium."

Sylvie had greater patience than I did, and managed to humor them a bit longer to make certain my irritation did not show enough to put them against us.

I had moved over to a corner of the fire alone, and, when she joined me there under the evening stars, I asked whether she was in the safari club already. "Just because they are not thoughtful people does not mean we should be less thoughtful when we deal with them," she said cheerfully.

"That's generous of you."

"It's not for them," she corrected me, as they grew drunkenly loud on the other side of the fire. "It is for myself, and how I want to be in the world."

I was always moved by the depth of her integrity, how she did not care how others were but remained always true to herself regardless of what there was to lose or gain, and tried hard to be the same way in every action she made and every word she spoke. It made me feel serene to be near, and I loved her for it.

Back in our room we closed the wooden shutters over the window, casting out the world and sealing ourselves in absolute night, and only the occasional sound of them still out on the lawn. But even that could not dispel the tranquility of that deep, certain darkness, the cool, ironed sheets and warmth of her there next to me.

The next morning we were awakened at dawn by the sound of the camp's grey parrot squawking across the lawn, and made our way to the canteen for a breakfast of *ugali*, the local porridge, fruit, and hot chai. The Coalition was hung over, complaining the food was not much to speak of, until we finally loaded our packs into a large, military lorry, built to move troops and supplies over the roughest roads, and were off, just after sunrise, across the plains.

We reached our next station by evening, a cluster of platforms high in the trees, covered in white canvas. After we unpacked they fed us again, and we climbed the ladders for an early night, in order to get a good start the next morning on the game in the lowlands.

32

We awoke high in the trees, and from our roost watched the sunrise; and under the sun, the savannah rolling into the far distance. At the horizon's edge the silhouette of mountains greeted the plain. The jewel-like dew in the grasses all the way across the savannah reflected back to us the minutes-old light like miniature stars, insufflating us with a feeling of indestructible well-being.

Looking out from the treetops was like looking back in time itself, and, from our ancient perch, the rising sensation of glimpsing with the spirit's own eye, for a vanishing moment, how people must have first looked at the world.

After joining the others for breakfast in the dazzling early stillness, we hoisted ourselves into the back of the lorry with our daypacks and set out for the plains. The brush was already awake with matutinal animals going to water: the rhinoceros, aloof with power; the graceful, anodyne giraffes; the unruly zebra herds; and everywhere the hyenas lurking, slick and lowdown in the grass.

By midday we still had not seen much large game, though, until we happened upon a pride of elephants plashing in the mud to cool themselves from the torching heat.

"Yes, they do bury their dead sometimes," Ali said, answering the inevitable question. "They use tools. They have names. They do everything we do."

The others thrilled and snapped photos with impossibly large camera lenses. I had been on safari before, and was content to soak in the landscape, and clicked sparingly when I had a good shot of the landscape, or animals, or Sylvie, beaming with joy from the bounty of the wide open land.

After the elephants wandered off we drove down to the lake, where a group of villagers had paddled in dugout canoes from the other shore, working their way up and down the banks, trading maize, meat, tin pans, corn liquor, and cloth on a floating market. We bought fruit and nuts from them, which were safe to eat, and took our lunch in the shade near the shore.

After supper that evening we saw our first leopard, dashing across the plains after a Grant's gazelle he had separated from the herd. "Look at the cheetah," one of the others called, before another corrected him.

The big cat gave chase, and in the truck some of us were for the leopard, and some for the antelope. When it started, and cut back toward the herd, the leopard seemed to flag, and those who were for the gazelle cheered, until the leopard lunged up in a great desperate leap to take it down.

The group recoiled or else thrilled to the sight of blood, according to their makeup, but were all primed and eager for more.

"Gazelle gets away, life continues. Leopard gets gazelle, life continues," Ali planed his hand evenly.

"Look, there's another leopard, up in that tree," someone called, as Ali brought the lorry to a halt.

We were stopped there beneath it for upward of half an hour, as the leopard slept through the hot afternoon, and the rest snapped endless pictures of the cat, and then pictures of themselves with the leopard in the background.

We spent two more days on the savannah like that, and every day was like the one before it. But Sylvie was happy, and what pleasure I had was in that.

The evening of the third day, as we headed back to camp for the night, the plain was heading to water and eat or else den down hungry. We stopped near a large mudhole, where the hippopotamus and okapi cooled themselves in herd, but suddenly all scattered amid a chaos of bleats and cries, as a dark rumble rolled low and powerful through the earth.

On the other side of the mudhole two colossal lions were circling one another, backing up toward the water. They were uninterested in prey. Off to the other side, a lioness in estrous watched them with supreme indifference.

The lions displayed their manes in turn, escalating the threat in stages until they filled the plains with echoing thunder, which terrified everything within hearing. Even at our distance, with the protection of the truck and guards, we feared being any nearer. The hair of their manes extended on end, until they were present in all their unbridled power and savage majesty.

One of them sprung an instant later, and it was clear, as they fought there, it was not for anything but the abundance of the future, which waited stoically for the hero of that contest, whichever of them it was. Even those in the truck were too awestruck by their battle to wager on it.

The titans rose and fought in the air on uplifted legs with gruesome ferocity, each clawing for the throat of his opponent, before crashing back to the earth, where they fought ever more violently in the dust. It was not long before one of them began to fade, the other to triumph over him. The vanquishing lion, sensing his victory, let loose a thunderous roar in the red evening sun, declaring his dominion over the plain and right to ride further on down time's arrow.

When he roared next his foe did not respond, but began stealing away in defeat. The alpha would not let him part, though, until he had sealed his conquest with a *coup de grâce*, which he did in a swift brutal blow that left the other denatured. The hero went off with the lioness after that; the other, back into the dry savannah grass to die.

The others snapped away with their cameras, never taking them down from their faces the entire time. Sylvie was gripped between watching and turning away in distress.

"It's horrific," she said, her face twisted in pain. "We should not be seeing this."

"It is the jungle," I shrugged my hands. "It is what we are here to see."

"Now I have seen it. I am ready to leave."

Ali heard her, and turned the engine and headed back to camp, as the others still thrilled and cooed like pigeons at what they had seen.

"When the lion goes off with the lioness they make love three days. Thirty times every day, and do not eat," Ali reported over the drumming motor.

"That is why they fought so hard," the others joked, as they reviewed the footage they had shot.

"What will happen to the one who lost?"

"He will die. Or if he lives he will lose his mane, and it is a bad life for him after that."

"That poor fellow," said Effie. "Isn't it awful, Edward?"

"I only hope," Edward said, still looking behind us to the lion in the grass, "when he had them, he let them swing a bit from time to time."

At camp there was a fire prepared, and the smell of roasting meat, which warmed against the oncoming chill. It was our last night at that station, so we were permitted showers to cleanse the red savannah dust, as the evening sun departed.

While Sylvie wrote in her journal, I returned to the campfire, where the others were already gathered, drinking the last of the cool beers, which Ali had put out.

"How did Ms. Sylvie like the big show?" Ali asked, coming over to where I was seated.

"She liked it fine, Ali."

"What about you, sahib? You didn't like it so hot?"

"It was something to see."

"You cannot let the others bother you so much, boss. Just focus on the land. On the first day you see the green and golds. On the first night the moon and stars. On the second day you hear the birds and insects. On the third day you can see the difference between the types of plants and rocks. On the fourth day the insects no longer bother you. If you stay out here long enough and look the right way, you will eventually be able to see everything and how connected it is. The rest won't bother you so much then."

"Thanks, Ali."

"You hear what happened in the north?" One of the Coalition cut us off, coming over to where we were.

"No?"

"They are all done for," he said. "They sent in planes from Brussels, and those rebel boys have nowhere left to run."

We gossiped until the beer was exhausted, and someone produced a bottle of the local spirit and passed it around the fire. The others added it to their chai, not knowing a bad bottle of the stuff could blind you.

We had dinner together sitting on dry logs, reliving the day's adventure, until one of the Coalition produced a ukulele and started playing it, not too horribly, but he started trying to sing and had no voice. Sylvie and I slipped away after that, as they began to carry on under the stars.

From our tent in the trees we heard Effie sing a Gaelic dirge as we tried to sleep, and I thought less meanly of them for it, and was even happy for the music.

We remained awake deep into morning, whispering and laughing idly under the stars, until I shifted myself toward her beneath the covers.

"You still want to, after what we saw today?" Sylvie asked, moving away from me.

"I do," I said.

"It was awful how he suffered," she said.

"He got to lord over things awhile," I replied. "It should not stop us from making love."

"Maybe," she allowed, as I cupped her breasts in my hands, "but only if we make love all the way."

"I thought we always made love all the way."

"That is not what I mean," she answered, moving her body back toward mine.

Her voice in the darkness was clear and sultry, and I felt her pelvis move under mine, until I could feel each vertebrae.

"Come," she said. "Make love to me all the way."

"I will," I told her.

"Until we make the world again?" she asked.

"No one can make the world again."

"I feel divine tonight. Don't you think it would be beautiful to make the world again?"

I thought how magnificent that would be. We made love and I told her we could try to make the world again. If we succeeded or even if we did not, it was beautiful and good to try. Again and again we tried.

33

We were spooled under the warm covers, still deep in the transparent hour of sleep, when the breakfast bell rang. We rose reluctantly into the morning chill, and climbed down to eat. We were moving up into the highlands that morning, which would entail a day's travel, so there was a full breakfast of hen's eggs, fried bacon, pineapples, blood fruit, sweet bananas, *ugali*, and bread toasted in the fire then slathered with raw cream butter.

Sylvie was trying to give up meat, but savored the smell of frying bacon as we sat on the night-damp logs and ate around the morning fire. It was still before sunrise when we finished, and barely light when we climbed into the lorry with our gear for the long drive across the country.

Instead of taking the main road, which would have consumed most of the day and taken us first back to the capital, the truck cut crow-wise through the countryside, so that we would reach our new base camp, up in the foothills of the mountains, by lunchtime.

The massive wheels made short work of the dusty road, and it was impressive to see the sixty-year-old vehicle still so reliable. The high beams carved a path through the morning fog, as the wheels found the ruts of a desired path the truck had etched out on previous journeys over the trail.

"It will last another hundred years," Ali boasted, driving with the genial self-possession of a man at ease in his world, as he began to tell the story of how he had driven the truck from Europe, across the top of Africa five years earlier, to get his start in life.

When he saw we were still full of sleep, however, and did not need to be entertained, he fell into an equally good-natured silence. I had thought him a buffoon when we met, but had grown to understand he was not even an extrovert, but a quiet man, wearing the mask the world required of him, and trying to make a virtue of that. When the world was not there he slipped his mask right back off, as easily as coming home from the office, and the man he was beneath did not suffer too great a harm from carrying the burden for the man he presented to the outside.

Sylvie rested her head on my lap, and I propped myself against the side of the truck, in a not too uncomfortable position, as we absorbed the juts and bounces of the road, until we eventually fell in the rhythm of our own breathing, and were able to fall back asleep.

I do not know how long we had been dozing, but time passed until we were roused by a violent jolt, bringing the truck to an abrupt halt. We had struck a cement barrier, hidden in the fog, and could see shadowy figures in the road up ahead, surrounding the lorry and speaking brusquely to Ali in one of the local languages.

I peered out the side rail, and was able to make out a group of men in military fatigues, brandishing a ragtag assortment of Russian, American, and Chinese rifles and machine guns.

"What is happening?" Sylvie asked, rousing from sleep.

Before I could answer, one of the men fired his rifle in the air, and pulled a dazed Ali from his seat. The rest of the bandits quickly streamed around back, where they trained their guns up at us, and began mounting the sides of the truck.

As the first of them boarded, Edward, who was nearest him, swung his pack like a shield into the soldier's midsection, sending him sprawling to the ground.

From the road one of the others let loose a staccato burst of rounds, which struck Edward hard in the chest. His blood spattered, and all afterward was the high shriek of terror in the ear, snapping each of us aware of nothing else but our own mortality.

They climbed quickly inside the lorry then, dragging Ali up behind them, as the one up front took over control of the wheel. None of us spoke when the engine restarted. They trained their guns at our heads, before throwing Edward's lifeless body down onto the plains, abandoning it in the dirt.

The vehicle gained speed, moving still in the direction of the mountains in the distance, above the cloud layer, as Effie shrieked in protest.

"We hereby requisition this vehicle in the name of the Army of the Revelation," one of them said, nervelessly ignoring her cries. "If you do not resist, no harm will befall you. If you do—" He looked toward the body in the path behind us.

"You killed my husband," Effie sobbed violently. "You killed my husband."

"You have driven into our territory," he replied.

Ali looked away guiltily, but dared not say anything.

"He was a good man," Effie challenged with the authority of her grief. "We haven't done anything. We are innocent."

He laughed. "There are no innocents. Only those too ignorant to see."

"We don't even know what your bloody war is about."

"You are American," he replied, not really caring what her nationality was. She was of the West. Effie was wise enough not to correct him. "You are in every war, and never know what they are beyond your own narrow interests, which you tell yourselves are justified that you are saving women from their men. Children from their way of life. One helpless brown body from another savage brown body. Isn't that right? By the great, loving hand of democracy. This was the lie of colonization, and you never tire of believing your own lie, which you now masquerade in a different play. It is ever the same. First you divide neighbors; then you divide families. But before any of this you must divide the person from himself. One so divided would do anything to himself, or his people, as the leaders you have imposed on us have. But if a man enslaves his own people, it is because he is a slave himself. Now we are a country ruled by your slaves.

"You have your own politics and your own histories of the world, and with these you replace men and women. But your world has forgotten the truth Rome taught to you, and your progenitors certainly knew: The only way to colonize a people is absolutely and for all eternity. If you do not have the stomach for that you are only stirring mischief. Freedom comes only through the voice and will and blood of the people themselves. Everything else is jerry-built. But you do not care what happens anywhere, so long as your dogs do your bidding. We choose to be men. Free and alive in our own country, or else dead and free in the earth."

"Fuck your bloody war. You killed my husband. You killed my husband!" She screamed in anguish of what only moments ago had been her life.

"If we have made a mistake, and your husband is collateral damage—I have lost many, so I know your pain," he said in a tone all the more disquieting for seeming sincere, as he looked at her with an eerie compassion.

"Monster," she screamed.

"Tell me what your custom is, and how much it will take to make you whole, or else, if you prefer, I will find you a new husband," he laughed.

Her tears subsided after that, overwhelmed by the fear of his threat. Her breathing was still erratic, though, until it seemed she might come apart completely. His menace and the dead man had cowed the rest, so that no one else spoke, or made eye contact, or tried to comfort her, until Ali spoke up.

"I am sorry, ma'am," he said. "It is my fault."

"It is not your fault, Ali," Effie answered, releasing him.

"My job is to get you there safely, but I got us captured. I was shortcutting. Now look what I have done."

"You put your own road where there was none but you needed a road to be. They just ambushed us, is all."

"Quiet," they commanded from the rails of the speeding truck, where they had entwined themselves like malevolent vines.

In the commotion I slipped the bracelet I always wore from my wrist over to Sylvie's, as we clasped hands. It was a string of different-colored wooden beads, I had picked up long ago, which she pressed her palm over, then began fingering like a rosary. Her head pressed tight into my chest.

"What is going to happen?" she whispered.

"We will be fine," I held her wrist. "Try to stay calm. But if anything too bad happens, the center one opens."

"What is in it?"

"A cyanide pill," I said. "If anything unspeakable happens, and we are not fine, eat it. But only if things are so bad you think there is no other way home."

34

We rode along silently as the drought-stricken plains turned to green hills, and the hills gave way to the gray mountain mist, with the peak of Mount Clarel, their last redoubt, poking up through the clouds. The angled light of the dying sun fell on us like their slanted guns, as our pulses tensed and beat faster in the cobalt air, and the soldiers watched like esurient hawks in the silence.

Our only measure of security was our value to them. We were their pawns and their insurance, to be dealt out and traded for safe passage in dire straits; sold for ransom, for food, for guns; or else deployed as shields to guard them, like talismans, from incoming fire.

Not that they believed they needed shields. They had other talismans, believing themselves to be protected from bullets by magical spirits, whose protection had been invoked with the ceremonial sprinkling of waters from the lake, applied to each soldier in turn by their commander when they first joined that army.

For some this magic seemed to work. They were not dead. The soldiers guarding us were the last of these, the final survivors from the bedraggled group of insurgents who had been in the field near three generations, as the men whose talismans failed them were used up. The wants of the war morphed with each successive generation in the field, and the war they inherited from their fathers' fathers was as different as their allies from outside, until they had no allies left, only themselves, and their reasons for fighting were no longer coherent, only the pent-up emotions of three generations of war and bloodshed and betrayal and still no satisfaction for their claims. They had been fighting since before any other part of the continent rebelled, and before the larger world rolled itself into the tumult, like dice, to find vengeance or oblivion in the chaos. Land to feed themselves, cloth to cover themselves, materials to build the machines of their desires and destinies, new dogmas to soothe their complaints, new ideology they might seduce themselves into believing to replace the ones that had come before, all were slaughtered when the magic of their talismans failed. They would fight from that mountain until the last talisman of the last man flickered out and perished.

Their first leader had been a notorious man, called Achilles Asha, who was taken from his village as an eight-year-old by priests, who came and snatched all the first-born children from that part of the country, after a minor rebellion led the colonial rulers to send the priests to help extinguish it.

There were no birth records and Achilles, second of twelve, was home while his brother was at pasture with the herds. His parents put him forth for sacrifice instead.

The children they abducted were then dealt out in the capital like playing cards, and Achilles ended with a group of Jesuit missionaries, where he was trained to someday return to help convert the others. By eighteen he had accepted this fate, until one night, as he read in the library, he found a copy of the *Malleus Maleficarum*, and it was like speaking to like; self communing with self without interdiction. Corpus and spiritus joined. Song of his own song. What was boy became warrior.

In the morning all the priests were found slaughtered. The boys were forced from the grounds, and scattered before the wind like seeds. "We are natural men, who have been spirited into an unnatural world, let us live as we were meant to again and forever. Return to your villages and bear witness to what happened here," he declared in his sermon that morning at Mass, before setting the campus ablaze.

When the fire was high enough that it glowed in the black of his eyes, he saw inside at the windows three novices who had not evacuated, but hidden in the dorms for fear they were dead to their people and would not be accepted back.

They escaped the inferno in time. Shadrach, Mesach, Abednego, as he called them when he enlisted them under his command, and set out with his army of ninth-graders to cleanse the world.

First they set out to rid the country of churches. Next they set upon government, then schools, jails, corporations, institutions of any sort.

Those who did not question on this first campaign, who did not buck, did not break, did not die, were elevated to be Achilles' lieutenants, as he himself was God's lieutenant on earth, holding court in lieu of the Almighty.

"Under what authority do you serve?" A new recruit once asked, challenging their leader's command, after his own village had been put to sword.

"The Society of the Virgin," answered Achilles. "She came to me in a vision, and revealed that I am the son of Christ. The Holy Spirit, it works through me."

"Which Virgin?"

"The Black Virgin. Mother of the Blessed. Protector of the Lost."

Sometime after that they were on maneuvers in the mountains, and he was pinned down by enemy fire, and Achilles knew he had been betrayed. They had just passed through the village of another of his lieutenants, and that man-child had sold out his brothers-in-arms in favor of the mother who first birthed him.

They fought through the night, outgunned and losing soldiers by the score, then the hundreds, between the edge of the jungle and the mountain's sheer rock cliff. He was a leader who, since he first understood his call, had known no doubt, but he meditated all that night on the fault of his ways, and made a vow before sunrise. If he emerged from that deluge he would purify and rededicate himself to his cause.

By miracle, they claimed, they lived to see the next day. His entire regiment had been decimated, save five others, four who were loyal and the one who sold him from weakness. They gave thanks nonetheless that morning, and in observance he bestowed on each survivor a new name, as the sun sprang its first pink knuckle from its nighttime grave, and the dew of first day seeped through their gear, chilling their skin.

Isaac he rechristened Jeremiah. Who was Esau became Obadiah. An albino boy, also called Isaac, he baptized as Isaac once more, and Isaac went after that by the name II Isaac. The fourth and most faithful he blessed with Daniel. These were the prophets of suffering, and the leaders of the First Army of Innocence, as they were then called.

The child called Chausiku at home and Uriah at school, he sprinkled with water from the lake, kissed him on the mouth, and called him brother. When he administered the sacrament he gave to him the new name Jude. The outfit that before had been the Army of Innocents was innocent no longer, and became thereafter the Army of Revelation. He himself he crowned Job, because he was come to suffer. Where they had been confused before, they knew exactly what they did now. They set out to reveal.

"Jesus forgives your sins, Jude, my brother," Job said softly. "They were caused because you love your mother and are a mamma's son. You thought the village mothers could save you from the wrath of the Father. Only repent and renounce Satan, who misled you, and all his Works, once again, and from this day forward."

"I renounce them," Jude said. "Satan, and all his works."

"Amen. But before you can sin again you must leave the earth for the kingdom." He dispatched him then, sending his friend to meet his Maker in a state of purity. "Here on earth I alone make peace. I alone create evil. I am judge of men, and judge of judges, and judge of kings. You I deny."

He no longer trusted those local to the region after that, and put out the call for recruits and comrades in all parts of the world, who would come into that jungle Eden with him, and reclaim it from wickedness. "The earth has become unnatural, and it is time for us to live again according to the laws of nature, and not Satan in the halls of power."

They heard his call, and came to him from all over the world. And he looked through the clarity of each eye, down until he could see the silver mark on every translucent heart; read the prayer engraved on each numinous, golden soul. Some he enlisted and others he sent away. Those he drew to him were culled from every war zone and every refugee camp and every ghetto, every occupied land and every crippled way of life. Whosoever was put upon. Whosoever was misunderstood. Whoever was wretched, and whose idols had been smashed, clung to him, to help pull down their oppressors in a cataclysm they said would equal the first fall.

They were all young as he, all veterans of other wars, and all saw visions of a new world, perfect and pure, to which they were devoted even beyond life.

In the most lawless stretch of the interior they laid hold to a city-state the size of Acadia, protected by the jungle, that in turn grew into a country the size of the Louisiana Purchase, in which they destroyed all roads, all telephone lines, all power cables, tax collection, any instrument of the modern world, to cut off contamination.

In the new land they fashioned fishhooks from bones, and medicine from tree barks and herbs native to the soil. They wove their own clothing, cooked their food in stone pots they carved from the mountain. There was no science beyond warfare, which they waged without cease on the corrupt world beyond their borders. Inside the republic they lived free and unstained.

From the center Job sent deacons south, west, and north to cleanse all corruption, while he himself held the eastern country absolute as the sun. "I am the sun," he would declare one day, as the rebellion began to unravel from within. "I will bring light to evil, and wash away sin with perfection."

He was thirty-two then, and had never known a woman's embrace, and made virginity a requisite for all his soldiers. Only those who were not stained by sins of the flesh could be pure, and those who were not pure existed to be cleansed.

He put his stone knife through those who were not pure, one by one, so they could die pure in the jungle Eden. "You go to heaven now," he proclaimed, in a madness so broken and scrambled it began to make a new sense. "Here I am ruler, and will commit this crime so that the next generation will abide no impurity."

Only the children were granted reprieve, to become the base of his new army and his new world. The adults he captured were put to work in mines, toiling ceaselessly by day to harvest ore, iron, copper, gold, coltan, and by night to produce soldiers.

"All good is built upon wickedness. From the broken world we forge a whole one." From the fertilizer of death sprang the new crop of purity.

To his army of orphans he gave the steel of arms to defend the new world, promising none should ever lord over them again. He was their Lord, permanent as the sun.

Five years more they raged through the jungle under his command. The more they succeeded, the greater the resistance from the outside became, until he needed stronger guns to defend against stronger enemies. These he acquired from what he could pay in gold from the mines, and all were eager to deal with him.

"Colonel," asked one of his lieutenants, who would become the head of the first breakaway faction, "does this mean we have come to accept the tenets of capitalism? Is it not an unnatural way to be?"

"War costs. We are only trading rocks from the ground that have no meaning to us, for guns that do. This one thing to Caesar, until he too can be cleansed. As for the capitalists, they are only babes, suckling in their nannies' arms, who would not survive a season here in the mountains."

"Are we in that case with the Communists?" A new recruit asked, bewildered.

"We are free, and beyond *isms.* To show how free I will baptize the souls of a thousand slavers, and we will have a feast to celebrate their ascension."

He could afford his magnanimity. By then he commanded a world larger than Charlemagne's Reich, and there was not an army on the continent the equal of his. He was thirty-seven then, the age we will all be in heaven, and he was at the height of his power.

When he died in that jungle his commanders found his plague-stricken body, and eulogized him, realizing how little they had known him. They did not even know what name to write on his grave. Some argued for Achilles Asha, others for Job, and another faction argued that though he had changed his name and changed it again, these were merely the fictions he had lived by in the world, and he also possessed a secret name. This died with him. And in death, as in life, he was powerless to change it. His true name.

While he lived the army went undefeated, but two generations after independence, what remained of the three armies that succeeded him was a single regiment, scattered piecemeal through the jungle, oblivious to borders, but reunited on the mountain where Achilles had made his first miraculous stand, and where they would make their last if need be—supported by a single mine, of copper not gold, and whence they would set forth again to claim and purify the earth.

They were virgins, and so long as they knew not the sins of the flesh God would be on their side, and their struggle was permanent as the blood red sun.

These were our captors.

"How do you live with yourselves?" Effie asked, as we neared their mountain in the late afternoon light. "Why do you hate so much?"

Their officer looked out over the receding jungle with the disquieting calm and self-command of those inured to death. "I do not have to answer this insolence, sister. But I will share with you a secret. Death is natural. Yours, mine, everyone's. I do not hate you, or anyone, even those I kill. All must die. Perhaps our enemies hate us, but to our view, the missionaries and colonizers—who came and stole the land from the old generation and then stole a new generation from the land—acted according to nothing but the perfection of their own purpose. To the extent they succeeded at that we salute them. They were excellent slavers, and excellent missionaries, doing whatever they thought was required of them to further their own way of life. We intend the same, according to a new purpose, to unwind history by our own thread. It is not personal. In another context I would be the implement of your desire—you would order me as you willed, Lord I Peter, stop blaspheming and fetch me a Tusker—so it is a question of subject and object. Who and Whom. "

The truck bounded over the broken road as our guards fixed their ears on their leader and their hardened stares on us. We continued up the mountainside, powerless, toward their camp.

"Why are you with the missionaries, eh?" their leader asked, picking me out from the others.

"I am not with them," I said calmly. He was nothing more than another sociopath, and I did not want to give him anything to seize on. "I am only with her."

"She is a nun," he laughed, looking at Sylvie with his red-rimmed eyes. He had spotted the bracelet on her wrist, which he now took in his battered hands, as a look of abject terror inched across her face.

"Why is she wearing the rosary?"

"It is from me," I said.

"A present must be of gold," he laughed. "It is a rosary." His voice contained a preternatural calmness. He was in his element, and it was nothing for him to kill. He only needed a reason, and he would take a life as simply as blowing out a match. Or no reason at all.

"It is just a bracelet." I feigned indifference, which I had for myself, but not for her.

"You are not a Christ bride, sister?" he asked.

"No. She is mine."

"You are a race-mixer, my brother," he grinned a demented grimace.

I did not want to give him fodder for his lunacy and stared straight ahead.

"The chief spoke to you. Answer him," one of his minions threatened.

"What you call race is a lie," I said.

"Ah. You are a white man."

"I am black as you."

"You are impure."

"Purity is a worse lie."

I did not want to debate the eighteenth century, and especially not with an armed madman. To my relief, though, he let go of her wrist for the moment, but as he turned away his eye caught mine in a different way. I saw him registering something as a flickering passed behind his thoughts. He saw me then, and that I was not afraid of him. I knew we were marked. He had released her wrist and the bracelet, though, for the time being, as we continued up the mountain, ascending to their base.

35

We were at the base of the mountain inside the damp clouds. Above us the lights from their camp were visible as a diffuse glow, refracted by the water vapor. The buzz of activity reached our ears from the camp, filling us with alternating currents of fear of the strange voices and fear of an unknown fate, as they forced us from the truck and started marching us upslope.

Sylvie was shaking as we climbed down from the truck, and I offered my hand to steady her in the condensed stillness, where all was quiet except the spray of pebbles from our boots as we ascended a narrow trail through the cloud forest.

When we had climbed more than an hour the path began thinning out even further, forcing us to scramble in single file up the steepest part of the slope, searching in the thickening darkness for handholds to help pull ourselves up when the ground fell away uncertainly.

We were slowed to a near halt, as the boots of the person in front cleated the dust down onto whoever was next, so that the line was stretched out forty feet against the face of the mountain. Two of the guards stood up ahead. To intimidate us, two were on either side of the group hectoring to speed us up, and another in the rear. Sylvie and I were near the last in line and the darkness was almost palpable by then, as we shivered from sweat and exertion.

The guards were growing agitated, visibly eager to get to the light and warmth of their camp, which could be seen clearly now, casting its steady glow out into the ravines opening below us.

"Whatever happens keep your head," I said, as we neared the two soldiers at the midpoint of the slope.

"Quiet," their shouts rained down on us from above. "No talking." They climbed like rams, and our slow-going was keeping them in the cold, away from their cooking fires, which we had started to smell. When we looked up we saw the front of our line had started to disappear into the mouth of the cave, and I grasped Sylvie's wrist to hold her there.

"Wait here."

The Aussie, who was ahead of us, looked back with annoyance, knowing we would only incite the guard's anger again, and that they would have plenty of time to take it out on all of us. He was right, but I waved him off, as the guard in back started yelling, scrambling angrily up the loose sides of the mountain to vent his rage. When he had closed the distance, and his hand raised to strike me, I threw myself hard down the slope at him, spiking my feet into his legs. My boot landed at his knee joint, and he tumbled over. Sylvie had already started scrambling down in a bolt of adrenaline as I grappled in the dust with the guard.

"Harper," she yelled.

I shouted for her to keep running and not to stop. I had caught the guard by surprise, but he was recovering from the initial shock, and searching with his hand for his holstered pistol. I managed to pin him briefly, but he freed himself, and we started to crash down the mountain as we fought and struggled, until we smashed brutally against a ledge. I managed to grab hold of a loose stone, and pounded it down as hard as I could to his head. He was stunned into stillness, and I claimed the pistol from his dazed hand, and scrambled to get away before his comrades could capture me and claim their revenge.

High above the others heard the commotion, and the soldiers began throwing themselves down the mountain in a rush to get to us before we were out of their grasp. I could see their silhouettes, but was uncertain if they had a bead on me, only that they were making steady progress. I threw myself off the ledge, diving headlong into one of the ravines below, where I crashed hard into the rocks and thorny underbrush.

The noise had let them know my location, and they began aiming their flashlights to track me down in the darkness. I aimed a shot right into the light, which went black and held them off for a time.

Sylvie was a good way down the mountain by then, and I began after her as another flashlight started to play over the ground. I heard shots ring from their guns and ricochet against the stones around me. I took careful aim, then fired again, trying to hold them back at least until I could no longer see Sylvie below.

The pistol was a forty-caliber Sig, and held a dozen shots. I only fired when I saw something moving, to make them consider how much it was worth it, and to know that if they caught me, it would not be with rounds left in the gun.

The darkness was gathering quickly; as I reached the cloud layer it grew near impossible to see, but I kept an eye trained for the soldiers and the other trained below to make out Sylvie's silhouette until she was out of range.

Around me several shots rang from above as I inched my way forward, but I had the cover of a boulder in the ravine and the shots struck some distance away, telling me they did not have a clear line of sight. I pressed myself against the ravine floor, and began picking my way down on my haunches. The spiny burrs stung my legs, and the rocks began to slide unstably down the trail with me.

The dust rose and rose as I slid, until all of a sudden I sensed myself falling straight down a gap in the pitch darkness, and it was then the shots burst closer. I suddenly felt something strangely warm pin me to the ground violently, and reached my hand out in the darkness to investigate, as the warmth turned fiery hot and began circulating through my body.

My hand groped its way to the hot center of heat, and I felt there the wetness of blood. I brought it instinctually to my face, as by some subconscious belief that it could not be my own blood, until I smelled its ferric familiarity.

I was overcome by pain, but knew I could not remain there, and pushed off the side of the mountain down the uncertain incline, unable to see more than three feet in any direction, and unsure whether they knew I had been hit. I started across the slope, knowing they would no longer have a straight shot down at me if I could get far enough away.

I could not judge distance in the darkness, but leapt from the ravine in desperation, banging hard along until I fell to rest again, against a bed of smooth stones, where I remained, unable to move.

I listened over the pain, and waited for the sound of their guns. I did not hear anything then except the pounding of blood in my own ears, until the tinkle of pebbles falling let me know they were still on the precipice above me.

Their flashlights reached down into the ravines, like transparent fingers, and I flattened against the rocks, as the light prodded and searched each gully in turn. They fired a burst of rounds into each trench when they were done searching it, and I began sweating with fever and freezing from the coldness of my injury, when the thick fingers of light began poking along the ground nearby until they finally let go a volley of rounds against the stones that rang in my ear like my own heartbeat. Then nothing remained and nothing could be heard but the darkness and evensong of the earth itself.

The lights brushed over the darkness above once or twice more, before bending down into my trench again. I do not know how long it took, but eventually the lights passed, and they started back up the mountain. I knew they would return at first light, if the hyenas and wild dogs did not pick up the scent of blood before that.

I was bleeding badly, and kept one hand pressed down against the wound to try and staunch it, and tried as well to control my breathing, and keep from crying with pain. I began down the mountain again.

I first picked my way horizontally across the face, trying to find the path we'd taken up. I could not separate it from the darkness, or see even more than a few steps of the trail I was on, until I was eventually completely lost, and on a different side of the mountain from where I'd started. Every opening in the vegetation seemed like a trail and every clearing seemed like salvation, but all were cruel tricks. The only thing for me was to head straight down, and try not to end up in one of the deeper *couloirs*, which I might never escape. Each step fell into a deeper darkness, and I poked at the air first with my foot to find the slope, then at the soil, testing the ground, to keep from falling off the mountain. I was hopelessly lost by then, feeling my way back in the direction I remembered, hoping I would not get taken by the hyenas or wild dogs, or else fall into one of the holes. And what I knew about where I was headed was only gravity.

When the slope evened out, I found a place to perch and managed a tourniquet from my shirt, which was soon soaked through. There were a lot of ways for me to die on the mountain then, and I did not know which I dreaded most, and I did not wish to acknowledge my fears any further, for fear of conjuring them, or giving over to them more power than they already had. I heard lizards scurrying in the brush and then a bark in the darkness, and that fixed my fear on the hyenas. The cats would come one-on-one nobly, and I had the gun and if I missed it would be a quick death, but the hyenas and dogs would come in packs, ganging up to rip and pick little by little, until I succumbed. If I fell into a ravine there was at least the chance I would break my neck and lose consciousness. Time I would lose against eventually, if not that night. The bullet I already had in me. I kept heading downward into the brutal blackness, keeping watch for hyenas and wild dogs.

36

The base of the slope appeared through the fog sometime past midnight. I was caked in dust and muddied with blood, and the pain from the wound throbbed with each heartbeat. The clouds parted midway and the dense stars were high and bright in the sky, along with half the moon, which made the going a little easier, until I realized how far I was from where we had ascended, and how far I was from the lorry, where I hoped Sylvie would be waiting and safe. I rounded the lower reaches of the mountain in another hour, before I spotted the truck below me in the platinum darkness. It was only half a mile away, but there were a series of plunging crevasses in front of me, and no way to cross over with the pain in my shoulder, and that hand unusable. I wrenched the tourniquet tighter, as I sat down to rest and try to plot a way down. There was no certain passage from where I was that I could see. The only safe thing to do was to climb back up, until I found the trail we had taken before.

I stood wearily and climbed uphill another hour, before finally picking up a ridge wide enough to pass over without falling into one of the ravines. From there I descended the remainder of the way.

By the time I reached the truck it was near two o'clock, and Sylvie was nowhere to be found. I was dead with worry, and tried to keep my mind from running off with bad scenarios, as I searched the cab of the truck for the medical kit and checked around for a spare key.

I did not find keys to the truck, and the medical kit was half empty, with nothing of use for the gunshot wound. I was overcome by thirst then, and went round back to find water and my gear bag, where I had some painkillers Doc had given me. It would be light in a only few hours and I did not think they could head back down before then without my being able to see them before they spotted me. I calculated if I slept three hours, and set out for Sylvie an hour before light I could still keep out of their reach.

When I climbed up into the back of the truck I was struck hard by something crashing into me, and tumbled backward, reaching for the gun holstered in my waistband.

"I'm sorry," I heard Sylvie gasp. "I thought they had caught you. They were so close." She threw her arms around me, crying with joy but drew back when she saw how I winced in pain, as moonlight streamed into the truck through the open flap. "Did I hurt you?"

"Not you," I told her.

"Let me see," she said, pulling away in shock, when she saw my arm and how bedraggled I was. "You're covered in blood."

She touched my shoulder gently, near the wound.

"It is better not to touch it."

"They shot you?"

"It did not hit anything major, or I would have known already," I tried to comfort her.

"You are just trying to keep me from worrying," she said.

"Worrying does not help."

"Does it hurt?" she asked.

"Like hell."

She found scissors and cut away my makeshift tourniquet, and made bandages from a clean shirt, and began to pour water from a canteen to wash away the blood, but I told her it was better to save the water. She began to redress the wound with the clean bandages, and I began to feel cold and clammy and parched. I was thirsty again and asked for the canteen, and drank deeply, until it was empty. She wrapped a blanket around me to help regulate my temperature, and refilled the canteen from a half-empty jug in the truck, and I drank half of it down, and swallowed the last of the pills.

We had not eaten since breakfast, and I had no appetite, but forced myself to eat an energy bar we found in our packs.

After that she fashioned a sling for my deadened arm, to elevate the wound, and make carrying the weight of it easier. There was nothing else for us there with the truck but danger. We refilled our canteens from the last of the water in the jug, found a bit of food, flashlights, a compass, and money from our packs, and started down toward the trees.

It was five treacherous miles to the lake by my reckoning. The hard night around us was infinite and deep, as we tried to keep watch for the predators and soldiers and whatever else might be out there in the jungle. I still had rounds in the gun, but not enough.

"From the lake we should be able to cross the border out of the country by water."

"Do you think we will be able to find a doctor?"

"No. There are none in places like this, and if there was one he would either have fled, or else have some connection. But if we reach the lake, we can get one of the villagers to row us across."

"I'm afraid."

"We still have the pistol," I said, calculating the chances of running into one of the rebels, or a predator that did not fear humans.

We were out of sight of the lorry by then, on the last stretch of fore mountain. Down below the tree line had come into view, and just after that a break, and a stretch of plain, where there were some structures visible.

"Look, there is a village over there," she pointed.

"I think it is better if we avoid it," I cautioned.

"They may be able to help us."

"Or harm us," I argued.

I did not want to take the risk, but we were not certain of our exact location or the lake's, and I knew she was right. We oriented ourselves toward the village, and kept focused on it as we came down the last stretch of incline onto flat ground, where the village disappeared in the darkness.

When we were finally off the mountain, we began quickly as we could manage across the open plain, toward the cover of the forest. We had no sense of shelter as long as we were out in the open, and no advantage over anything else out there, except for the few shots left in the gun.

We thought being back inside the forest would offer a greater sense of protection, but when we entered the trees again the shadows quickly brought home how many more places there were for danger to lurk, as we began to worry about what might be above us as well. There was no choice, and we picked our way carefully through the strange forest, trying to control our fear as the trees swallowed us in the denseness. The vegetation was equally impenetrable, and we fought through with our hands, using the compass to navigate a straight-enough line.

There were no stars visible anymore, only the occasional break in the clouds and gilded light of the moon, which shone sharp into the forest, playing intermittent tricks with the shadows. I felt every sense grow acute, and the fear at least deadened the pain. We made our way through the darkness by feel, a few feet at a time.

My shoulder was in terrible shape after a while, and there were no more painkillers, so I tried to focus on my steps to take my mind off the shoulder. After an hour the forest seemed to thin out, and we could get a glimpse ahead, where the outline of the village came clear again, but was soon swallowed by darkness when the clouds passed across the face of the moon and fog began rolling in over us, swelling the night with a perfect darkness and perfect fear.

We continued on until we startled, hearing activity in the leaves ahead. We froze where we were, listening to a rustling of the ground moving steadily toward us, with the confidence of feet familiar with the forest. Whether human or animal was impossible to tell. We crouched against the trees, and tried our best to remain calm. The sound grew steadily nearer with slow intent. I kept my hand on the gun, hoping for the advantage of surprise over whatever it was I was going to shoot.

A moment later we heard the meaningful patter of human voices crystallize, but the words did not separate out one from the other. We knew what we faced, at least, and hoped it was a villager out looking for wood for the morning fire, and not something more nefarious out there at night.

The steps grew closer until we were certain it was more than two people. We did not wait, but quickened our pace in the other direction, to run before they could reach us.

Their movements were confident in the strange landscape, and when we heard them stop, we stopped as well. A voice called out to us, but we did not know the language nor trust the voice we heard, and did not leave the spot where we hid against the trees, until the nearby branches stirred with a movement too near. I stepped out with the gun drawn, and saw in the break of the moon three children passing in near silence.

They startled when they saw the gun, and paused, looking at us, and at the gun. We did not say anything at all, and they broke out running in the direction of the plain.

When they were gone we kept in the opposite direction as quickly as possible. There was something about them that did not seem like children. Perhaps I was only being fearful, but it was not a time to second-guess the instinct telling me I did not want to find out what they might have known that gave their faces such hardness and courage in that jungle.

We circled back toward the village, checking nervously every time anything stirred in the underbrush to make certain no one was following us from behind and nothing was tracking us from the trees. The forest felt empty, yet they had come from somewhere, so I was hesitant of going to the village after that, but Sylvie still thought it the best option to get help, so we kept going undeterred through a darkness and silence so deep the only thing we could hear was the age of the earth.

We eventually reached a clearing on the open plain again, out of immediate danger. The fog had dissolved and the clouds had cleared and we could see a fair way in all directions, but search as we might, we had lost sight of the village.

Sylvie was more at ease having cleared the forest, but I was still tense with edginess, trying to ignore the fear, as the insects in the high savannah grass called from the distance, and the forest sounded from behind us, and my own pulse still beat hard in my blood.

"Do you smell something?" Sylvie asked, stopping midway across the clearing.

"No."

"It is fire."

I still did not smell it, but a few feet further on the wind caught it and carried it toward us, acrid and distinct, but impossible to tell where it came from.

"If there has been a ground fire it will be good," she reasoned. "The animals will have been frightened from the area."

"What makes you say it is a ground fire? Isn't it more likely from the village?"

We debated again whether to go to the village, but we were lost and had no choice. She wove her fingers through mine, and I laced my hand in hers briefly, before putting it back on the pistol. The stars burned away overhead and the partway moon gave some partway light, but not enough.

We could not tell whether it was more dangerous for us in the village or whether there was more danger there in the dark. That is what fear is and it is what we felt and the only thing moving us forward was desire to escape the fear.

The village came into view again not long after Sylvie first smelled fire. We could see everything that had been there was burned down to embers and ash.

As we navigated the charred earth we saw bits of what had been there before, stones from cooking fires, and posts from buildings. It was after that we started to see pieces of bone scattered on the ground, and at first they looked like the bones of cattle, because that was what we wished, but my foot kicked something and it was not.

"What is that?" Sylvie asked.

"Do not look," I said. "It is not something to see."

We hurried to get out of that place of death. It was only a small village, and most likely a temporary settlement for the herders moving their cattle over the plains to summer pasture, but the ground showed clearly where the houses had been, and they were not there. The people were not there, and, as we crossed out of that place, we could smell nothing except fire. They had purified that place, and when they were done making it pure only the atoms remained.

The forest soon grew up severely all around us again. The herders had probably chosen that place thinking it safer than the wide-open plains, but it was not for them and it was not for us.

We picked up a trail at the edge of where the village had been, and hoped it would take us on to the lake. Without that we had no chance in all of hell.

We were relieved to be out of the village, and the forest felt safe to us, or just less unsafe, as we pressed through, not knowing where, but believing that it could become no worse.

A hundred feet into the forest again we saw a shape ahead of us, crouched low to the ground. We stopped in terror, then began backing away slowly.

The creature in the road did not move toward us, but nor did it run, so I pointed the Sig at it, and Sylvie stood behind my shoulder, and we searched for another way but the trees were dense and there was no other way forward.

I yelled out, and still what was there did not move. We inched forward again, my finger tight around the trigger, until I saw a pair of eyes staring at me, and squeezed off a shot that exploded in the dirt.

The thing did not stir, and I yelled again, inching close behind the gun, until my stomach heaved at what a monster of a thing it was: a human baby dead and burned up and wrapped in cloth and left there in the jungle for the animals.

"Don't look."

She had seen it already, and clung tight to my arm, then buried her face, as tears coursed from her eyes. I went up to it and knelt to close the dead child's eyes, but the eyelids were burned away and it kept staring at us.

"What an awful thing." She was crying hard, and I could not comfort her.

"It was meant to be humane. Whoever did it was trying to spare the child. To sacrifice it to whatever they were and believed in, and not whatever enemy wanted to cut them from it."

We walked in silence, but our breathing was loud over our emotion, and the pain in my shoulder seemed to breathe again too as the pills wore thin.

"How is your shoulder?" Sylvie asked, from concern, as well as desire to dispel the silence.

"It is fine. It does not hurt as much," I answered flatly, to mask my worry about the bullet still being inside of me.

"Oh, you are suffering."

"I will be fine."

"You don't have to be brave for me."

"I know. But I do if I want to keep going."

There was nothing else to say about it, as the forest called around us, and the earth sounded beneath us, and our fear rose a little but soon so did our hope when we realized it was nearly morning. The darkness was not yet burned to the blue light, but the crepuscular window between night and morning was starting to open.

Nothing was different but a feeling in our cells, and then there was the sound of the river, not yet seen, but the clear swell of water rushing somewhere down below, which we knew would lead us to the lake.

As we pressed on we heard a single bird call and beat its wings from high in the trees, but we did not know if it was of the night or of the morning, but soon after that the buzzing of bees, as a colony of them moved somewhere in the still darkness.

"It is morning," I said.

"It is still dark," she answered. "There are at least another two hours before day."

"It is morning," I said with relief.

"How can you be sure?"

"The bees are matutinal. They are up with the day."

"Like monks," she said.

"Yes," I nodded.

I felt her heart lighten a little, and she tried to buoy mine as well. "Do you think they can marry us?"

"Monks cannot administer rites."

"Their abbot can," she said. "Just promise you won't make me a widow. It would not be right, after you made me love you like you did."

I rested the gun in my waistband and took her hand for comfort. But she stopped dead all of a sudden, screaming with fright as something larger than us moved out of the jungle directly ahead.

Before I had time to get the gun it was rushing right in front of us without fear and, at the sound of her scream, only answered it with a long, low cry, and was right on top of us before we saw it was nothing but one of the cows from the village.

Our chests collapsed with relief, but we were put on guard again, seeing how easy it was for anything out there to come upon us.

"We should hurry. This is still their territory. As soon as it is light they will come for us."

"They will not bother with us now."

"I'm afraid they will," I said. "We know where they are."

37

We kept along the river's edge through the last of the cloud forest, the trees growing shorter and shorter, turning first to shrubs, then to grass. The red earth of the plains began to show, and the sky grew slowly lighter, as the morning flowers began to open and spread their perfume, masking the rotting jungle.

We were in an area with only a sparse copse of trees here and there, and could make our way through easily. The air sweetened and I had the sensation we were nearing the lake, though in truth, I had had that sensation many times already, from wishing it so.

The sound of the sluicing river off in the distance was soothing in our ears, even as the trees thickened around it. The ground was flat, at least, and it was light enough that we could see plainly. We hugged the sound of the river, and hoped just to whistle down the darkness until daybreak.

Our phones did not have reception, making it impossible to map our location or call for help, but we felt sure the lake was getting closer, and even the throbbing pain of my shoulder had turned to a white noise against the blue darkness. It was sufferable as long as I did not think about it but stayed focused on walking and fighting off the weariness and creeping hunger, until I ceased to care anymore about what would happen.

Sylvie looked at me tenderly, and tried to mask the pain in her eyes as she took my free hand in her hand. "Just walk with me," she said, holding my hand and leaning into me, trying to ease my weight as best she could.

"Do you want to rest?" she asked, as we came upon a place a little further on that was open and dry.

"Just a little while," I agreed.

We sat down in the dew-jeweled grass to take water and rest. It was good to feel my muscles relax, but the pain in my shoulder had started throbbing with greater urgency.

Sylvie handed me the canteen, and the water was cool from the metal and sweet to taste, making me feel we would make it.

We sat there awhile in tranquility, collecting our strength. As we prepared to leave, though, the air became charged with the sense we were being watched. We scanned in opposite directions, and when Sylvie stopped moving I turned slowly to where she was focused, and saw in front of me a pair of deep black eyes, staring at us in pensive silence.

It was a massive blackback, with an enormous head and those preternaturally large eyes contemplating us without blinking, nailing us to where we were. We did not have the sense to be afraid at first, it was so uncanny an intelligence behind them, making us feel less threatened than that we were made of glass, and being turned around in the sun to see how we were composed. When fear finally stirred, it was bone deep, and I moved my hand slowly toward the pistol without thinking. The gorilla saw my movement and charged, shrieking as she rose up onto her two legs so that she was half a head taller than me, and roared close enough that we felt her breath. If I had moved any more she would have taken me from life, but I stayed still, resigned to the worst, as my fear settled and there was nothing to think of except how my life had been. Whatever unfolded, so it was and so be it.

She stopped when I did, and I realized her vocalization had been a warning, as she dropped back to all fours with slow composure, all the while keeping me in her gaze, with a stare of fiery intensity that seared the wall separating us. I was glass and the wall was glass, and the glass thinned and thinned until I felt seen through completely, and it was only a bent note across.

I stood held in her stare, not knowing if she would attack, but feeling at peace with whatever happened. I released the breath I had held, and she let loose a ferocious screech that wakened the birds, making them flock from the trees overhead as she soared up on her feet again, before returning back to all fours on the ground, still staring at me. But I had lost my fear of her, because there was no life beyond that point, simply what I had already had and already was or had been and the shape of her claw. I was content for it to go either way, but knew somehow, or thought I knew, we would be let to pass.

When she settled on the ground, she started moving away in a great rush, until she was twenty feet back, where she stopped at the wall of trees by the bank. We saw the rest of her family then, which we had not before, another blackback, and two infants, who rushed to her and began crawling on her, which she indulged. When she had made it to the far field we could see also another figure in the dirt, a gigantic silverback stretched out immobile, in a snare.

She sat in front of it, pulling the leaves off a branch, which she gave to the juveniles, and did not move any further. We knew what she did not, however, that the poachers would return soon, and we could not be there when they did.

The two matrons both looked at us as we began to back away, and started to rush toward us, but they stopped short and wailed to end the world, before returning again to the corpse and the cubs, who did not understand and wished still to play.

It was the damnedest thing I ever saw.

We were transfixed and watched them, and the matriarchs watched us, until we took another step away and they paid us no mind, but stripped the leaves from a low tree and fed their young. We were like that for one second or else one year, until the light made it clear we had better keep moving.

When we felt safe to turn our backs they hooted again and began fleeing up the mountain, in the opposite direction.

"They are people," Sylvie said, as we pressed on toward the lake. "I did not know they were people."

"Yes," I said.

"Those poor people," she said. "They look so wise, like ancient old people. Those poor people."

"It's a rough business," I said.

"The poaching?"

"Peopling."

"They are gentle, and it is the same thing that happens to all wise people."

"Yes."

"Do you think they have souls?" she pondered.

"I don't know," I said.

"They do. I know it. I felt it. They *are* souls. They rise from the earth, just as we do, and have the same spirits, just like us."

"That's for the cosmologists," I said.

"That's just something clever to say. You think I'm being irrational, and are damming it off. But I don't care how clever anybody tries to be. They have souls."

"Maybe."

"God—"

"I don't believe in God."

"Don't be petulant, honey. God is a metaphor. I thought you knew things.

"And the same God holds them, just like us, and rocks them, just as whatever you want to call It does us, in the hollow of His hand." Her eyes were bright with tears, which she wiped away as they slipped down her face. "I don't care what else anyone says. I know it. The way you just know some things. The same way I know I love you."

38

The sapphire water of the lake twinkled in the distance. The sky blazed with bands of teal, saffron, red, and the pure gold of first light in that part of the world, as the wavelets on the water rippled in the dawn, reflecting the sun like veins of fire.

We reached the bank, and began searching around for a boat to hire or borrow without too much fuss. But there was no one on the shore, and we walked the rim a long while in silence, before we spied a low line of houses, set back among the trees. We stopped in front of the first one, where there was smoke rising through a hole in the roof, and called out.

We did not know who the people on this side of the lake were—what part they had in the fighting, or how they kept themselves out from the vise of it—but there was no other way. We called at the door until a little boy came out, staring at us in a moment of dazed wonderment before running back inside for his parents in fear.

From deep inside the smoky room a tall thin man, wearing a red sarong around his waist and a T-shirt that had been washed to a single cellular layer of material, walked out to us. The man was blue-black, like the boy, and looked at us with the same bewilderment, trying to figure out where we had come from.

"We need a boat to take us across the lake," I explained.

The man looked at me, and it was clear he did not understand.

I pantomimed what I wanted until he grasped my meaning. He shook his head, though, making clear he would not take us anywhere, and did not want anything to do with us.

"Where can I find a boat?" I asked, scanning the horizon, then paddling the air with my hand. As I made the motion I saw him look suspiciously at the bandage around my shoulder, and wag his finger no. He was fearful and I tried to make him understand I did not need him to risk his neck for us, I just needed the boat.

Still he shook his head no, and began walking away. I pulled out the stack of notes from my wallet, which I held all out to him. It was a little more than a thousand dollars and, I would wager, more cash than he had ever seen in his life. Still he refused.

As I offered him the money Sylvie pointed to my shoulder and made him understand we needed to find a doctor. He looked at both of us, and nodded once, slowly, before leading us around to the back of the hut, where there was a dugout that did not look too unsafe.

"*Hii ni bei gani?*" I asked in Swahili. "How much does this cost?"

He panned his hand flat across the plane of the ground. He would not take money. I did not want to be in his debt, and thought it was stupid of him to refuse, and held out again the mixture of currencies, pushing them toward him. We stood staring at each other, neither of us yielding to the other's way, but trying to figure each other out.

"It is of no use to him," Sylvie shook her head, grasping his position. "They do not have money."

"They do on the other side," I said, refusing to believe he could not make use of it.

"Give him the gun."

"No," I said.

"He is giving us his boat."

"I am trying to pay him."

"He cannot use money here."

"Somewhere he can."

"How will he get there without his boat?"

"We may need the gun."

"The boat is how he feeds his family."

She pointed at my waistband, nodding to the pistol. He followed her gaze and nodded at it.

"It is a fair trade," she said.

I took the gun reluctantly from where it was holstered snug against me, and slowly began handing it over, and I could see he saw what I thought, which was if I wanted to have the boat by force I could easily overpower him. But he had already given it to me and I felt guilty for my thoughts. I think he saw that, too, as I turned the barrel, and put the stock in his hand. He closed his fingers around it, feeling its metallic weight.

He turned it over several times, then nodded solemnly. I was not sure if he would use the gun, or barter it for something or bury it in the earth, but it was his now, and without it I felt immediately our vulnerability.

I was seized then by second doubts and fear, chagrined I had done the trade without further barter, and opened our pack, to offer him the camera instead. But Sylvie stopped me. It was the fair thing.

"We have the boat," she said, seeing my worry. "That is all we need now."

As we completed our transaction the little blue-black boy came out to the yard, trailed by a scrawny goat, so I saw how poor they were and did not feel so badly about the trade. The boy pulled at his father's clothing, and said something in their language. The father nodded and asked in Swahili if we were hungry and wanted food.

"Yes," Sylvie said. "*Ndio.*"

"We should find out what it is."

"Poor, fatherless, motherless child. You cannot ask that."

I asked what there was.

"*Ugali.*"

"*Ugali* is very good food." Sylvie beamed. "We would like some very much. Thank you. Tell him thank you, honey. Tell him thank you very much."

"Thank you," I said, nodding.

The blue-black man spoke to the blue-black boy and the child went to the house to tell his mother.

"I will go help," Sylvie said. "Do you think that would be okay?"

"Yes," I said. "I think it would be fine."

She followed the boy inside the house as the man showed me how the boat was outfitted. He was proud of it, I saw, and I was glad then he had gotten a good price for himself. Afterward, he started to drag the boat toward the water, pulling it down a worn little path from the side of the house toward the lake. I attempted to help, but he pointed at my shoulder and solidly refused, as the boy returned, along with two smaller children, who giggled and were shy of me as we headed toward the water.

It was time to go, but I did not see Sylvie, and it was only when we reached the bank I saw she was already there waiting. It looked as though she had been crying, but I was not sure and did not say anything.

The sky was ablaze, red-golden by then, tearing through the final darkness as we loaded ourselves into the boat. The sun fired harder, rose-gold and copper over jeweled water, and the iron mountains in the distance were beginning to glow, as the fog draping the silent water slowly burned away. Soon it would be full light and beautiful, and fill all the people along the shore and all those out on the lake with the awe and wonder of how perfect and well loved they were, in the way certain mornings make you tremendous with the knowledge of just how beautiful life is, and how connected all life is—everything that has been alive and everything that ever will be alive—and how magnificent it would be to live forever.

Sylvie was holding the porridge, which was wrapped in a broad leaf, and still steaming in the morning chill as the heat rose from it. My shoulder was beating full of pain, so I knew I could not suffer it much longer, and was anxious to go.

Sylvie saw I was hurting and trying to hide it, and I knew she knew it. I smiled at her, and we thanked the blue-black man for the boat, and the blue-black woman for the food, and the blue-black children just for being, in a state of thankfulness.

It was our boat now, but for one piece of business. As he pushed us off into the water, the blue-black man paused and made a staccato chanting we were not expecting, which was a prayer and blessing, or at least I took it to be.

He shoved us from the shore then, pushing us out until the water came to his waist.

"I will row," Sylvie said. "You need to rest."

"No, it will go faster if we both do. At least until it becomes too difficult."

"Do you remember the way?"

"I think so. Do you?"

"Yes."

"We are safe now."

There was a dull, brass sheen to the air at the horizon, and to the smooth white stones and pale birds all along the shore and the mountain's blue iron still in the far distance, as Sylvie arranged herself facing the shore, and took the port scull. I faced the prow, with the other scull in my left arm, which when I swept the water did not aggravate the wound too much.

"You will tell me if it gets any worse," she said. "You don't have to be afraid to tell me."

"I will be fine."

"Do you promise me you will be fine? This time I really will not know where home is anymore without you."

"We are headed north," I told her. "The sun should always be at the right, and we will only be about eight and a half miles to the other side. If we stay on the hypotenuse it will only take three or four hours."

"That is a long way, what with the bullet still inside of you."

"It's not far," I said.

"If anything happens to you—just promise me you will not die."

"I promise," I said. "I will never die."

"Don't make me cry. We have to take care of each other, just as they do. It is what our lives are for. If you die we won't be able to, and everything will be meaningless."

"I won't die. I promise."

"I believe you."

"May I ask something?" We had finally pulled beyond sight of the shore.

"Anything you wish."

"When did you first know you loved me?"

"When I first saw you," she said. "You were in your boat, just like this, and I knew we were going to meet. And then you came to dinner. Do you believe that?"

"Yes," I said.

"When did you figure it out?"

"At dinner, I think," I replied. "Except before I could accept it, first it had to get through all the parts of my heart I did not know, until I could see it was all of love."

We plunged the sculls into the water and watched it ripple, feeling how alive and fortunate we were.

"We might have died," she said.

"We did not," I said.

"How is your shoulder?"

"Holding on. Are we on the hypotenuse?"

"I remember the way."

"Okay."

"Can I tell you something?" she asked.

"Whatever you wish."

"It sounds foolish, but when I was waiting for you at the shore, I felt in my whole body the energy of my feet plunged into the earth, and every particle within me started to disintegrate and pull toward the sun, and then all of my energy and all the energy in the world were flowing through me, and all of you, too, and I wept."

"You had a moment of grace."

"Have you felt such a thing?" she wanted to know. "I mean, really felt it?"

"Not before I met you. I think before I only knew the rapture."

"Honey, what happened with your other woman?" she asked.

"Who?"

"The one before me. The one you loved, and never talk about."

"I told you."

"You told me the story, but not what it did to you. I know that you loved her."

"How do you know that?"

"Because I was afraid to ask about her before. Now I am not. Because I know we are together."

"It is the past."

"The past does not frighten me, unless it frightens you."

I reflected a while, remembering deeper, an open window down a summer corridor, where a birthday cake cooled on a side table. *I walked toward its wafting aroma, a pilgrim, to my own first memory. Outside, a truck parked in the middle of the street with sirens that do not sound, but glow bright as candles on a winter night. I walked into the house, sensing something was the matter and asked where she was, and was told not to worry. And the way in which it was said made me ask again, and I am told again not to worry—She has only gone to visit friends. I pressed further and no one answered, so I submitted to those in charge. Later, when I would not stop asking, they told me she was in the hospital, and I asked what that was. It is for people who are sick. I asked what was wrong; what had happened, and when would she be well. No one answered. They were in charge, and I submitted.*

But later they confessed, She is not coming home, and I asked, Why?
Because she has gone home. I thought this was her home, and asked
where else her home could be, and they told me it was where God is. I
asked about God. He is the Lord who made the world, and everything
in it, and where we will all go one day. She is with Him, and is happy
now. When will she be back? We all go to the Lord someday. And it is
awhile before I unravel it. Heaven means death. And I remembered
the song they sang in church, because it was her song, and her mother's
song. And the cake that day is the last I had of her sweet breath in
my face and sweet smell of her skin in my nose when I pressed to her
bosom. And that dessert was the last sweet bite in my memory's mouth,
and it was still sickly sweet. I did not have a mother after that, nor
trust what my father said. I knew later all fathers were liars, the world
demands it of them, but found out too soon, and wished for one more
memory, but had lost all memory before that, except the light from her
eyes sometimes, in dreams, in my cells themselves.

I did not know if the self we sometimes claim to know is truly
the self, but I felt my entire being on a great ocean flowing into
everything around the lake as I looked down and saw myself in
the boat, and saw Sylvie, and saw the lake and both shores. I saw
the errors of my life, and they fell all away as the overflowing price
of being alive, and I saw its triumphs, and they enfolded me as its
bounty.

"Sweetheart?"

"Yes."

"It is okay, dear. You can tell me. Nothing will take us from
each other. Don't worry about that. And if you loved her, and she
loved you, well, then you don't have anything to regret. Even if it
made you feel afterward like no one ever loved you at all, and no
one could love you again, because not even you knew the depth of
your aloneness. I am here for you. Harper?"

"Yes?"

"Stay awake, honey. Please stay awake."

I heard her from down at the other end of the shore, as the pain pulsed and surged. "Maybe we will not have to row all the way, but will see a boat that can tow us the rest of the way to shore. See how fast we are going and how wonderfully the boat is holding us up and the water is holding the boat. Don't fall asleep, honey."

"No. Not yet," I said. It was too painful to row, and I put the oar inside the boat, and let my hand fall in the cool water, and splashed some to my face.

"I wish I could hold you now," she said sweetly to me.

"You already are."

"Promise me you won't die."

"Yes."

The sun was firing gold and copper in the distance, as it created and enthroned the new day, and the fog was burning away, and on the far shore light had already broken so beautifully, suffusing everything with crystal fire that seemed to burn from inside each thing alive as far as could be seen, filling the people everywhere around the lake with the awe and wonderment of certain mornings that make you see how good life is, and how eternal love is, and how perfect it would be to live your own life your own way, and how fine and beautiful it would be to live forever.